D1201523

THE FIVE DAYS

A man is on the run among the mountains, fells and moors of Northern England. He is trying to escape both from capture by the police and from the impulse towards goodness and unselfishness which has pursued him over the years. Always he has eluded it, or it has failed to hold him. His childhood was marred by the harshness of his father, a loveless, egocentric parson. His love affair with the wife of a famous playwright brought him only to a barren place of pain and jealousy. Always impulsive, he takes a momentous step, but finds himself insecure and uncertain; and when first the daughter of the woman he loved and then the woman herself come to him for help, he, in an attempt to redeem what he thinks are his failures, becomes the instrument of disaster for them and for himself.

By the same author

Joanna Linden
The Small Rain
Between the Stirrup and the Ground
Strangers' Gallery

THE FIVE DAYS

DIANA RAYMOND

CASSELL · LONDON

UNIVERSITY OF TULSA - McFARLIN LIBRARY

CASSELL & COMPANY LTD.

35 Red Lion Square
London, W.C.1

and at

210 Queen Street, Melbourne; 26/30 Clarence Street, Sydney; 24 Wyndham Street, Auckland; 1068 Broadview Avenue, Toronto 6; P.O. Box 275, Cape Town; P.O. Box 11190, Johannesburg; P.O. Box 435, Lagos; Haroon Chambers, South Napier Road, Karachi; 13/14 Ajmeri Gate Extension, New Delhi 1; 15 Graham Road, Ballard Estate, Bombay 1; 17 Chittaranjan Avenue, Calcutta 13; P.O. Box 23, Colombo; Denmark House (3rd Floor), 84 Ampang Road, Kuala Lumpur; Avenida 9 de Julho 1138, São Paulo; Galeria Güemes, Escritorio 454/59 Florida 165, Buenos Aires; Marne 5b, Mexico 5, D.F.; Sanshin Building, 6 Kanda Mitoschiro-cho, Chiyoda-ku, Tokyo; 97 rue Monge, Paris 5e; 25 Ny Strandvej, Espergaerde, Copenhagen; Beulingstraat 2, Amsterdam-C; Bederstrasse 51, Zürich 2.

© *Diana Raymond* 1959
First Published 1959

Set in 11 pt. Bembo type, and
printed in Great Britain by Wyman & Sons Limited, London, Reading, and Fakenham

F.259

For

ERNEST RAYMOND

with much love

'Lord Buddha, was your gospel true?'
'True and false.'
'What was true in it?'
'Selflessness and Love.'
'What false?'
'Flight from Life.'
'Must I go back to Life?'

G. Lowes Dickinson

CHAPTER ONE

HE still kept his head down. It was the gesture of a child who goes past some frightening shadow on the stairs: 'If I don't look, it isn't there.' But he was not, he thought, exactly frightened; on the whole he was walking more easily; perhaps as a man might walk who'd simply tired himself on the hills. It was hard to tell.

The curious thing was that for moments at a time he felt safe, as if he were no more than he appeared to be: a man in early middle-age, not tall, wearing the rough clothes of the climber, limping along the fellside path, making for home. These moments made him afraid: he had to keep his danger clear in his mind, to be aware all the time of the tremendous task he'd taken on. Once he lost sight of that he might do something foolish; he might throw away all he'd achieved so far.

I have to keep going, he told himself. That's all: it's easier if you have one thing in your head, one important thing. It stops you being afraid, if you know what to do. . . . These words had an echo; he thought, Someone said that to me once; when? At a moment rather like this, when I was doing something that I knew at heart couldn't turn out well. . . .

He paused, his pack hanging from one hand, his head bent. It made him dizzy to try to remember; he had learnt that by now. He had to keep within the present, a man, as it were, born two days ago, standing here in the afternoon sunlight, with the hills about him.

Familiar hills; in that past shut away from him he had known them well, could give all their names from one glance at their shapes. Now they teased and puzzled his mind; the names slipped away like fish. Some of them he still knew: that was High Moor whose stony bulk butted towards the sun on his right. But these were not the tallest hills; those lay further to the north, where the distance showed a frieze of varying iron-coloured shapes weighted with cloud. Here the track under his feet was made of rough warm lighted stones; the whole scene painted with the brilliant economy of April: space and the wire-thin shadows of unfledged trees. The sky was clear. So far the sky was clear.

I

A wave of sickness forced him down to the grass at the side of the track, head between his hands. 'Trouble is,' he said, 'I'm hungry. Need food.' A bit frightening that, like a warning twinge of cramp, far out of your depth at sea. Perhaps if he rested, just for a few moments . . .

He looked towards the sunny buttresses of High Moor. Those could be climbers or sheep on the far summit. He went on looking while the brief rest restored him; he hoped they were climbers. So far distant, he was in no danger from them, merely comforted by a touch of something human in this wide stony silent theatre of rocks and hills. He had always needed the praises and love of his fellow men; now that their love was lost to him, reassurance came from those distant shapes; they had to do instead of the love.

He pulled himself to his feet, felt the shining sky sway above him. 'Well, I have to go on,' he said to the stones.

Once walking again he felt easier; gradually the sickness passed. He glanced down at himself: legs in the worn corduroy trousers moving precisely, like any other man walking; the trousers flapped about his ankles, were a little large: he wondered whose they had been. The memory of his taking them stung him, but it was one sin amongst many; he was far gone, out of sight of hope. He glanced to the distance where the high mountains were iron-coloured; a different day over there. Which way was the wind? There seemed none, but he thought perhaps the clouds were spreading a little, beginning to climb the sky.

'If I can find food,' he thought, 'I can get through another night.' One night lay behind him: a confusion in his mind of cold, and shredded sleep and the iron-hard ground; a long loneliness under a sky that at last swam slowly into light.

He passed his hand down his face. Grime came away with the sweat; he wondered when he would be clean again. The bathe in Heron's Tarn seemed far off; a splendid baptism, naked in the clear mountain water under the early morning sky; foolhardy, his heart beating heavily, yet fear couldn't quite spoil the delight as he lay cradled in the cold bird's-egg-green water, splashing tired grimy limbs.

Now the heat of the day had brought out the ingrained dirt; he hadn't the courage—or the foolishness—to stop to bathe again.

Sometimes he thought he heard sharp voices not far off; sometimes the brisk, eager barking of dogs.

§

The whitewashed farm buildings looked unattended in the evening light, and under quiet, continual smoke, gave no sign of danger. From the shelter of higher ground he had spied on them for some time. A shepherd, a woman in an apron, a farm labourer with a bucket. A distant, surely harmless company, reminding him of small lead figures from his childhood. 'Well, I'm going down,' he had said.

For a few moments he hesitated in front of the cottage. The door was propped open by a mountain stone; on the small table within the dark narrow passage lay post cards of steep crags, a chalked card offering teas and soft drinks; and a brass bell.

I expect this is a silly thing to do, he thought; because most of the things he did seemed to have an edge of foolishness; they seemed all right at the time, but later on he saw them clearly: impetuous, muddled, un-thought-out.

He rang the bell.

There was a mirror in the narrow hall; he glanced into it in curiosity. Hair greyer than he'd expected; the stubble on his chin not, perhaps, as noticeable as he'd feared. Large, clear, grey eyes; not much else to be said for the face, which held a certain trustfulness. A sap's face, he'd once called it; the kind you pass dud notes on. He turned a little tiredly away from it, as from a man who'd not done him any good.

'I'd like tea, please,' he said to the girl who came from the kitchen, 'if it's not too late.' He kept his eyes on her, watching for any sign of surprise, but she showed none, merely nodding and flicking straight brown hair aside from her face which was still a child's face.

'All right. Like an egg?'

'Yes, please. Everything there is.'

'Done a long walk?'

'Yes.' He hoped that would end it, for he was uneasy with her, but she seemed to be waiting so he lied quickly. 'From Bannerdale.'

'Aye, that's a fair walk.' Still she lingered; he could hear a

voice out of his past saying with a mixture of wonder and irritation, 'People always *talk* to you; what an extraordinary thing.'
Once he'd been glad of it; he didn't want it now.

'Look,' he said, forcing into his voice a quite alien avuncular
cheerfulness, 'I want that tea.'

She gave him a wide smile that in a year's time would be flirta-
tious. 'O.K.' She nodded to a room on his left. 'You go in
there.'

He opened the door, then stopped abruptly. Something in his
head said, 'Oh, hell, here we go. Here's the first mistake.' He'd
counted, at this late hour, on the room being empty. His heart
began to throb; he thought, Shall I go without waiting for the tea?
Go quickly, now? No, that wouldn't be any good either; the
child will come back with the tea, and then . . . Nothing to do but
ride this one as well as I can.

'Good evening,' said the man by the window. Round-faced,
grey-haired, smiling, sports jacket and a dog-collar. A clergyman.
He had time to wonder why half the population on the fells were
schoolmasters or clergymen.

'Good evening.' He sat at a table in the far corner; the deep
cottage window curtailed the light; here he sat in shadow. His
eye rested for a moment on the clergyman's face, as if it fascinated
as well as disquieted him.

'Been a lovely day,' said the clergyman.

'Yes, it has.' He seemed, now he was sitting down, to be waist
high in a mire of weariness; he leaned heavily on the table, his
head in his hand.

'Tired?'

'Yes. Yes, I am rather.'

The clergyman's eyes were on him, speculative above his pipe.
'Sometimes one can overdo it. Especially in fine weather. Been
a long way?'

'Yes.' (People always *talk* to you.)

'On your own?'

'Yes.'

'More tiring that way, for some reason. You'll be glad of your
tea.'

(How soon would he go? His teacup was full and steaming;
the plate of scones untouched.)

4

He nodded, leaning more heavily on the table.

'You don't feel ill, do you?'

'No.' He made an effort at a smile. 'No, I'm all right.'

Silence now for a little. A blessed silence; all he wanted now was to make no effort of any kind. A large round Victorian clock ticked at a matronly pace on the mantelpiece; the room was small, plushy and dark, contrasting oddly with the pale cloud-shaped hills seen through the deep-cut window, like misty water at the bottom of a well. The child brought his tea; he knew he must go carefully, taking the food like any other man. His hand shook as he poured the tea; the liquid stained the cloth. He wanted to say, That doesn't mean anything; I've always been clumsy, always knocked things over and spilt things, I don't know how it is. . . .

'If I were you,' said the clergyman, 'I'd take quite a long rest. Seems to me you've overtired yourself. Easy to do. While you're walking you feel you can carry on for ever, but when you stop to rest you realize the damage you've done.' Bland, smooth voice, a little too soft, modulated to reassure, the professional voice of a man who was selling security. How well he knew that pitch of voice. Odd to hear it now. It went on. 'I've had to learn my own strength—or my own weakness, rather; as a young man I could do twenty miles in a day, but now I'm afraid it's nearer ten. I don't enjoy myself any the less, you know.' Yes, the professional line: an upward twist of optimism at the end. 'Don't be afraid to admit your limitations.'

'No.'

'One doesn't get much exercise in one's job as a rule. Where d'you come from?'

'London.'

'Ah . . . yes, well . . .'

(Sorry, but I can't talk. I really can't talk.)

He ate hungrily. The light at the deep window began to change; the first flowers of shadow grew tall in the valley; evening, like a drift of smoke, was blowing into the sky.

He put down his cup; prepared to rise.

'I really do advise you to rest a little longer, you know. I've had some experience of men at the end of their tether, and you look to me pretty done in.'

'I have to go on.' (Had he said that aloud? Yes, it seemed so, for the clergyman was leaning forward.)

'You've got far to go?'

'Yes. Yes. To—to Blencaller.'

'To-night?'

'Yes.'

'Then if you'll allow me, I'm going to make a suggestion. I'm staying at Caudale farm—it's on your way. If you come along with me, I can give you a whisky. I keep some for emergencies.'

'It's kind of you. I don't think I've time.'

'It would hardly take a moment.'

'No, I know, but—it's really not possible.'

Silence. The clergyman was smiling, as a determinedly charitable man smiles at an unexpected rebuff; then lifted his head, as if to ask a further question——

The child came back, an empty tray hanging from one hand; she stood looking at his table, with the tea stain on the cloth, banging the tray lightly against her knee. 'Finished now?'

'Yes.'

'That'll be two-and-three.'

'Yes.' He could hear the clock; the girl was collecting his cup and plates, piling them noisily on to her tray. The clergyman was looking towards the window. The girl finished collecting the plates and stood waiting with the frank bored patience of a child.

He fumbled in his pockets, ashamed of the artifice, aware that the clergyman was turned towards him again. The child's boredom had changed to interest. He said, 'I seem to have lost my money. It must have dropped out somewhere on the hills.'

'You sure?'

'Yes. If you'll give me your name, I'll see that you——'

'Just one moment!' The clergyman was on his feet. 'No—no, I insist. I'm only too happy. It happened to me once; found myself in exactly your position; dropped my purse without knowing it on my climb.'

'It's very kind of you. I'll see that you get it back.'

'Let's look on it as a gift. Small enough.' The bland voice wore a dust of weariness. He gave the girl money for the teas and added, when she had gone, 'I'd like to explain. Would it interest you?' He put a tip tidily under the plate, made his way out of the cottage.

Nothing to do but follow him; he took his almost empty pack, and met the colder air of evening.

The sun was behind the hills; they walked in a flat clear light; the beck at their side carried through the rough grey grass traces of the sky. 'I don't know if I *can* explain,' the clergyman said. 'It's the difference, I suppose, between words and truth. Between the thing as it is, and how you say it is. I don't know if I'm making myself clear. I'm not a clever man.... Are you cold?'

'No ... no.'

'You're coming with me, aren't you? Perhaps I could lend you a jacket, or something. You're travelling light, aren't you? Not much in that pack, by the look of it.'

'I trusted in the day.'

'One can take cold easily, after a climb.... I've been in the Church for more than thirty years. I may have been some use, I don't know. I pass for quite a good fellow, I believe. But I've never been really able to help anyone, not as I used to dream of helping them. Perhaps I'm too lazy or not clever enough or too selfish ... I don't know. But I can't help wishing sometimes, that I could ... well, that I could *really* be what I'm supposed to be.' He smiled towards the ground. 'You say nothing. Don't you understand?'

'Yes. Yes, I understand.'

'D'you know, I thought you would. Odd, isn't it? After so short a time. After barely exchanging a dozen words.'

The evening wind, rising, tuned the telegraph wires beside the road. He began to shiver, a hard, inward shivering that he could not control.

'You *are* cold, you know. My place isn't far ... just there where the road bends.' He made a gesture with his pipe. 'Yes, it's odd how one can be certain about a man so quickly. I'm a lazy man, as I say, and I've never been one of the clever ones, but I've got a sort of ... well, call it intuition, if you like. I *know* about people. How they're feeling. What they think. It's a help sometimes.'

The wires sang louder. The clergyman paused for a moment

7

on the rough, empty road. He seemed to be half-ashamed, half-pleading. He said after a moment or two of difficulty, 'As I told you, I've always wanted to be of some use. How much help do you need?'

Panic smothered him like a black cloak flung over his head; he said urgently, 'I don't need help, not any help'; and went running towards the thick covering of the woods.

§

It was hard going; the ground sloped uphill, the boulders tripped him; once his ankle twisted sharply on a hidden stone. Breathless and in pain he leaned against a tree trunk, turning to look back. Surprising how far he'd climbed; the road below him was diminished by distance. It seemed empty. Was he being followed? He listened. No sound but his own breathing and the rising wind, and far off, the barking of a dog.

He sank to the ground. Blind and stupid to run like that; he should have carried the thing off, even gone and had the whisky, borrowed the jacket. For a moment he saw clearly the clergyman's face, ashamed and pleading: 'How much help do you need?'

'Oh, hell, I'm sorry,' he said.

He lay back. The rough ground hurt his body, but the hushed shelter of the woods gave him peace; he was hidden; he was alone. He looked about him; the racing of his heart gradually slowed. The light here was thicker, murky with shadow; the rusty bracken smelled of evening. The coming night imposed upon leaf and grass a delicate stillness, a cave of quiet below the swaying tops of the trees. Along other roads the climbers were coming home, the fells abandoned to the dark.

He had nowhere to go, no one to turn to, no hope of rest. For a moment it seemed absurd; the kind of absurdity that had always attended him, a man who went through life missing appointments by confused mischance, before whom the lift gates always closed a fraction too soon, who seemed continually confounded by a mixture of his own weakness and his good intentions. . . . Can't be true, not really true. It's a nightmare, the old one you always had of hiding and being hunted, while the shadowing fear came closer. . . .

He rubbed his face with his hands. No, it was real. The stony floor, the coarse, scented bracken, the rising, hunting wind, were all real. He was a desperate man, but for the moment he could not feel so; panic was dulled—by weariness, perhaps, or mercy— and his mind seemed strangely free to wander and surmise and remember, as a man, walking idly through a gallery of pictures of his ancestors, sums up their sorrows and fears, sufferings and deaths with a casual word.

Somewhere in a valley church a bell was ringing, a small harsh sound, beating on the large silence. Idly he listened; the sounds, measured and rhythmic, were like steps, going back, crossing time and distance, until he stood beneath the sound of that other bell, not hunted as he was now, not even a man, but still afraid.

CHAPTER TWO

HE had forgotten to bring the flowers. There was no question of his father being angry; the Reverend Anthony Harvist was seldom angry; nevertheless he had at his command some other power than anger, of which the young Mark was afraid.

'Yes, I'm a bit scared of him,' he had told an astonished school-friend who had replied, 'But he's always so darn jolly!' Mark could not find words to express the conviction that his father's good cheer was in some way inhuman; large, marvellous, shining and uncommunicative, it blazed, giving no heat. Faced with wrong-doing, the light did not lessen, but somewhere behind it was the chill fathomless dark of disapproval. Unvoiced, it was therefore unanswerable: if Mark cried out, 'But it wasn't my fault!' Anthony Harvist would reply, 'My dear boy, no one has blamed you for anything'; and from there on you'd had it; nothing but a cold frustration, of which his father seemed entirely unaware.

Anthony Harvist was admired by his parishioners, but not loved. His large firm body flowed through space with the smooth authoritative movements of a man in command of circumstance, a man whose bearings have been secretly oiled for him in a way that other men's have not. When he crossed himself (as he did frequently, for the church of All Hallows, Wrenfield, was as high

9

as may be) the movement distracted your eye by its perfection, but did not seem somehow the gesture of a man, small and humble, before his Maker.

In the presence of pain or grief, he showed a calm shining certainty that was impressive, like a monument or a cathedral, but not immediately comforting. On these occasions—when young children died, or sons were killed in war, and people found themselves face to face with insupportable anguish—it was his wife who wept.

Lucy Harvist, in fact, wept easily and often; it seemed sometimes less the result of grief than the only protest she dared make at the position in which she found herself. She was pretty, fair, absent-minded, loving, ignorant, but not entirely foolish. As a vicar's wife, she failed. She forgot people's names, their birthdays and what it was they had rung up about urgently two hours ago. Faced with these lacunæ, her husband showed an endless, infinitely reproving patience, which only unnerved her more.

'I don't really understand—' she would say—to Mark or the housemaid or any woman friend who might be near, for she talked as she thought and whenever she wanted to; to herself if no one else was by—'he is so *good*. I ought to be more ... to find it easier ... to feel quite happy with him. ... He's never been angry. Never angry! And yet I don't feel ... any *love* coming from him. Oh! I shouldn't have said that. How dreadful!' She would fly to the mirror, as if fearing to see in its depths some avenging shadow, but once there she stayed, beguiled by her fair yet highly-coloured prettiness. 'But of course—' turning away—'he loves God. He has it all clear, I mean he knows how to do it. Religion to him is ... isn't difficult at all. It belongs to him. And yet ... sometimes I can't help wondering—isn't it perhaps larger—great and terrible—in some way quite beyond us?'

Mark, listening at ease, would nod with grave sympathy. His understanding was intuitive rather than exact; she spoke his language in a way his father did not.

Lucy Harvist, finding that her demonstrative, verbal, happy but easily wounded form of loving rebounded from the shining armour of her husband, directed it towards her son. Mark received it with warmth, and the exaggeration of the child who needs to be able to say, 'This is the person I love,' and to stand aside from himself and say also, 'That is me loving the person I love.' As he walked, a voice in his mind would say, 'That's Mark Harvist; he's devoted to his mother; he'd do anything for her.' It wasn't quite true; he was as little likely to sacrifice himself as any other boy of fourteen, but she became his harbour of warmth and comfort, especially at moments like this.

He came slowly towards his father's house in the hyacinth-blue spring dusk. The church clock was ringing the hour; the noise, close above him, made his heart beat; it sounded like a moment of reckoning. He let himself cautiously into the house. The hall seemed built of foreboding. He had thoughts about lying, but decided against it; he did it clumsily and was always found out.

He trod lightly, postponing the moment of reproof. His crime, with each moment, seemed to grow heavier—'Old, widowed, crippled Mrs. Lines, *waiting* with the flowers, and I never came. Never *came*.' In spite of himself, he gave a mildly hysterical giggle. It was like the time he'd knocked the best teapot off the tea table into the grate; so awful that——

He paused. The door of his father's study was open, and he could see his father sitting at his desk. He was leaning forward with his head in both hands. This seemed so astonishing an attitude for his father—though normal for other men—that Mark felt, there in the dark hall, the apprehension of one whose customary world has slipped its moorings. At this moment his father raised his head, and passed one hand across his eyes.

'Oh ... Mark,' he said in an unrecognizable voice. 'Yes ... go along and have your supper.'

No word about the flowers. No explanation of that odd, unrecognizable voice. Mark fled.

Later that evening he went to his mother's room. In answer to his question, she said she had gone to bed early with a headache. He could not feel that the cause of his father's concern lay here, nor that she suffered much, for her colour was high and her eyes bright.

'I hope it isn't bad,' he said politely, 'and that you're better now.'

He was surprised that this purely formal expression should bring the tears to her eyes. 'Oh, yes! I'm better. ... I'd like you to stay and talk to me.'

He made an embarrassed movement in his chair. He was quite

prepared to talk to his mother, it was one of the things he enjoyed most, but to be asked to do it made him feel uneasy.

'To-morrow . . . is Sunday,' she said.

It sounded like a question. 'Easter Sunday,' he replied, his uncertainty growing.

'So pretty when Easter comes late.' She was looking from her window as if some brilliance showed at the far end of the dusk. 'Lilac with the flowers, and the church smelling of it.'

Now seemed the time to say it. 'I forgot to bring the flowers. From Mrs. Lines. Father asked me to, and I forgot.'

'Did you, darling? I don't suppose it matters; there will be plenty. We always have more than we need.'

'I like Easter too,' said Mark, encouraged and clasping his ankle; perhaps nothing was wrong. In his mind was a confused impression of soft winds and white sunlight on the morning table-cloth, Easter Eggs and daffodils, incense and the crowded candles with their shivering wings of flame.

'And yet—' his mother's voice broke in—'it always worries me. A little. Your father isn't worried about it, of course. I often think of Easter as an enormous wave and your father rising to the top of it quite effortlessly and preaching a really splendid sermon *from* the top.'

Mark giggled, beginning to feel happy.

'Yet for me . . .' his mother's eyes fled from him, as if she oughtn't to have made him laugh, 'I feel sometimes that I'm not really thinking of the right thing. It's all so large and tremendous— oughtn't it to roll over one and leave one with nothing else in one's mind at *all*? I'd like to feel like that, but I never have. I once tried to tell your father how I felt, but he looked . . . I don't know exactly what—*offended*, I think—no, more than that; stricken but not showing it. I must have been a great disappointment to him.'

Mark said nothing, and became aware that this sojourn with his mother was somehow different from others: that he both wanted, and did not want, to leave her.

He made an effort. 'I don't think of the right things, either. Football . . . arithmetic. . . pocket money . . . .'

'You should try talking to Jim Elliot.'

'Father Elliott is . . . a different kind of priest from Daddy,' Mark hazarded.

'Oh, yes.' His mother seemed gently unconcerned. 'An easy, bending kind of person who's never shocked by what you say. Awfully restful.' She paused, seemed to hesitate, then said, 'If you're ever in any kind of trouble . . . I should go to him. He'd help you.'

Mark felt his skin prickle; for some reason the words were uncomfortable. 'I'm practically always in trouble,' he said, trying to turn it into a joke, but his mother merely smiled, then closed her eyes.

He sat for some time, waiting for her to say more. He could hear movement in the house downstairs; the chime of a clock. He leaned nearer to his mother, and saw that she was asleep.

This disconcerted him, for he could not remember its happening before. He waited a little longer, but she did not wake, and he got to his feet and went uneasily from the room.

§

'It's all quite different now,' Mark wrote some days later to his school-friend, Guy Furness, who was away for the holidays. 'Mother's ill and I'm not often allowed to see her. She is going away to hospital, my father says. He says she will be better.' He was, he found, incapable of expressing his more savage fears: he did not believe she would be better; he grew frightened.

His father, he perceived, though expressing grief, presented an unmoved shining serenity, travelled with as much billowing authority, crossed himself with the same gesture, too perfect to be humble.

'One quite understands, Mark, that you should be distressed,' his father said to him, finding him red-eyed one evening, 'but you must realize that it shows a failure in faith.'

Mark thrust his hands into his pockets, kicked a chair leg, and said sulkily, 'No, it doesn't.'

After that there grew between them an inexpressed hostility; Mark became rude, untidy and even clumsier; Anthony Harvist wore the tired, patient expression of a man who is carrying one burden too many.

Three days after Mark's fourteenth birthday, his father called him into his study. The room was unwarmed, barren with morning light and pale, heatless flames, wooden surfaces wearing an antiseptic skin of polish.

'It happened last night,' his father said, after the first bare announcement. 'She died about eleven o'clock.'

In the silence that followed Mark was uncertain whether his father had more to say, or was waiting for some word from him. He could supply none. His father raised his eyes, and there passed between them a glance which Mark found fathomless, but seemed, at base, to convey some deep, unalterable hostility.

Later that evening, he walked carefully into the church. It was empty; the candles on the altar unlit. Something vulnerable about the place as though he spied on it; he could smell leather, wood and stale incense.

Tentatively he came into the church, knelt and crossed himself. All the time a small distant Mark watched in some shame. He stayed determinedly on his knees, like a writer with a pen in his hand, waiting for enlightenment: for it was this or nothing; he needed help, and from all everyone said, help might be here.

After some moments, somewhere in his brain, or in the darkness behind his closed eyes or in the church itself, he was aware of a faint stirring of comfort, a slight, indefinable pulse. Encouraged, he waited for more.

The sound of steps on the flagged floor distracted him. He glanced up, to see his father, pacing this way and that, apparently waiting for him.

The thread quite broken, he scrambled to his feet. 'Ready?' his father enquired; Mark nodded dumbly. The atmosphere was heavy with unexplained guilt. They walked out of the church in silence; the heavy door creaked and swung.

'I think one has to realize, Mark,' his father said after some moments, looking away to distances over Mark's head, 'that there's a certain amount of showing off in some people's religion. Don't feel I mean this unkindly; I just think it's best to get this sort of thing clear in your mind. People, even in great grief, can partly *enjoy* it, you know; enjoy the drama and make a show of prayer and sorrow.'

Mark did not reply. He looked back at the church. The spire close above him drove steeply towards the clouds, the windows gave back a little of the yellow evening sky. It had begun to take on the shape of a sanctuary whose doors were shut.

14

CHAPTER THREE

SO far, so good. That brief resting place in the bracken was an hour behind him; while there was still light he'd climbed the slope of Caudale Fell, and down the other side into Dartford's Coombe, a sheltered valley, carved into the steep fellsides. He was coming nearer to the central mass of mountains; here he was still amongst the early foothills, but the crumbling, disused sheep-pen near the beck would give him shelter for the night. More than he'd bargained for: shelter from the cold; water close by.

He looked about him. The hills made a hem of absolute dark-ness, beyond which the sky, though dark itself, showed pale. The beck ran with tireless urgency, with the whispering roar of swift shallow water; the sound soothed him. I might even sleep, he thought. Yes, perhaps I shall sleep.

He lay in a grassy hollow, against the crumbling wall. The apparent softness of the ground did not deceive him; it would grow fangs that bit painfully into shoulder, hip and thigh. The cold touched him, like the lick of an icy tongue. Yet in some way these things carried less hurt than comfort. This, it seemed, was where he wanted to be; bruised nerves eased by the great distances; by solitude and silence.

He lay for a long time, until weariness at last dragged him down towards sleep, away from the hard ground and the cold. Some-where at the edge of sleep, there seemed to be a great clamour, like the sound of men's voices, shouting in urgency and triumph, but the noise faded and became nothing more than the hollow sigh of the mountain beck, then nothing more than sleep and the violent dreams.

§

'The damnable part of it is,' said Major Fellowes, running an exasperated hand over thin grey hair, 'that nobody really sees my point of view. There are chaps who want to turn the whole place into a recreation centre, and others who want a Venetian dungeon, chains, water and all. And they're *both* wrong, you see.'

15

His Chief Officer, a smart young man, anxious to agree, brushed a speck off his uniform and said, 'Yes, sir. Aye, that's about it.'

'They pick on me for everything, of course. A well-deserved sentence in here, all that's humanly possible done for them—God knows, I'm not a vindictive man—oh, God knows I'm not—and when it's over, what happens? Out the bastards go and write a book about it. Talk as if they'd come back from some lower region. Hell, I mean,' he added.

'Aye, they do.'

'And I can't answer back. That's what's so damnably unfair. Oh, chaps get up in the House and say Three cheers for the Governor, *he's* a jolly good fellow (or Fellowes—ha!) but nobody believes them. Anyhow, they don't say the right thing.... God, it's warm. He's had the devil's own luck, hasn't he, not a drop of rain.... They make it sound simple. 'T'ain't simple—oh, God knows it isn't.' He rubbed his face all over with his hands and sat back looking defeated. His eye travelled over his room, over the carpet and the glass-fronted bookshelves and the plan of the prison on the wall, as if they formed part of his defeat.

'No, sir. You're right there. Personally I've no sympathy with these lads who write books about how badly they've been treated. Whose fault is it they get sent here?'

'No, well...' The Governor looked as though he ought to like this remark, but couldn't quite. He sighed and looked out of the window; the large grey courtyard was filled with the shuttling of grey prisoners, pushing hand-carts, carrying buckets and planks. At the end of his vision was the steep, unyielding wall. 'Things aren't pretty here at Scarside. One can't really expect them to be. I don't hold any brief for the way this place is built—nor where it's built, come to that.' He continued to look from the window, as if he could see the rising distances of Allen Moor. 'Mountains... never cared for 'em. Make one feel shut in... have I made a joke?'

'Well, sir, *shut in*. After all...'

'Oh... I see. Yes. Different kind of shut in, though... no, things aren't what you'd want them to be here. But—Heaven help us—what *is*? In this world. What on earth is? They talk as if I worked here with a whip and a thumb-screw. Oh God, sometimes I think I'm the only reasonable man. The only fair man—seeing both sides. . . .' He hunched over his desk. 'What made him go, d'you think? Him, of all people?'

'Don't know, sir. Don't know at all. He was never any trouble.'

'Not always the best sign. Talk to him at all?'

'No, sir. Not much . . . wasn't exactly an easy chap to talk to.'

'No, he wasn't, was he?'

'There was just one thing, sir.'

'Yes?'

'He didn't like being shut in.'

'Didn't like it—how?'

'Looked scared when you locked the door. Looked . . . as though it hurt him, somehow.'

Major Fellowes sighed. 'Well, I know, but we've got to lock them in. Well, here, you have.' He sighed again. 'Didn't like it. . . . Difficult to talk to. . . . Yet he must have been a very remarkable man—surely he must?—to do what he did. Change his whole way of life in midstream. . . .' He brooded over his desk. 'Funny thing is, I thought I was beginning to make a bit of headway. The last time I talked to him in his cell, that is. . . . Wonder where he is, don't you? Hiding? Frightened? Hungry? Oh, well . . . Yes, that last time, I thought he really looked on me . . . oh, I'd say as a friend. I felt he—well, God knows, I'm not a snob—oh, God knows I'm not—but I felt he was glad to talk to a man who spoke his own language. He talked . . . even made a joke, I think, though I can't remember what it was.' He looked worried, trying to remember. 'Made me realize he was the kind of man who *could* have made jokes. . . . Something about wearing a different uniform to the one he was used to—God, what a story. And now this. How'll it end, I wonder?'

'He'll be back here. The next day, or the day after.'

'And when he is . . . lot of good it's done him. Bread and water, loses his remission. . . . Oh, I'd give a lot to learn what made him go. An intelligent man—intelligence must come into it—surely it does? An educated man. Not some poor foul-mouthed tough who can't sign his name. What did he think—good Lord above—what did he think he'd gain?'

'They don't think, sir, when they break a working party like that. They're desperate.'

'Mm, yes, I suppose so. Desperate . . . then he won't get far. Unless the Almighty's taking a personal interest in keeping him at large. You need your wits about you, to keep going——' He lifted the telephone as it rang. 'Fellowes here . . . yes . . . yes . . . I see. Well, it gives you a line, doesn't it? . . . Yes . . . thank you. Good-bye.' He put down the telephone, and said to his blotting pad, 'Climber's clothes and pack missing from the drying room of an hotel near Leader's Fell. A sweater and corduroy trousers. Could be him, I suppose.'

'Bound to be, I should think, sir.'

'Yes . . . yes . . . Funny, can't fit it in—can't see him doing it.'

'Stealing?'

'Well . . . no.'

'Seems to me, sir, if he was desperate . . .'

'Mm . . . desperate . . . and dressed in stolen clothes. Where's he making for, I wonder?'

'They usually make for home, sir.'

'Yes, the old excuse when we get them back: "I was worried about things at home." But in his case he can't exactly say that, can he?' A prisoner in a white jacket brought in tea on a tray; the Governor said, 'Thank you, Davies,' and waited for him to go out before saying, 'After all, he must know how lean his chances are. Even if the police do little more than block the roads and sit and wait, he can't keep going for long. And yet he goes and grabs some other chap's clothes and hides and runs. . . . What does he expect to find? In the next twenty-four hours? Because he won't have much more than that unless he's *very* lucky.'

§

At first Mark thought he was being held down by strong hands, while lights flashed in his eyes. He flung one arm across his face and gave a shout, half protest, half fear. The shout seemed to choke him, and he sat up coughing. He looked about him. No hands, no lights; only the sun staring levelly between a gap in the hills, and sharp areas of pain in his body. No one near him; only the morning lifting up, and the broad silent hillside.

Morning. Another day coming towards him, large and formidable as a ship. He said aloud, I don't think I can go on.

When he had said it, he sat and thought about it. No, I can't.

18

Of course I can't; the whole thing was mad from the beginning; I haven't any hope. Better to go back, to stop hiding; it'd be easy. Except . . .

No, there was a snag. Difficult at the moment to focus on it, but it seemed that any hardship, hunger, thirst, fear—even death—was better than going back. These were large claims, but true.

He looked up. The lazy, increasing growl of a plane? They used planes, didn't they? He wasn't sure exactly how they would hunt him; in his mind was a confused image of the mechanism of the chase: dogs and spotter planes and men on motor-cycles, swooping over the roads in their strange and sinister balance, like a swarm of noisy birds. He shielded his eyes with his hand, searching the sky. The sound faded; he could see nothing. Not yet.

A snowy pelt of mist lay on the lap of Fallon Ridge; he stared at it until his eyes hurt; until he was in that other mist, hearing the voice inside his head which said, 'Now. Go on, now. Anything rather than go back. Now or never.' The diver's plunge, away from the working party in the quarry, in that split second after the mist came down and before the officers called the men together. As he ran he could hear the voices, sharp voices, calling orders; they didn't know yet that he'd gone; in three—five minutes they'd know; he had to go on running. Behind him was Scarside, with the long, spidery galleries, echoing with the sound of keys, the cell door that shut flush with the wall, so that the cell was like a tomb, a sealed place on which a man could batter his body and tear his hands and nails, but from which he could not—could not—could not escape——

He had to keep running. He had no idea what the two officers would do; they couldn't both chase him, that'd leave the rest of the prisoners free to escape too. One of them, he supposed, would come after him, the other staying with the men. But the mist was thickening; he had a start; if he kept running——

There was a moment when he thought he was finished; he could see no one, but the harsh breathing of a man running seemed right behind him. His heart beating, he crouched down beside a boulder that would scarcely hide a dog. If the mist should lift, magically in a moment, as it sometimes did——

His pursuer muttered to himself. 'He went this way—*know* he went this way—I heard him—oh, this bloody mist——'

Burrowes, the junior officer. Mark could feel the man's indecision: whether to plunge deeper into the mist or to turn back.

'Don't know where—can't see a bloody thing—oh, hell.'

Still the sound of breathing; footsteps going a little way and then retracing themselves; silence, as if the man stood with an ear to the mist, listening. Somewhere not far off, a scuffle of movement; a sheep, Mark guessed; a smothered exclamation from Burrowes; the sound of his feet plunging away. Growing less. Wait to count ten, wait, you've got to let him get out of the way, wait, one, two, three, four—no, I can't, I've got to move—on, into the deep white enclosing substance of the mist, running, running, until he had to pause and listen, and at first could hear nothing but the strained rasp of his own breathing. Then as his lungs grew quieter, the triumphant silence about him. Only a faint sound that might have been the shuffle of hidden water, or the stumbling of a sheep.

On then. In hope of what? He didn't know; nothing but the need to run; the future was the next few minutes, the space of the mist, the breath and energy he had to keep running. The mist seemed to welcome and embrace him, further and deeper; it gave, as he went on, an illusion of safety, like sinking deep below the surface of the sea, like a child in a tent, pretending that no adult can find him. His prison clothes were soon damp with sweat and the mist's moisture; his legs seemed weighted with stones; still, at the heart of it all, was a little germ of triumph. 'A mug's game, that,' they all said, 'no one ever makes it, chum, not ever; putting your money down the —— hole if you tries that'; but he'd got away, got *away*; into the soft, yielding comfort of the mist.

§

That had been the beginning. Now, with two nights behind him, he got to his feet and looked about him. Westward the hills stood, carved in low morning light, but to the east they were dyed blue and purple, their heads blunted in cloud. Storm? He leant against the wall of the sheep-pen and stared at the darkness shouldering up against the sky on this bright morning.

Little hope for him if the storm came. And it would come sooner or later. Then why go on? Because I have to. Because I can't go back till I'm dragged back, pushed behind the locked door, to sit and remember——

Yes, that was it. He had it now. That plunge away into the mist had stopped him thinking; since then the weariness, the cold and the hunger had all blunted and deadened his mind. Alone in the cell, with the hours stretching ahead, the memories swarmed through his mind; all the worst memories, and that last memory, the worst of all, played themselves round in his head, till he thought he was losing his reason.

Perhaps he had been a little mad; lots of them went a bit queer in prison. Certainly both the Governor and the Chaplain had made efforts, but he'd not had much to say to them; they had looked, he thought now, disappointed. 'If we could restore your faith,' the Chaplain had said, and to that he had smiled as politely as he could without raising his eyes from the ground. The Chaplain had felt at a disadvantage, everything about him betrayed that; he came into the cell with too brisk a step and spoke with the determined clarity of a man who fears he may stammer. Well, who could blame him; a hard enough job at the best of times.

So now? He pushed himself a little way from the wall. I can't have much longer, he thought; the odds are too heavy, it can only be a short time.

Somehow he didn't seem quite able to grasp it; perhaps his brain was too tired. He began to move on. Not much time, he said, to convince himself; but there was a small nerve of content, even of excitement, in his head, as if this short space of time contained things of great moment, as yet hidden from him.

§

By the shadows on the rocks he thought it must be late afternoon. He'd left the Coombe, made his way by small tracks across the valley, climbed again to the ridge of Divers Moor. The higher hills were closer now. To his left the coarse blond grass and the grey stones broke abruptly, changed into the dark vertical splintered rocks of Tower Crags. Lichen and black moss grew on small, dizzy, slanting platforms.

He'd had plenty of water, little rest, no food. This did not seem to trouble him. Perhaps I can do without food, he thought; I didn't eat much in prison; perhaps I need less and less. But now and again the hills and the coloured clouds swam, as if he saw them through watery glass, and he passed his hand before his eyes.

He began to talk aloud, as he did often now, as if to a companion. Somehow, it made it easier to talk.

I used to come here a lot, you see; that's what's so strange. In those days I used to see Scarside in the distance, in the early shallows of the mountain country; it drew your eyes, in spite of all the loveliness around you; you couldn't help wondering about it. I was never close enough to see anyone moving there; it was just a harsh structure of grey stone. The first time I saw it, I didn't know what it was, and the man I was with said, 'That's Scarside,' and for some reason I stopped to stare; my companion, climbing ahead of me, had to call me on. . . . Yes, I climbed all over these hills . . . another man in another world. Oh, such a different world, you can't imagine how different. . . . A good world, as worlds go; I pulled it down about me. Why? Oh, I don't know. Hard to trace things back to their root, isn't it; weakness, vanity—something like that, perhaps. I meant no harm, but I caused it. Yes, great harm. . . . I expect you've heard of Gerald Minestaff . . . yes, the playwright; I knew him well, and Lorraine, his wife . . . who was his wife. And their daughter: I knew her too, Daphne; yes, I knew her. . . . I only mention them, because I want someone to say that they've all forgiven me, yes, forgiven me, please, in their mercy——

He paused. His words died; he stood there amongst the sunlit stones and the rough grass, dry with shame and surprise.

The girl crouching close—surely far too close—to the brink of Tower Crags, was turned to look at him. They were some yards distant, in the wide emptiness of sky and evening hills, and her face was unreadable. For some moments they stayed, both silent, looking at each other across the stretch of stony ground.

CHAPTER FOUR

HE wondered whether to walk on, but she still crouched there, staring at him, and it seemed difficult to go past without speaking. He moved hesitantly towards her. She wore the uniform of the young: the raw, hacked hair-cut, loose shirt and canvas trousers, but, drawing closer, he saw that she was thirty, perhaps more. His mind fumbled for some word that would bring her away from the brink of Tower Crags. When he spoke his tongue felt dry; he had to swallow between the words. 'If I were you, I'd come a bit further in. You must have a head of cast-iron.'

She did not answer, but continued to look at him. Her eyes were large and dark; her face pale; her expression alert, even hostile. She must, of course, have heard him talking to himself; perhaps she thought him mad. Perhaps she had recognized him; there might have been, somewhere in the newspapers, a photograph of him, not beyond recognition. He stood his ground with an effort. 'Those crags are dangerous ... well they've always frightened me, anyway. Most people keep away from them, and the climbers won't play because the rock splinters. One man tried to climb in Hunter's Gully down there, but he was killed.'

She gave a glance down at the dark, fanged fall of rock below her, sighed, stood up, paused for one moment braced against the sickening space of sky. His heart tripped. She moved a little way towards him. 'Got a cigarette?'

'No—I'm sorry.'

'Have to do without, I guess.'

'You American?'

'No. I've been over in the States quite a lot, and I use their language when I want to feel some other person than I am.' She thrust her hands into her pockets, still looking levelly at him. 'You were talking to yourself just now.'

Her directness made him stammer. 'Was I? ... Well, yes ... I daresay.'

'Do a lot of that?'

'Sometimes—when I climb alone.'

She nodded. He was surprised to see, as she withdrew her hand from her pocket, that it was trembling. She sat down on a large boulder, leaning her forehead in her hand. 'Sorry. I'm a bit done in.'

'Come a long way?'

'You might call it that.'

He stood looking down at her. She was slight and boyish; her breasts scarcely marked her shirt. Something vulnerable in the way she sat, in the unsteady fingers and the firm, pale face.

'Can I do anything to help you?' he said. It seemed, in the circumstances, an absurd thing to say. Some part of his mind chalked up one more mistake.

'I don't know.' She raised her head and considered him. 'Where are you making for?'

'I . . . just . . . the Hardgill path.'

'Rather I didn't ask you where you're going?' She grinned faintly. 'Think I'm going to tag along and talk all the time and then attempt your virtue in a coombe?'

He said, on a laugh, 'No, of course not. It's just that I'm . . . a bit done in, like you. I forgot my food to-day. I've had nothing since—since breakfast.'

Again she considered him; he became more and more conscious of the sunlight on him, defining his weariness and pallor and rough clothes, and his shoes that weren't climber's shoes.

'You've climbed all day without food? That's a mighty silly thing to do.'

'Yes, I know.' Anxious now to get away from her, he took a pace or two to his left.

'Want to go on now?'

Again her directness disconcerted him. 'I . . . well, perhaps.'

She nodded, accepting him and his desire to go on with a marked, adult calm. 'Mind if I ask you something?'

He swallowed, wanting to go, to be done with this; yet held by her, in some way he couldn't explain. 'No.'

'Why were you talking to yourself like that?'

'Habit—a bad one, I suppose. Gains with age. A comfort, sometimes.'

'But like *that*?'

'I forget what I said. I say all sorts of things.'

'Making you shy, am I? Talking too much?'

'No. No.'

'Don't go yet.'

This is the beginning of being frightened, he thought; seeing the threat growing up suddenly, where you'd expected none. He stood silent.

She stared up at him with enquiring honesty. 'D'you think I'm a menace? Someone to get away from fast?'

He said with pity, 'No.'

'You're apprehensive and you're being polite.' She seemed to weigh these facts from some standpoint of her own. 'I don't know why you should be either; I can't hurt you, and to be polite's a waste of time. Are you in a hurry?'

'I . . . yes, in a way.'

She frowned at the lame answer. 'I need someone to talk to. D'you think I'm nuts?'

'No.'

'I'm not. Not altogether.' She seemed more and more vulnerable, crouching on the boulder there. 'I just need someone badly.'

(The threat growing, closing in. And how to get free without hurting her? The conflict locked him in silence.)

'I'm not asking you to stay and talk to me here. I'm not as crazy as all that. Anyway, the kind of thing I want to say's best said in a room; all kinds of trouble are best spoken of in a room— don't you agree; out in places like this it blows away, doesn't take. You say you've had no food. If you come down with me to Bleadale, I can take you to my father's house and give you food.' She searched his face, then said, as if divining a fear, 'There's no one in the house. My father isn't there.'

For a moment there swam before him a mirage of comfort; of rest, shelter and food. He said, after an effort, 'I'm afraid it's impossible. I have to go on. To get to——'

'I can give you anything you need—food or drink. It shouldn't be a very difficult thing for you to do.'

She put the offers down firmly, like coins, without pleading. She remained, in the midst of her vulnerability and her need for company, oddly independent, oddly dignified.

'No, it wouldn't be difficult,' he said. 'It isn't that. I don't want you to think——'

'Let's say politeness is out, shall we? Leave all that coming and going, "When I say this I don't mean" and "You must understand that what I really"—all of that. No time for it, see?'

'All right.'

'Well, then . . .?'

He was frowning, following a thought of his own; something

that had been there since the first moment he saw her, only now becoming clear. He said, 'Why were you so close to those rocks?'

She shrugged. 'I was looking down, I guess.'

She continued to sit, her face lifted towards him, with the expression in her eyes of enquiring honesty. 'What have I said?' she asked. 'Something awful to you?'

'No.' His eye traced the distance from here to the edge, met the sudden fall of space, the misty air. 'Looking down?'

She shrugged again and said nothing, bending to pick a handful of small stones from the ground, running them from one hand to the other while she waited.

He could feel the moments going past him; a wind sprang up; though here they remained in sunlight, a tide of shadow ran over the surrounding peaks, giving enmity to the distance. He nodded, as if recognizing the prospect of bad weather, or perhaps his own foolishness in what he did. 'All right, I'll come with you. Just to the house.'

'Fine.' She rose to her feet abruptly, the matter settled. She put her hands in the pockets of her trousers, looked once over her shoulder towards Tower Crags, then walked with a firm stride down the path a little way ahead of him.

§

By the time they reached the valley, cloud had overflowed the sky; only for a few moments a bare, silver-antlered ash showed itself, printed in light against the dark hillside. A gleam at the edge of shadow, a thin echo on the wind, spoke of coming storm. Their path took them near to the beck; without light, its waters were grey, with foam the colour of dusty cream.

Mark plunged on, his legs seeming to move by some force other than strength. What a fool thing to do, he thought, but there seemed no way out of it now. Something he did not like about being in the valley; in this clear grey light the fellsides closed a little way in on him; the boulders, throwing no shadows, seemed all the more places behind which a man might hide and watch.

The woman was a little way ahead of him; he spurred himself, caught up with her and said, 'Have you seen a paper—a newspaper to-day?'

She paused, looking over her shoulder. 'No. Not seen one for a week. Not been interested. Why?'

'Just that I haven't seen one either . . . wondered what was happening in the world.'

'Nothing and everything as usual, I guess. How're you doing?'

He rested his hands on his hips. 'Not too badly.'

She eyed him carefully. 'All the same, next time you damn' well bring your food or go back for it. We're nearly there.'

Vaguely astonished, he looked about him at the steep, rough fellsides, the beck and the scattered stones. 'Here?'

'My father was . . . I'm not quite sure what he was; he liked to be on his own. Eccentric? A recluse? He wasn't any trouble to anyone, he just liked his own company, I guess.'

'Was?'

'He died a little while ago. We don't have to talk about it now. We turn off there, by that gate. The house is behind the trees.'

He looked ahead. Through the light green stitches of young larch trees he could see a trace of grey rough stone. Some such house as a family might take for the summer; he did not know why he was a little afraid of it. A sheep-dog barked on the fells and his nerves sprang.

'This way,' she said.

She pushed back the large wooden gate that led on to the rough stony road. As he caught up with her he saw her suddenly for the first time as a stranger; up till now, striding ahead of him, she had been in some odd way familiar.

'O.K.,' she said a little wearily, after a glance at his face, 'you don't have to stay long.'

'Don't have to——'

'Your look said, Oh, Lord, what have I let myself in for? You haven't let yourself in for anything. Only to eat and listen for a while and then go.'

'Do all women——'

'Do all women what?'

'Know the thought inside your head?'

She shrugged. 'They get plenty of practice. That's where most men keep their thoughts. Or the ones I've met, anyway. Come on. This way.'

The house was square and simple, with a roof of locally quarried slate. An old car stood on the rough ground beside it. 'I use that,' she said, 'to get food.'

'Over these roads?'

'So far it's stood up. Come along.'

He looked behind him before he went into the house. There was no rain. The hills, royally dark, purple and blue and violet, were draped for the ceremony of storm.

The house echoed strangely. In the hall were coils of climber's rope, a rucksack, climber's boots.

'My father's things,' she said, looking at them with a tranquil respect. 'This seemed the best place for them to be; I didn't know what else to do with them. He hadn't climbed for years, but he always kept them there; he never threw anything away. So I keep them too. Come in here.'

The door opened on a small explosion of silence: something about the atmosphere of this house, with the dead man's climbing gear and darkness at the windows, that made his skin prickle. She lit an oil lamp and the light reached out gently to the corners of the room. She stood, the light on her cheek and side; her face looked exhausted, as if she'd been struggling with a task beyond her strength. She pushed her hair back from her face. 'If you'll make up the fire, I'll go and get food. I'd better tell you my name. It's Gillian. Gillian Fairfax.'

'Mar ... Martin,' he said, trying to think fast, 'Martin—Henderson.' His eyes were searching the room; he could see shadowy bookshelves, leather armchairs, an oil painting of a stony summit; the little golden fire that came from the lettering on the spines of the books.

'Want something?' she asked.

'I wondered if you had a radio.'

'No. Father had a thing about wireless. He saw it as a kind of monster that pursued him everywhere.... Put some more wood on the fire; the room's cold. When people had it on in their cars, he used to shout after them to turn it off, but they never heard. Because of the wireless, I suppose.'

He smiled, and crouched before the fire, making it up with pine logs. He watched the young shoots of blue flame and dusted his hands together.

'Why did you want a radio?'

'I don't want one. I wondered, that's all.'

'I'll get your food.'

When she had gone he stood up, took a pace or two about the room as if trying to come to terms with it, then sat in one of the leather armchairs. The wood burned freely now; the sharp scent mixed in some way with the unstressed glow of the lamp to make a place of comfort and refuge. Distantly he could hear the noise of the beck travelling urgently through the growing dark. He leaned back in his chair; difficult to remember that all this comfort had an icing of danger. His eyes closed; his brain, just this side of sleep, heard the noise of plates, knives, forks and cupboard doors shutting from some other part of the house.

§

Gillian lit the Calor gas stove and found eggs, bacon and beer. She said to herself, tray, knife, fork, plates. . . . Odd, like doing tasks in a dream. Was he really sitting there? The man in the shabby climbing clothes, his skin so oddly pale for a man on holiday in the hills?

Crazy thing to do, asking him home. A strange man . . . in just about the loneliest house from here to Carlisle. That's how women get raped and have their throats cut. . . . Why am I so sure it's all right? Why can't I be afraid of him? Might be I'm past being afraid, could well be that, of course. But . . . something about him that's reassuring, though I can't begin to make sense of him yet.

She sliced the rind from the bacon clumsily; she did everything clumsily now.

He was talking to himself when I saw him; that was the first thing. Used to frighten me when people did that; not any more. It made him the kind of person I knew something about, that I could talk to. He was a thin line of hope, something to hang on to, that's why I asked him. Not a normal thing to do, but then I don't do normal things any more.

If I hadn't met him . . . She stood transfixed, staring at the bacon. Would I really have done it? Not just a thought in the mind, but *really* done it? I honestly don't know. While the balance of her mind . . . Don't feel overcome with misery, can't be absolutely raving, else I couldn't cook bacon and eggs. Just

... instead of life and hope and wanting to do things, there's a space. Nothing there. Knock, and no answer. Don't want to climb or eat or read or sleep with anyone; just a blank. Bit frightening, that.

She thrust at the bacon in the pan, turning it. One edge had caught; she prodded unhappily at the shrivelled blackened shape. Well, that's one hell of a way to cook a meal. Never was my best line, jobs about the house. Maybe that was one of the reasons——

The pain jabbed hard and suddenly, biting through.

Now then, she told herself, none of that. She put her hands in her pockets, rocked back and forth on her heels and whistled between her teeth. This, she had learned, however absurd, was a good thing to do. The spasm passed; she was once more in the kitchen, with the strange neutral emptiness of heart. The man waited in the other room; meanwhile a premature dark brought the fellside closer to the house.

If he'll talk to me ... don't know why he should; he's got his own troubles; that was clear. But there's something about him, behind the stress and the abstracted look; a trace of ... what? Can't quite get it; if I had to find words for it I think I'd say 'a world elsewhere'. As if, having once known some place of peace, his eyes gave a hint of it when they looked at you.

How long will he stay? That's the thing, of course. When the people go and the silence starts.

Well, if you didn't want silence, fool, why come here?

Seemed the only place. Hidden, far off, no one to see if one behaved badly; decent, like going away somewhere to be sick.

The meal was ready; on her way to the door she paused to glance at herself in a small mirror on the dresser. It was so long since she had looked in a glass with any kind of interest, that she looked longer in surprise. The face was that of a stranger, a pale, bony prospect; not really like the picture I have in my head of myself: more like a woman policeman who's just failed to make an arrest. Here we come, Mr. Henderson, bringing food and drink and a load of trouble ... and I'd give a lot to know what your particular territory of trouble is. Perhaps, before the evening's done, I shall have your history too.

She kicked the kitchen door with her foot and went to him with the tray.

§

When he heard her come in, Mark gave a convulsive movement in his chair.

She said, 'You were asleep.'

He rubbed his face with his hands. She stood before him holding a tray; he was astonished and alarmed, for a moment remembering nothing. 'Asleep——' he said stupidly.

'I brought you this. I'm sorry it isn't better, but it's food.'

Sense came back to him; he looked gratefully and tiredly at the food before him. 'Has the rain started yet?'

'No.'

His eyes went to the window; little light remained. 'How long have I been here?'

'Twenty minutes. Perhaps more.'

He pushed the tray a little towards her. 'You too?'

'No, thanks.'

'You've been very kind.' He tried not to fall too wolfishly on the food. The rain whispered suddenly; the fire spat. He had to brace himself against the comfort and warmth here; not to give way to it. Thunder sounded far off, a distant altercation that did not yet concern them. 'Are you ever afraid here, alone?'

'Not of things like thunder.'

'Or people—strangers?'

She shook her head. 'All I've been afraid of——' She stared at the tray as if calculating to an ounce the food there, then said, 'All that's frightened me has been *me*, d'you know that one?'

'Perhaps.'

'When the ordinary person who's been you all your life and done the ordinary things suddenly stops, and someone else takes over.'

Comfort and food seemed to be sending a sluggish amiable warmth through his blood; he said easily, 'Takes over and does what?'

'Oh . . . talks to strangers, asks for help . . . hasn't any way of giving the right answers or making plans for the next day. Someone with her communications cut.'

He tore off a piece of bread, frowning. 'Comes to most of us, I suppose, one time or another. What happened?'

'Hard to explain. No, not really hard but . . . Hard to explain, isn't it, how it feels in your head; you want to say to the other person, Come in and be *me* for a moment, see what it looks like from here, and then tell me what to do. I can say what's happened, and you can tell me it's all right, that lots of people have been through the same sort of thing and got over it. I daresay they have—perhaps they were braver than me. I'm not brave. Or perhaps like Mrs. Gummidge, I just feel it more than other people. Anyway, whatever it is, I've met the thing that's larger than my courage.'

He looked up sharply; for a moment he thought he heard shouts on the wind; even a thud on the door. . . . The sounds came again, without menace; nothing but the storm. 'What happened?' he repeated.

'I'd like you to understand, I'm not complaining.'

'No,' he said absently, 'One doesn't complain.'

'This is how things work out; one asks for it, I guess. I bought it, this is what it cost, and this is all the change that's left. Fair shares for all. But the way life looks to me now, I don't want it.'

It seemed a flat statement, not the flourish of a dramatic flag. He stared away into the fire, and then said at last, 'What kind of life was it before—when you did want it?'

'I had a job on a woman's magazine. I spent half my time in America and I made money and I got the reputation for being pretty spry and tough and smart and free with my bed—all the things I despise, and am not.'

She paused. The rain clamoured down; it was like a third person there at the window. He said, 'Go on.'

'I had ideas about being honest with people. It seemed to me the most important thing. When I was young I shared rooms with an American girl. She used to say, "Never let yourself be serious with the gentlemen, Gill. Weep, and bite your pillow when you're alone, but give them your brightest smile and your tightest sweater, that's all they want to see." I said it seemed mean not to say what one felt, and she said, "Honey, all of life is learning not to say what you feel".'

'So?'

'Maybe it is. If so, it's a lesson I never learned.'

'I don't think one learns much—except, perhaps, how to live with oneself. One is one kind of person, or another. Nothing really alters that, however much one may change one's skin—or one's uniform.'

'Uniform?'

'A man can dress as all sorts of things . . . a lawyer, for instance, a doctor or a priest. But *he* doesn't change—the man inside. . . . Go on.'

'For about five years I lived with a man called . . . his name doesn't matter. He was one of those people who do a lot of different things, so many that you wonder how they have time for them all—writing, lecturing, a bit of acting, bit of broadcasting. Sounds a bit tatty, and so it would have been if he hadn't carried it all off with a kind of lethal charm, like someone going so fast over a rough surface that they seem to travel smoothly. Do you want some more beer?'

He shook his head. For a moment his sympathy failed; he'd no stomach just now for some hackneyed story of man and woman, at odds in love.

She had paused, her eyes on his face. 'Boring you, is it? Too much like everything you've heard before?'

He ducked his head. 'Why . . . no.'

'Well, I can see that it might be. But listen a little longer. I do need someone to listen.'

'Yes,' he said, and smiled in spite of himself, as the words were so familiar. 'I'm listening.'

'For me it was the sort of loving where every cold look, every hard word is a kind of death—impossible to explain, and also, to anyone who knows, impossible *not* to explain—if you get me. There were other people besides me, but I didn't mind that so much, because he always came back to me. He couldn't tell the truth, and I minded about that more than anything, but I still kept going, without too much fuss. I suppose I thought at the back of my mind that in the end we'd get married. Yes—I know I thought that: it was the kind of certainty that you never speak, even to yourself, but which stays deep at the bottom of your mind like a stone under running water.' She shrugged. 'You'd say, I suppose, I wore blinkers. Maybe I did. But after five years you begin to have some kind of certainty, you can't help it, it grows on you like moss. Pity, really. Because nothing, after all, can be certain, and you're better without it.'

'And he?'

'I don't know. One doesn't really, does one, ever? Even after so long, even after being so close. He said things, sometimes made me believe . . .' Her eyes went to the window and the loud evening rain. 'One can believe anything, of course, if it fits a pattern one has in one's mind. One builds up a shape out of so little; it's usually wrong. One finds out, of course, sooner or later. The finding out . . .' Her voice trailed. She put her hands in the pockets of her trousers and swung one leg back and forth. 'Well, it's bound to be painful, isn't it? I started a child, you see, not on purpose, it was a mistake—sorry, is this making you shy?'

He said with conviction, 'Oh Lord, no.'

'Fine. Well, I suppose I thought it'd be all right. I mean that we'd go ahead: I'd have the child and we'd get married. Not in that order, if you follow me. . . . Self-pity plus, this, isn't it?'

He shook his head, and bent to put another log on the fire. . . . People always *talk* to you. Well, don't they? he couldn't help thinking. And what am I doing here, listening, anyway? It all seemed for a moment confused and unreal. Well, but, like it or not, he thought, some part of you wants to stay and listen to her.

She went on. 'I was awfully slow in grasping what was happening. Surprises me, now I look back, but at the time . . .' She shrugged. 'He said we couldn't have the child, and I minded about that, but I did what he wanted.' She caught his glance. 'Can't quite see me in this, can you? Don't sound like the love-them-till-death-and-after type . . . well, maybe I'm not any more. But I was then. Oh boy, was I not. More to eat?'

'No, thanks. Go on.'

'He was kind and gentle, and especially loving, and I thought he was pleased with me for doing what he wanted, and we'd be closer together because I had. All this makes me sound pretty simple.'

'Better to be simple. Better to believe everything.'

'Better for whom?'

'Oneself—in the long run.'

'A *very* long run, brother; longer than I can make.'

'It does no harm to be simple—to believe—to be loving.'

'Sure it does harm——'

'No, no, none,' he repeated.

'Think not? I found out bits and pieces here and there and in the end he had to tell me, just before I went into the nursing home, that he was going to marry this girl ... yes, she was a girl, I know that, nineteen or twenty; I don't remember her name.' She looked at him in vague astonishment. 'That does seem odd, doesn't it; how could I have forgotten? ... Perhaps he never told me.'

He said nothing, looking down and drawing one thumb along the other.

'That's all. That's the whole story. You look as though you were thinking how small it was.'

'No. I was thinking that, a year ago, I'd've known what to say to you. Now I don't.'

'If you get to the point where to be you isn't endurable any more; when you're nothing but a structure of flesh and bone that hurts, like a piece of stiff armour, the only thing is to get small and wriggle out from inside and leave it there. But I can't.'

'Courage?' he said tentatively.

'I've told you. Courage's given out.'

'Endure without it, then.'

'Did you?'

He pushed his plate a little way from him. 'We were talking of you.'

'Well, sure. But chaps don't walk about talking to themselves like that unless something's hit them pretty hard. ... Nothing to say?'

'Not about myself, no.'

'Pity. Might help.'

'You or me?'

'Both of us, I guess. What's the difficulty? Confidential stuff? I was known as Little Miss Clam in my working days.'

He shook his head. 'However boring it sounds, I can't explain about myself.'

'Play it your own way.' She stood, one arm on the mantelpiece. 'Still think it's a pity, though. After all, *why*——'

He got to his feet. 'Among other things, because I have to move on.'

She glanced at him with a slight smile. 'You have, have you.'

'Yes. It isn't that you haven't been so very——'

'I said we'd cut that kind of fritter. Why must you go? Been getting boring, have I? Talking too much? Yes, I suppose so. That's the worst of being in trouble, one does such dull and unattractive things—sad, because it's the one time—the only time— one needs people.' She pushed a calendar straight on the mantelpiece. 'Won't you really stay? Just a little longer?'

He said tiredly, 'I can't do anything for you.' For a moment he saw in his mind the pleading eyes of the clergyman who had said 'How much help do you need?' The desire to run was as sharp and urgent as then. He stood perplexed. His ear caught the sound of the lessening rain; outside the window the stony prospect had a steel-blue shine; flowing apricot clouds stained a darkening sky. He said gently, 'I just have to go, that's all.'

She crossed to the window and stood looking out, as if she already watched him walking away. 'Where?'

'Blencaller.'

'An hour's walk—if not more.'

'I'm rested now—thanks to you.'

She nodded, one hand playing with the curtain. Some of her rough independence seemed to have ebbed from her. 'Where are you staying, at Blencaller?'

'I—I don't know yet. I shall find a bed for the night somewhere.'

She said over her shoulder, 'There's one here, you know.' When he didn't answer, she put her hands in her pockets and said, 'When I say a bed, that's all I mean. I'd say at a rough guess that to sleep alone is all you want for the present, and it's all I want, too.'

'Aren't you being very trusting?'

'No, I don't think so. Whatever you've got on your mind, it's a long way from a tumble in my bed. If you stayed, we could talk for a little longer. Then sleep.'

He shook his head. 'I shouldn't be any help to you, you know.'

'We could find out.'

Again he shook his head, and took a step or two towards the door. He paused, and looked back at the room, seeing it as it would be after he'd gone, the remains of his meal, the bright, wood-scented fire, the silence. 'Before I go,' he said, 'you must just promise me not to climb again to Tower Crags.'

She leaned against the window-frame and said, 'Can't promise that. Sorry.'

He said under his breath, 'Oh, hell.' A sudden weight of responsibility when he'd no heart or strength for it. An insoluble, head-splitting conflict: he couldn't stay with her, and couldn't leave her.

She looked a little ashamed. 'I don't say I'll bring it off. Maybe I'll get cold feet and turn round and come home again and see the evening out, here alone.'

He shook his head as if at some question, thinking, That isn't any use. He said aloud, 'Why me? Of all people?'

But he knew the answer; it was the challenge that must come sooner or later to the man who runs into the mist; it was the moment of reckoning, escaped from in one place, that met you again in another.

His mind considered this, while she stood there, not answering him, passively waiting for his next word.

CHAPTER FIVE

'LONDON looks so beautiful on a summer evening.' Mark went on up the steps of the club; the words were not addressed to him; they were spoken by a woman to the man beside her, a couple who passed on brisk feet, a couple as vastly unknown to him as the spaces between the stars. Nevertheless he gave one glance over his shoulder at the street: lemon-coloured lights and a bright yellow sunset sky, dry bluish pavements, grey stone in tranquil shadow and a glitter on the surfaces of cars: he supposed it was pretty, but he'd no time for it now.

'Mr. Minestaff is expecting me,' he said to the porter, a little out of breath. 'Mr. Gerald Minestaff.'

'Mr. Minestaff is in the Morning Room, sir. Can you find your way?'

Yes, he could find his way. The sombre brown and crimson of the club enclosed him; the pale iridescent summer evening was shut out. He had a sense of guilt: he was late, he was wearing too many clothes for the warmth of the evening, there was a small ink-stain, only just perceived, on his cuff. Moodily preoccupied with these things, he climbed the broad staircase with his head down, not seeing on the walls the shadowy oil paintings of dead actors and actresses, either posing with self-conscious splendour, or, in the heat of the drama, with outstretched arms or drawn swords, caught for ever in some gesture of alarm, defiance, or despair.

As he reached the top of the stairs, he heard Gerald's voice and laugh; some nerve of apprehension within him withdrew at the sound, and he stood, smoothing his ruffled hair and looking at a bust of Thackeray. How does it feel to be dead, chum, he thought, with all your problems solved? Not to have a question, nagging and burning in your mind? Not to have ink-stains on your shirt? The calm white marble face looked back, a shade supercilious. Mark hesitated a moment longer; no trace of Lorraine's voice; perhaps she wasn't coming. Well, better so. He went in.

The large Morning Room, tall and draped in sombre green, held three or four small groups of men and women; they had, as they took their drinks, a hushed reverence, as if some religious ceremony were being performed within earshot.

Gerald was the only one on his feet; he was talking, glass in hand, as Mark entered; he looked as if at any moment he might give some word of command which all in the room would have to obey. 'You're late!' he called to Mark, and continued to talk. Mark felt a twinge of comfort; if Gerald was going to irritate him, perhaps the whole thing would be easier.

Then he saw Lorraine. In these gentle lights she looked no more than thirty; she was sitting, chin in hand, her eyes down, somehow a little bored and inattentive, as if she'd entirely lost interest in the woman who'd put on her make-up and pulled the seams of her stockings straight as though her life depended on it. No woman, he thought, put so much into her appearance, and so soon forgot about it.

'Yes, I'm late,' said Mark. 'I'm sorry.' Traces of the summer evening lay here in the large room; a few torn wings of light amongst the dusty brown surfaces.

'Doesn't really matter. Pleases me rather in an obscure way

that I haven't time to go into now. Large gin and——? French? Italian?—if you say so. Cigarettes and all that kind of olive nonsense are there on the table. Lorraine, you haven't welcomed our guest.'

She looked up and gave Mark a faint salute; like many bad actresses, he thought with compassion, her movements off-stage were beautiful. Gerald was striding down the long room towards the telephone to order drinks. The room, though large, didn't look too large for him, Mark thought; his heavy but not unwieldy bulk travelled with authority, like a ship making for the open sea under a skilled captain. He might have been any age between forty and sixty; when he laughed and heaved his thick shoulders he looked young, but there were moments when he seemed to withdraw behind a shaggy, shadowy look, with lines in the heavy pouched face and drifts of grey in the abundant untidy hair, and then you might have called him an old man.

When he had ordered the drinks he came and stood above the small table, looking down on his wife; his face just now had the broad, jovial yet heavy lines of the sad jester.

'See that man over there?' He sat in and obscured a chair, waving a hand towards a group in the far corner of the room. 'That's Aldous Brayne.'

'Mark isn't really interested in actors,' said Lorraine. 'He scarcely knows one from the other.'

'Oh, he should be, he should be. I like the famous. Why not? I'm famous myself. Been famous for years. No wish to be anything else now; I like the bang of flash-light bulbs and the sort of snarl that critics give when a man goes on being successful in spite of all they say. . . . I like the money too. All this I confess each Sunday at Mass. . . . Why were you late, Mark? Trouble of some kind?'

'No . . . not exactly.'

'Sounds like a reproof. Aren't I allowed to ask? I like to *know* things. That's why I write such good plays. All the time I'm writing, I want to know what's going to happen next, that's why the audience wants to know too.'

'Well, there was a collection of things,' said Mark, rubbing his forehead, and seeing the kind of harassed muddle which constantly hampered his days, and which was quite alien to Gerald. 'I thought I had plenty of time, but then I thought I had so much time that I wrote a letter, and then . . .' It was beginning to sound exactly the sort of thing Gerald didn't like.

'An important letter? I like to know things.'

'No . . . yes. To my father.'

'Oh . . . fathers. The ancients of the tribe. Essential, I suppose, in youth, if what the psychologists tell us is true, but expendable in age. Finish up your drink, Mark; what a chap you are for suddenly dropping out of sight into a sort of cloud of unknowing. . . . Where d'you go when you do that? Would so like to know.'

Mark gave a faint smile. 'Just thinking.'

'If I were you,' said Lorraine, 'I'd stop asking Mark questions.'

'You would? Oh, very well. . . . Where were we? Fathers . . . Well, yes. I have a loving and devoted daughter, but the time will come when she'll wish me in my grave, I have no doubt.'

'She's coming here this evening after dinner. Or so she said.' Slight bitterness crossed Lorraine's face. 'She made one of her rare and sudden phone calls from her digs.'

'Is she? Our lovely Daphne? How very surprising. Must be to see you, Mark; she doesn't come here as a rule. Won't go anywhere where she can't dress like cheap slave labour in the Caribbean.'

'Wouldn't be to see me,' said Mark, making an effort to hide the ink-stain on his cuff, and dropping an olive on the floor. Confusion seemed to be gaining on him. He went on, 'She's in a world apart. The young always are——'

'For a man not yet forty——' Lorraine began.

'Oh, yes, but good gracious, *forty*. She's—what? Eighteen? Nineteen? The most frightening age of all, frightening as a fleet of arrows. I saw her coming out of her dramatic school place not long ago with five others, all of the same age, and all beautiful. Shining and lethal. I ran the other way.'

'No, that's quite wrong,' said Gerald. 'You should stand your ground and look them straight in the eye, like lions, and then they turn and limp off.'

'But even when I do talk to her, I say the wrong thing. I can hear my talk as she hears it: a lot of middle-aged clichés, thudding on to the carpet.'

'Daphne crosses swords with everyone.' Lorraine threw a glance at a group who had just entered; towards one of the men she gave an outline of a wave with her fingers. 'So full of aggression and independence; she's like someone armed to the teeth.'

Gerald looked as though he disagreed, but said nothing.

'She'll get where she wants to get,' said Mark, on a sigh. He saw clearly his own present uncertainty: his guilt and his hope. Beside Daphne's clear-cut ambition he felt like a man who'd bound himself with ropes.

'Yes, possibly.' Gerald drained his glass. 'That's what *I* want for her. A stage career with more ha'pence than kicks.'

'So does Daphne,' said Lorraine. 'An overwhelming single-mindedness that by-passes parents as if they weren't there. Rather disturbing.'

'Single-mindedness is the root of all success,' said Gerald. 'Trouble only starts when one's single-minded about the wrong things . . . such as women. . . . Are you ready, Mark?' He rose bulkily from his chair, casting a look over the room as if it suddenly bored him. 'Dinner, and I'll tell you my plan.'

§

Their table stood close to a window. The long Coffee Room glinted with the gold tooling of candle flames and high chandeliers, and the deep watery gleam of polished silver, but the London street out there had its own grey light, a different place. Mark's head kept swinging towards it, as if it were there he wanted to be.

'Are you listening, Mark?'

'Yes.'

'You keep looking out of the window.'

'Habit. I'm sorry.'

'Well, I don't know exactly that you need be *sorry*,' said Gerald, crumbling his bread. 'If you find my conversation dull, it's a pity, but not your fault. . . . Lorraine, you're wasting your food.'

'I'm on a diet.'

'Slimming? What on earth for?'

'*Pour passer le temps.* Gives me something to live up to. A belief. Like yours. A discipline.'

Gerald, chewing his bread, said, 'A diet is worth a Mass? Confession after a bun and chocolate? I suppose it's a line of thought.'

'You make it sound very childish.'

'Well, let's face it, it is childish.'

'The other person's thing always sounds childish. I have to be *me*; sometimes you forget that. I'm not you—or Daphne, come to that, blazing all over with faith and artistic integrity. I wander through my days indulging myself. I've never worked hard *enough* at anything in my life.'

'More's the pity.'

'Well, certainly, from your point of view. But from mine . . . that's what I say, you have to understand what it's like to be me—doesn't he, Mark? There's something amateurish and inefficient and slipshod about me, there always will be. Those things make *you* very angry, because you're a professional to your nerve-ends——'

'It'd be interesting to know where the money would come from if I weren't——'

'Oh, sure, sure, I've nothing against it; I'm just saying I'm too bored or too lazy or too altogether ungrown-up to be it myself. I can never make a final effort at anything—getting my hair right, or making all my clothes match—sorry, Mark, this seems to be a private quarrel; you'd better get on with your food. . . . I like the theatre, and I liked life backstage and putting on make-up, but when I played Lady Macbeth in some hideous place that was cold enough for the Arctic Circle I suddenly got bored half-way through and thought what an awful ass she was——'

'That might account for a certain lack of conviction in your performance.' Gerald spoke evenly.

'Oh, certainly. Give me credit for this: I never thought I was good.'

'Better, in that case, to leave the thing alone. To pay it the tribute——'

'Give me credit for that too; in my later years I have done that also. Not altogether without help; in spite of being your wife, the offers of parts get fewer.'

'Understandable——'

'Just what I've been saying.'

The brief civilized quarrel spent itself; a silence followed, in which Mark felt like an umpire who had failed to give a decision. Gerald said, breaking the silence, 'Now seems the time, Mark, to tell you my plan.' He appeared unruffled, as if the quarrel were something he had eaten and digested without trouble, leaving him serene. 'I am going away. I will tell you why. There are two reasons. First of all, I'm being sniped at——'

'He's only——' Lorraine began.

'Oh, look now, let me tell him, will you please? My last play—I don't know if you saw it——'

'Yes, I did,' said Mark.

'Oh, did you? Did you? What did you think of it?'

'I enjoyed it.'

'Not more than that? I think you must try to say either *more* or *less*; enjoyment is such a flavourless word; it needs peppering with adverbs.... Never mind. There was a character in it—I don't expect you remember—called Jerome Holly. Of all the names. An actor who took drugs.'

'He killed himself in Act II.'

'Makes it sound a lousy play, doesn't it? Well, anyway, there *is*, believe it or not, an actor called Jerome Holly. I expect he's a sod, all actors are sods, or if they aren't they walk like sods.... And he's suing me for libel. Has Lorraine already told you this?'

After the faintest hesitation, Mark said, 'Yes, she has.'

'Oh, well, never mind. The only reason I tell you is that the whole tedious business is coming up in court in the near future, and the idea irritates me so much that I've decided to go away.' Gerald made shuffling movements with his shoulders as if the idea of the libel action were an irritating skin. 'I don't think he can possibly get away with it, because the whole thing is such palpable ... let's say, nonsense, but when I think about it I get cross in my head, and I can't work if I'm cross. And I have to work, got a new play that's being difficult. So I'm going to Scotland. On the advice of our friend, Jim Elliot, who says it's the place for unravelling. I'm driving through to Kyle of Lochalsh, and then across to Skye. I want someone with me who doesn't chatter too much, but who'll drink with me at six o'clock and listen while I talk out my ideas for the play. It seems to me that you'd do all of those things admirably. All expenses paid. Well?'

Keeping his eyes on the window, Mark felt Lorraine shifting slightly at his side. He hesitated. 'It's a very handsome offer——'

'Yes, it is rather,' said Gerald evenly.

'I—could I let you know? Think about it?'

'Well, certainly, if that's what you want.' Gerald now wore

the muffled impatience of a man used to getting his own way. 'But I really can't see the difficulty. Don't want to bring up painful subjects, but after all the publishing house *has* come to grief, hasn't it?'

'Oh, gracious, yes,' said Mark absently. The large disaster no longer had much power to hurt; it lay behind like a landslide which just hadn't crushed him; when he looked back it seemed inevitable, his kind of thing. 'I was a mushroom publisher, and as mushrooms go, I've been gathered. Nothing left of Harvist and Page but a lot of note-paper.'

'And at the moment you're—as we say—resting.'

After a brief hesitation, Mark said, 'Yes.'

'Well, aren't you?'

'I've been having ideas about what to do.'

'You can have them in Skye. Publishing ideas?'

'Not exactly.'

'For a man who likes to know things, Gerald,' said Lorraine, 'you're not doing very well this evening, are you?'

'Yes, Mark seems to have gone into his cloud; we shall need radar to find our way through.' He rose with a grunt, dropping his napkin on the floor. 'You two will now sit here with heads turned away while I go and perform the obscene little task of paying the bill.'

When they were alone, Lorraine said, 'Not going on the grand Hebridean tour?'

'I don't know. Who was that you waved to?'

'Who did I what?'

'Waved to. Upstairs, before dinner.'

'Up . . . the Lord knows. A face that keeps cropping up whenever I come here. I don't even know its name.'

Gerald returned, putting his cheque book into his pocket. He looked sombrely thoughtful, as if thinking he'd been overcharged. 'Coffee, I suppose,' he said. 'Upstairs, don't you think?'

As they moved down the room to the door, men and women greeted Gerald, and Gerald moved on, ducking his head and saying 'How are you?' and not waiting to hear. Lorraine gave each of these people a rather sad smile, like a consolation prize. Mark walked behind; a blurred, anonymous friend, he told himself: well, that's how the cards seem to be stacked for me. He wasn't greatly concerned; just now the tremendous dream kept lodging in his mind, and when it was there such things as failure and success grew small.

They drank coffee in the large Morning Room; Lorraine was doing most of the talking; Gerald was filling a pipe with devoted interest, and Mark felt himself struck by a sudden curious fatigue.

'Ah,' said Gerald, interrupting Lorraine, as if he'd been paying no attention, looking down the long room. 'Daphne Laureola. In a skirt. A bit gaudy, but a skirt.'

His daughter came down the long room, confident, light and dangerously youthful. When she was sitting with them, Mark thought, she changed the atmosphere; it was like entertaining someone who'd come down from a mountain height.

'Coffee,' she said, in answer to her father's question. 'And brandy. A *fine*. Don't look disapproving, Mother; that's what wealthy fathers are for . . . on my own I drink coke and eat buns, and how I keep my figure the Lord in his mystery knows.'

'Coke?' said Mark.

'Coca-Cola,' replied Daphne, looking aside, a little bored with an adult who was out of touch. 'Don't you go to the movies?'

'Very seldom——'

'And then I suppose you call it the cinema and see Norma Talmadge in *Passing Through* or whatever it was.'

'Rude, Daphne,' suggested her father.

'No, I'm not, I'm only living up to what's expected of me.'

'In any case,' said Mark, 'I'm post Norma Talmadge.'

Daphne giggled. 'Like early for Christmas? Oh, Lord, I can feel the atmosphere growing cold: spoilt child taking up all the room on the sofa.' She sat back in her chair, let her glance swing over the room. '*What* a place, really and truly. No, I don't mean to be rude, but honestly, everything dark green, except for the pictures which are dark brown——'

'Let me remind you,' said Gerald, 'that this club has the most famous collection of theatrical pictures in the world——'

'Well, sure, sure, but what's ever duller than the most famous collection of *anything*: eggshells or Spanish combs or prehistoric razor blades . . . Oh, sorry, sorry, perhaps I've gone a bit far; mustn't jeer at grown-up things, be old myself one day. Dinner been good?'

'Passable,' said Gerald. 'You would have been welcome to come——'

'Couldn't. Work. I work and work, did you know that?'

'We know it,' said Lorraine.

'Mean that I blow off? Shoot a line? Well, but why not? I want to get to the top, well near it, anyway; that's very difficult, it needs heaps of work and nerves like steel; I can feel my nerves stretching and hardening like arteries, and then in the end I have to talk and talk or burst into tears.'

'Sounds exhausting,' said Mark. 'Personally I——'

'Oh, but you don't understand. "Sounds exhausting." Nice detached grown-up voice. Dismissing the emotional young. You don't under*stand*. Oh, talking too much, am I? But you've got to care a lot about things to get anywhere, make a noise about it——'

'So it seems.' Lorraine was unmoving.

'Oh Lord, let's leave it.' Daphne changed her position violently in her chair, leaning awkwardly on one elbow; her hair fell across her forehead. Gerald sat pulling at his pipe, eyeing his daughter with a mixture of humour, interest and indulgence.

'Anyway,' said Mark gently, with some idea of getting Daphne afloat again, 'you're wrong if you think I don't know anything about wanting to get to the top. I climb mountains. They may be small and English at that, but——'

'Oh, yes, you climb, don't you,' said Daphne, suddenly interested, leaning forward with both fists under her chin.

'—when you're on your way up it's the one thing that matters. Mountains are——'

'There are mountains on Skye,' Gerald reminded him from behind his pipe smoke; he seemed aloof from the argument.

'Somebody,' said Lorraine, 'might allow Mark to finish a sentence——'

'But climbing. Now that I should like,' said Daphne. 'Something stony and difficult and high up.'

'Like the paths of righteousness,' said Gerald.

'Mark was talking about mountains,' said Lorraine.

'Our faith has moved them,' said Gerald and heaved silently; his remark seemed to put him into a good humour.

Lorraine gave a faint giggle, but said, 'Not religion to-night, please, Gerald. My worst subject; I score minus every time.'

46

'Not your subject either, Mark?' asked Daphne.

'I wouldn't say that.'

'But Roman Catholics like me and Pop are out?'

'I didn't say that either.'

'Oh, my dear girl,' said Gerald, 'you've got him quite wrong. He's very tolerant.   No, more than tolerant, interested.   He listens. He listened to me once on the subject for an entire evening.   D'you remember, Mark?'

Yes, I remember, thought Mark.   Gerald invited me, soon after we first met, and I expected to see Lorraine.   But she wasn't there, and all the time I was waiting for her, only half-listening to Gerald. It was a bloodless summer evening like this, and he never mentioned her; it was as if she had died unspeakably.   She didn't come, and I began to listen to Gerald talking about his God, because there was nothing else to do. . . .   He seemed, I remember, quite extraordinarily happy, untroubled by questions and self-dislike, accepting himself with all his sins, splashing about in the love of God like a porpoise in a sunlit sea. . . .   Perhaps on that evening, without my knowing it, the dream began.

'Tolerant?' Daphne was saying, looking at him under raised eyebrows.   'Are you tolerant, Mark?'

'I'm——'

'To excess,' Gerald cut in.

'*Tolerance*——' Daphne began.

'A grown-up virtue,' said Gerald.   'Not for the young.'

'Not so sure that it *is* a virtue.   In fact I'm pretty sure it isn't.' Daphne swept a hand through her dark fringe so that it was left slightly on end.   'It makes everything into a kind of easy mush.'

'Oh, now look here,' said Mark, suddenly warmed into irritation, 'doesn't your church tell you to be tolerant?'

'Not as I see it.   For me religion is kind of tough—as we said just now—stony and difficult and high up——'

'I thought,' said Lorraine, 'that we weren't going to discuss it.'

'Apparently,' said Gerald, still placidly non-participating, 'it's a difficult subject to keep out.'

'I manage O.K.,' said Lorraine, giving a sudden small frown as though she didn't like her words now she'd heard them.

'Alone against the Powers of Darkness?   With no help and no comfort?' Gerald shifted bulkily in his chair. 'It sounds brave but bleak.'

'Lorraine doesn't believe in the Powers of Darkness,' said Daphne. 'She thinks it's all a lot of phooey.'

'*Not* fair, Daphne,' began Lorraine.

'Look, does this have to be a quarrel?' Gerald made a vague gesture towards his coffee cup, saw it was empty and left it alone. 'There must be some way in which we can meet as a family—divergent as we are—and *not* quarrel. Surely there must?' He leaned across the table and knocked his pipe out into the ashtray. 'Haven't you any suggestion, Mark?'

Mark found they were all looking at him; he felt uncomfortable, fumbled with a packet of cigarettes and dropped them. 'No, I haven't—any idea,' he mumbled towards the ground as he bent to pick up the cigarettes. He didn't like the way the evening had gone; he still felt irritated with Daphne; he still had to make up his mind about going with Gerald to Skye.

'No idea; oh, what a pity,' Gerald was saying; he looked suddenly bored and pushed back his chair. Mark was glad when they rose from the table; his endurance for this evening had given out; his bedroom, book and reading light began to look like a haven. . . .

He became aware that Daphne was lingering by his side, while Gerald and Lorraine went ahead. She made a small, awkward gesture with one hand, and said, 'I want to talk to you.'

His heart sank a little; he said, 'Well?'

'Oh, not here. Long serious talk—well, serious to me.'

'All right. When?'

'I go to bed late. Come back with me now?'

He could see the top bed-sitting-room in Lancaster Gate, the late night quiet, the sort of conversation he did not want. He said on a sigh, 'Very well.'

They all went down the steps of the club together. The heavy doors swung, shut off the leather and oak, the chandeliers, dead actors, good food and old books. Outside lay the long open streets, washed through with the cool, lightly dangerous air of summer darkness. Neon lighting lay about like tinsel.

Lorraine pulled her coat round her. She was standing close to Mark, and for one moment she leant against him, with a small tired sigh. A familiar nerve in his head began to prickle and ache with apprehension.

He shook his head when Gerald offered him a lift.

'Not? Oh, very well. Daphne I don't need to ask; it's part of her Plan of Independence to travel by tube.' He climbed into his car; If he'd been an unsuccessful man, thought Mark, the doubling up of the large body would have been absurd; as things were, it wasn't. As if he knew it wasn't, Gerald smiled in a pleased way at the driving wheel. 'Let me know about Skye, won't you? Soon, if you don't mind.'

Lorraine gave Mark a sad smile as the car slipped away; it was like watching her slide into some dangerous journey.

'Ready for me now?' said Daphne.

§

Her room made him feel he had crossed into a foreign country without his passport. Amongst the bright clothes and the toy rabbits, the gramophone and the large pots of well-known face creams, the crucifix on the wall seemed a touch of bravado, no more than a pose.

'Mind if I change?' She disappeared behind a curtained alcove; reappeared in what seemed to Mark a matter of seconds, wearing black trousers that stopped short below the knee and a bright yellow shirt. She said, hitching at her waistband, 'I talk better like this.'

'Why?'

'More comfortable.'

Some of his remaining irritation drove him to say, 'No; because you see yourself as you're talking——'

'I *don't*——'

'I didn't mean to make you angry.'

'You haven't.'

'I do as a rule.'

'If you mean you're not my kind of person, you've got it in one.'

His energy to keep on with this gave out; he said, 'Daphne, look: could we not fight this evening? Or at least work our way up to rapiers and daggers slowly?'

'Oh, Lord, I'm so awfully tired of all this soft stuff. It's just a kind of laziness; anything for a quiet life, leave me alone to do what I want and I'll never say a harsh word to anyone. Tolerance—what we were talking about just now. A good-sounding excuse for not running the risk of being disliked.'

'Nothing is as simple as the young can make it sound.'

'Oh, *look*. I get bored with people telling me I'm young. So I am, but I know things, some things that are true.'

He said gently, 'Yes, I'm sure you do.'

'You don't have to be under*stand*ing about it. *Sorry* for me. Everything's on my side.'

He felt anxious only for peace, a truce from this. 'Well, of course; no one's denying that.' He took a toy rabbit from the dressing-table and played with its ears. 'What did you want to say to me?'

He could see her face out of the corner of his eye: challenging and blank with youth. She curled her legs under her on the bed and grasped one ankle.

'Father's trip to Scotland.'

A chorus of screaming little nerves in his head seemed to be shouting, 'We don't want to talk about it.' He said, 'Well?'

'He said he was going to ask you to go with him.'

'Yes, he has.'

'Because you listen, or something, and he can talk to you.'

'So he says.'

'Well, what's so grand about that; don't we all listen? . . . Well, no, I suppose we don't.'

He waited, with his head down.

'See in a way what he means: things seem to go a long way into *you* when one says them; go in and stay there; with other people they bounce off. All the same, I don't want you to go.'

'I see.'

'Oh, look . . . *honestly* . . .' She took a handful of cushion. 'Larry and you . . . *Lorraine* and you,' she corrected herself, as if the nickname didn't sound serious enough, 'everyone knows about it. Except Father; well, that's how it goes. I let the whole thing ride, but when it comes to going on holiday with Father——'

'Doesn't that lie between him and me?'

'No, I don't think so. That's a pretty out-of-date line of thought. Things have changed; they have to make sense now. All that kind of gay, over the windmill frenzy that you had when you were young doesn't go any more. We can't just shrug things away; we've got to take ourselves seriously.'

'People of your age have been taking themselves seriously since Boadicea.'

'Oh, you don't understand. I know what Larry's like. I know her through and through. Oh God, do I know her! She's had it. She went after the wrong things and now they've all turned bad on her and she's nothing left. I'm not going to be like that. Pulling all the heads off the flowers and wondering why they don't stay alive in your hand.'

'Which play does that come from?'

'It doesn't come from any play.'

Acting, he thought, all of it's acting; she's conscious of her face, the gesture of her hand, of the pattern of her body. And yet he was moved. 'I'm sorry,' he said.

'What for?'

'Saying that about the play.' He found he was directly facing the crucifix. He tried to imagine Daphne at prayer, at confession; his mind refused.

She was sitting forward, her hands planted on the bed before her. 'And you'll say no to Pop?'

'I'll think about it.'

But a final sourness had settled on the evening; the dream was far off, nearly lost to him; his thoughts were grey-coloured, moving in a dull cloudy wakefulness; he wanted to be gone.

He came out of his thought, to see that Daphne was staring at him. She said after a few moments in a surprised voice, 'Why are you sad?'

'Oh . . . not sad, exactly. Tired, perhaps. Disappointed.' The word escaped him.

'Because I asked you not to go with Pop?'

'No.'

She went on looking at him, puzzled now. 'You look . . . odd, Mark. Sort of . . . sick.'

He smiled. 'I'm all right.'

'If I said . . . if I made things difficult——'

He smiled again. 'No. Or not more so than they were before.'

She got off the bed in a smooth trained movement. 'Oh, hell! Why is it so difficult to hate people?'

'It is, is it?'

'Oh, yes! I had it straight. I hated you, everything about you; not only because of Larry, but the way you didn't seem to work hard enough, or to care about anything; the way... oh, just everything. And then a few minutes ago, suddenly I didn't any more.'

She was standing up straight, legs apart, still acting a little, he thought, yet meaning it as well. 'Why not? Because I looked sad? It couldn't have been a very substantial hate.'

'No, not only sad. More than that. Bleak and lost. How I'd try to look if I were playing Oedipus Rex.'

'Now that I'd like to see.'

'You know what I mean.'

'I think so, yes.' He was grateful for these moments of truce. 'People in trouble lose their irritating edges and blur into something likeable ... that it?'

'Just about ... are you in trouble, Mark?'

'Not exactly. Yes, perhaps.'

'Is it something to do with Larry?'

'Not quite.... In a way.'

'Meaning will I stop asking questions? All right, if you say so. Couldn't I help?... Well, no, suppose I don't seem to you the right person.' She put her hands in the pockets of her trousers and swung one leg back and forth. 'All the same ... I do think about Larry—worry about her.' She stood before her dressing-table, a slight, gaudy figure, absurdly dressed, suddenly still and heavy with thought. 'Don't go yet, Mark.'

Now she wasn't acting at all. 'All right.'

She spoke with her head down. 'I can't talk to Father about Larry—don't know why, but I can't. But I wonder sometimes ... what's going to happen to her.'

'What d'you mean?'

Daphne made a gesture with one hand as if she were throwing something away. 'She hasn't got anything. I think of that sometimes and it frightens me——'

'She's got you.' Something prevented him from adding, And Gerald.

'Me?...' Daphne put her hands in her pockets and looked with a mixture of amusement, pride, doubt and excitement, at

some image of herself set at a little way from her. 'Don't think
I'm an awful lot of use—we're too different. I'm not trying to
say she's a bad mother or anything, but I don't honestly think I
mean a great deal——'

'If you believe that, you've got a surprise coming.'

Daphne shook her head. 'No, I burnt the parental boat when I
came to live here. There was one blazing row, and ever after a
kind of frozen gulf between us.'

'Only because she misses you like hell and won't admit it.'

'Think so? No, I don't agree. Nothing means an awful lot to
Larry. Work didn't. You've seen her act, haven't you?'

'Once or twice.'

'God help me, I'd rather die than see it again. It isn't that she's
so bad; she just misses, all the time. Like having the wireless on
not quite loud enough to hear. And she knows she's no good—
you heard her talking to-night—and she just shrugs it off. As she
shrugs everything off—any sort of faith, any sort of purpose in
anything. If you do that at her age, what have you got? What
keeps you going on?'

'An awful lot of people manage to keep going for no very
apparent reason. Quite small things can do it, like bird-watching
or an interest in stamps.'

'But for Lorraine?'

He stared at the floor. 'Love, perhaps . . . friends.'

'I don't think she's got friends, not the sort of friends who mean
anything, anyway. As for love . . .' She drew one finger over
the surface of the dressing-table mirror, as if she were making a
sign there. 'I suppose you'd say that you loved her. But that
can't really make her happy, can it? It can't be a thing she can
rely on . . . believe in.'

Once more the nerves were jumping in his head, saying, 'Oh,
please stop.' He said, 'You don't think so?'

'It wouldn't be, for me.'

'You are—as you've said—very different.'

'Yes, but, I understand her . . . more than I want to. I *know*
about her——'

'You think you do. But you don't. You make her sound . . .
like someone who's failed, as if there were nothing for her in the
future.'

Her eyes widened a little; she said, 'Is there?'

'Yes, of course.'

'With you?'

'No, not necessarily.'

'How then? If you think she's going to land the right part by a stroke of good fortune and crash through into the bright lights, you're——'

'No, I never said that. She's got other things—more than you realize. She's lovable and kind——'

'So long as it gives no trouble——'

'You're unfair to her!'

She looked for a moment full of anger, but then turned aside, drooping a little, and said, 'Perhaps I am. Perhaps because all the time I'm fighting not to become like her.' She picked up the cushion from her bed and threw it into a different place. 'So you think she'll be all right? Move on to a serene old age, her grandchildren round her knees?'

'Of course,' he said, and shut his mouth firmly, as if in certainty.

'Very well. If you say so.' She stood regarding him, legs apart, brow furrowed; someone not quite an enemy. 'You still look sad.'

He smiled. 'An habitual, middle-aged expression. Having no special meaning.'

She shook her head, and he was aware of a light, easily perceptive glance, a precise tuning-in to his thought, disconcerting as a piece of magic. That at least, he thought, she shares with her mother. 'You really wouldn't like to tell me?' she said.

For a moment he was tempted, but then foresaw some disaster, with Daphne making him see, perhaps, how impossible his dream was. He shook his head. 'Can't. I'm sorry.'

She accepted this without rancour. 'Very well.'

'About Lorraine . . .' He hesitated by the door. 'Try to understand her. Don't cut yourself off from her.'

She was thrusting her hair into small spiky plumes. 'No. All right.'

'She needs someone to rely on. Someone who'll be *for* her, in spite of everything.'

'Well, I know. Don't we all?'

'Yes,' he said, and added as he turned away, 'you needn't worry about the trip to Skye. I shan't be going.'

§

Two days—perhaps three—before the beginning of the heat-wave, and the meeting with Lorraine in Regent's Park.

He walked, black-suited, in the dark green clarity of shade; there was a long avenue of shade beneath the trees like a long, cool tent; beyond it the light burned, soaking into the delphiniums and the hot, scarlet poppies. Grass sprayers sent up cool whispering growths of water in the shadow; it looked a different territory, out there in the sun.

'Not our kind of day,' he thought; usually when he came here the trees wrestled under tired grey skies; sometimes a light rain touched his cheeks and the backs of his hands. Better like that; the park was all the more their own, and warm places of shelter waited under the thick trees. Now it was alien in its bright beauty, and the people were wandering through.

Not that he saw them; his mind as he walked to meet Lorraine was turning the pages back, finding the day when he'd first met her. Dinner at old Father Elliot's, of whom his mother had once said, 'If you're ever in any kind of trouble, I should go to him.' Lorraine and Gerald there for dinner; how extraordinary to think that he'd first seen her amongst all those crucifixes and pictures of the Sacred Heart; Jim Elliot was a man in a thousand but his taste in art was deplorable. Gerald and Jim Elliot talking together, so that Lorraine was left a little outside, and turned to him as if for comfort. And, as he watched her and talked to her, his own desire and love coming to life with one bound, like the leap of a large nerve, so that when the evening was over he could have told nothing of what was said or done; only that he'd met Lorraine. . . .

'That can't really make her happy, can it?' Daphne had said, speaking of his love. It seemed a sad summing-up; couldn't he, at this loaded and crucial moment, think of a better one? But the images that passed through his mind were confused.

For one thing, the image of himself, as a man in love, kept changing. Sometimes he had been the one in command, loving her with tenderness and pity. These were the times, he thought, when he noticed the small signs of age on her face, when she was tired or a little 'high' after a party. Or when, sitting curled at his feet, she became childishly confiding, pouring it all out to him, telling him of innumerable theatrical failures and near-failures, making him laugh. Laugh, and at the same time feel a little sorry for her, because her failures strengthened his arm. He would go away, glad and happy, hazy with success in loving, pleased with himself, the one who held the strings; and loving, as this one always does, the little less.

But there were other times. Times when some word, some expression on her face, momentarily and unexpectedly guarded, would switch the whole thing round, and he'd be lost in the dingy corridors of mistrust.

It wasn't that he'd much to go on. It was simply that she had once said, 'I lie; I've always lied, lied to everyone, different lies, to make the picture come right.' After that no ground beneath his foot was certain. Sometimes the logical part of his brain took over, asking questions:

'Got any proof?'

'No—not really proof. But I *know*—I feel I know.'

'Know what?'

'Well—that she's interested in other people.'

'That's a bit vague, isn't it. So are most of us. A few more facts.'

'Her own admissions——'

'All before your time.'

'That's only what she tells me.'

'You have to believe something.'

'But she lies——'

'So does everyone.'

'Not as she does.'

'We still haven't got any facts.'

These were uncomfortable things to remember; he tried to put them away and recall some other, less sour, aspect of his loving. 'For,' he told himself, 'I do love her very much; it's been all along, as far as possible, the real thing; wrong, of course, and hampered by lust and selfishness, but as near the real thing as may be.'

And suddenly, as he told himself this, he was struck by a shaft of loneliness. It was not the simple loneliness of walking alone through the park; it was large, as if he found himself walking, not on earth, but through some draughty distances of space; as if all power of communication had been taken from him, and he had no means of making any gesture of friendship, enquiry or pity to the other people walking not far off. It was a loneliness so profound that he wanted to cry out for comfort.

He paused, trembling slightly, in the sun; aware of his absurdity: a forked creature, dressed for town, carrying his hat in his hand, suddenly dwarfed unbearably by the tall, unloving spaces of the universe. . . .

He lifted his head and saw Lorraine. He walked slowly towards her, not yet clear of his isolation, so that he seemed to see her as one sees a figure on shore from far out at sea. She had pulled her canvas chair in the shadow of a plane tree whose strenuous black skeleton of trunk and branches seemed at odds with the summery leaves; she looked tranquil, with the wide-eyed ease of those who have come in out of the sun.

She waved a hand. 'Hullo, there.' The sound of her voice dispelled his mood; he was Mark Harvist, bounded by his own clumsiness, with a difficult half-hour in front of him.

'Hullo.' He sat in the deck chair beside her. There was something a little absurd about the confining frame of the chair; he moved impatiently; the canvas creaked. She was turned towards him, placid, faintly amused; if he wasn't careful they'd start this off the wrong foot.

She said, 'You look as if you hadn't been enjoying yourself. Too hot?'

'No.' He put his hat down beside him on the grass, staring at it, trying to think of the right words.

'You can't possibly be cross. I haven't done anything to make you cross.'

'No.'

'I've had the dullest sort of day; I bought two vests in the morning, and then had lunch with a woman who only stopped talking to eat. And that wasn't very often because she was on a diet. I don't know what she——'

'Oh, Lorraine. Please listen.'

She looked vaguely startled. 'But I am listening.'

'I really have been——' He was appalled at the difficulty of communication: hours and days of thought, of pain, of indecision; now he didn't know where to begin. 'I've had to make up my mind about something.'

57

He did not look at her, but he could feel the difference in her silence.   Not far from them two elderly women had sat together in chairs; they gave penetrating exclamations of relief, then began to talk.   Their loud, educated trivialities went over his mind like birds.   He went on, 'It's the most difficult thing I've ever done.' He tried to give the words the right depth, but they seemed light and without meaning, spoken into the large cool shadow of the tree.

'Well?'   Her voice was muffled; he could make nothing of it.

'Please try to understand——'

'Well?'

'I want—no, I don't *want*, but I do ... think it'd be best if we ... well, if we ceased to be lovers.'   That hadn't been what he wanted to say; it conveyed nothing of the pain and difficulty and sounded pompous into the bargain.   He stared angrily at the grass.

After a brief silence she said, 'Mark.   What an extraordinary speech.'

'I know.'

'Do you mean it?'

'Yes.'

'I really do feel ... I don't know what I feel.   Astonished, I think.   Not able to believe——'

'Please listen to me.'   The loud South Kensington voices of the two elderly women went on, a frieze of noise round the edge of his mind '... And on *Friday*, my dear, they all come to tea.   That was the day I met you in Harrods in the morning, when I changed my library book, that horrid one by an American——'

He bent his head.   'Don't think I'm saying this ... lightly——'

'Well, no, I suppose not.'

'For a long time I've been——'

'Restive?   Bored?   You didn't show it.   Or perhaps I'm slow——'

'If you'll try not to be angry——'

'I'm not precisely angry.   I don't *think* I'm angry.   Let's say it's just that in my world people only stop making love when they stop wanting to, and I can't conceive of any other reason.'

He stared at the bright liquid light beyond the shadow's edge. 'I want you as much as I've always done.'

'Well, then?'

'Try to help me.'

'Help you to do what?' She gave a small, social, unmusical laugh. 'To give me the push? To show a clean pair of heels? You ask a lot.'

'I don't think I imagined it would matter very much to you, if I went.'

'Oh . . . so you thought that. You *can't* have thought that.'

'Isn't it true?'

'No. Of course not. Oh, *Mark*. Honestly. Mean you really thought you could just go . . . and I'd be pleased? Something like that?'

'What will you feel?'

Her next words were unsteady. 'You make it sound as if . . . as if it's settled. Final.'

He said at last, 'Yes, it is.'

'Perhaps you would . . . explain. Try to . . .'

'Please don't cry. Please don't. I love you with all my heart— you're the only person I ever have. No, please stop. I never thought—I didn't think it would mean so much.'

Her crying was orderly and civilized; no one noticed. She said, 'Why not?'

'I always thought . . . there were other people, for you.'

'In the past.'

'I thought—even now.'

'I told you—often and often—there was just you.'

'Yes. But you said other things as well——'

She wiped her eyes quickly and nervously as if she were worrying about her make-up. 'Yes, I see. I told you I lied to people, to everyone; I was trying to tell you all about myself, the whole truth; you were the one person I did that to. But of course . . . I do see. Once you've admitted to lying, no one believes you, even if you say, This is the truth I'm saying now. Bit crazy, isn't it? Reminds me of a story we used to tell at school, Somebody the Cretan said that all the Cretans were liars. . . . You built up something quite different out of what I told you. Was that it?'

'Yes . . . I suppose so.' The elderly women had rather surprisingly taken out vacuum flasks and a small tin of biscuits.

'How awfully . . . well, frightening, in a way. One's a prisoner of all one's done and been; one can't escape from it. Is that why you're going? Because you thought there were other people?'

'No.'

'Why, then?'

'If it sounds pompous or priggish, will you try to understand?'

'Yes, I'll try.'

'For a long time I've had an idea, a hope at the back of my mind.' He paused, staring at it, for a moment losing sight of the park and even Lorraine beside him. 'I thought at first it was nothing more than a cosy fantasy. But lately it's grown stronger.'

'What kind of hope?'

'I can't tell you yet. Not till I'm sure.'

She was looking aside to a bed of tall delphiniums. 'It isn't a very good explanation.'

'No, I know. It's the best I can do.'

She let her eyes travel to the crimson luxury of the rose-bed; their velvet petals seemed weighted with sun. She looked dazzled, confused. 'You mean that you're not bored—tired of it?'

'No. Oh, no, never.'

'But that seems ... so odd. I can't understand why you're not tired. You're not my sort of person at all, really; I see how much you're not, now you've said that about going. You're quite different, entirely different, walking miles and miles through parts I don't know anything about to get to the same place. So why should you like me? I'm not even young any more; naked I'm too thin.'

'I love you.'

'And yet you——'

'I'm going to part from you—yes, I must.'

She made a sudden angry and desperate movement, leaning forward and putting her fist against her forehead. 'Oh, goodness; this seems to me Department of Self-Inflicted Wounds.'

'Don't be angry. Please don't.'

'Oh, honestly. I am angry. Or hurt. Or frightened. I don't know which. But whichever it is, I'm entitled to it; God knows I am. You come, out of the blue, no warning, no real reason, and tell me we're through, and thanks for the ride; yes I am angry; yes, I am.'

'Hasn't anything I've said——'

'No, it hasn't been any good. Words, high, grand-sounding

words; the kind of thing men talk; women know better. You look as if I was hurting you.'

He did not answer.

'Well, fair enough; you hurt me. Is it over now? Do we move on? I mean, away from these chairs? Do we walk together? Better not, I think; don't know how it is, find it terribly difficult to walk beside a person if there's a *thing* between us; you don't know where to look.'

He put his hand on her wrist. The elderly women were being polite over the last biscuit; a light wind swept through the leaves overhead, and broken filtered light fell into their laps like different leaves. He said, 'I can't bear you to go.'

She rose, pulled her hand from him. 'But I have to, all the same. *Yes.* Because I don't want any more . . . nothing more of this——'

'Please believe—I shall go on thinking of you and loving you, and if ever you want anything, you can ask me and I'll do it.'

She paused for a moment, her head down. The heavy leaves sifted again overhead; she put her hand to her hair, standing in a transience of light and shadow.

He waited, looking up at her. After a moment she said, 'Yes, I see. That's very nice. Sort of thing one's quite glad to know. However, just for the moment, it's not enough. Oh . . . not nearly enough. Good-bye, Mark.'

He got to his feet, but made no attempt to follow her, though his heart, a small painful thing, not free of her, seemed to be dragged along the grass behind her.

She walked quickly and well, holding her shoulders back and swinging her arms, like any other woman, walking away from the park.

He watched her until she was out of sight, and the park was a different place with himself alone there. Then he sat back again in the canvas chair, staring unseeingly at the girls who were watering the flower beds with long hoses: the jets of water through the warm air made a sound like the light distant clash of metal.

He'd taken the first step towards his hope. Something difficult accomplished; there should have been a kind of triumph somewhere. He looked about in search of it, but all he could find was a small knot of misgiving as if he'd shut his ears to a cry for help.

This seemed to make it difficult to move, and he sat for a long time, while thin cloud climbed from nowhere and blotted the sun, and quiet shadow began to invade all the park, which had already, though it was not yet late, a look of evening.

CHAPTER SIX

MARK shut the door of the mountain house quietly behind him. Large breakers of mist filled the valley; a frail blue morning sky showed here and there, lighting a bare, scalped mountain head with its hieroglyphics of snow.

He sat on the doorstep; his limbs trembled with the effort of moving quietly through the house. He pulled his shoes on hurriedly and tied them with fingers swollen with clumsiness. The quiet seemed heavy and menacing, as if far off a drum beat.

Gillian, he was sure, still slept; he had tip-toed past her door, his shoes in his hand. His heart was heavy as he remembered it.

'I've written a letter,' he said to his accuser. 'There was nothing else I could do.'

'Nothing?'

'I stayed with her when she asked me——'

'Not long enough.'

'As long as I could; longer than I should have done.'

'No, not long enough. She needed you, and you were the right person. The right person at the right time; a very rare thing. One might almost say, a God-send.'

He stared at the word as if it angered him, turned abruptly and filled an empty bottle from a tap at the side of the house. The bottle overfilled, spraying out and darkening the stony ground. He said, 'Fine kind of God-send. A criminal on the run,' while he wiped his wet hand on the worn corduroy trousers, and the echoes of Gillian's voice went on in his head. Standing there in the quiet with the bottle in his hand, he could see her, wearing the rough climber's clothes, sitting on the floor, angular yet graceful, smoking and talking to him. As it grew later her voice had roughened, as if with exhaustion.

'So you think there's something to be said to me?'

'Yes. Of course.'

'You think there's no place beyond repair, no point of no return?'

'There may be, yes; but you haven't reached it.'

'Isn't that for me to say?'

He said, after thought, 'No.'

'Reasons?'

'Because the worst thing hasn't happened to you.'

'That being?'

'Hurting someone else beyond repair.'

She was silent, her hands still. 'Oh, I see,' she said at last. 'That one. Kindness to others. Quite a good line for those whose minds turn that way. Doesn't take account, though, does it, of the kind of pain you can't endure.'

'There are worse pains,' he repeated stubbornly.

Her glance, alert and questioning, focused on him. 'You believe in God?'

'I'd rather not answer that.'

She sat, her eyes calmly on him. 'Why have you changed?'

'I haven't changed.'

'In your voice . . . careful, somehow. Different from anything else you've said.'

He shook his head without answering. She hesitated, then went on quickly, as if she didn't want him to change the subject, 'I played with the idea quite a lot. When I was at my worst, I hovered outside churches. Once I even went in. I couldn't help feeling a bit mean; it seemed like only going to see someone when you wanted to borrow money.' She sighed, made a small grimace. 'But I needn't have worried. I didn't get anything out of it. Maybe there was something there between the pews and the coloured glass and the candles, it didn't reach me. Missed my wave-length altogether.'

He sat staring at a match-box in his hands. 'Where did you go? Which church?'

'Oh Lord, I don't know. I was beyond knowing about places. I just walked and walked, and went through a door. That sort.'

'Was there a service going on?'

'I don't think so. A woman praying, as if there were some point to it, as if it meant something. I envied her.'

He gave her a smile. 'You could have done it.'

'Could you?'

'It was different for me.'

'It always is——'

'I'd done something that couldn't be forgiven.'

'Oh . . . I shouldn't think that was true. Seems to me we all live on mercy and forgiveness, like an overdraft. You have to accept that.' After a moment or two of his silence, she looked directly at him. 'Have I said something surprising?'

'Not exactly surprising. Perhaps true.'

'I think it's true,' she said calmly.

'This church you went into. What kind was it?'

'Kind?'

'High—Low—Roman——'

'Oh, I wouldn't know anything about that. I don't know an apse from a nave or an incense-burner from a high priest. You do?'

'I know that much, yes.'

'In the world of glossy magazines you don't get far with theology.'

'Didn't you have it when you were young?'

'Oh, no, none at all. Progressive school, no church, parents of the utmost enlightenment: never hit me, never bullied me, always reasonable——' She raised one eyebrow; 'In fact, now I come to think of it, they were Christians *par excellence* about everything except going to church. You know a lot about it?'

'A fair amount.'

'Through the usual channels?'

'That and—my father was a parson.'

'Oh, *well*. Did you swing right away when you grew up? Most parsons' sons do.'

'In a way.'

'And now?'

'Now?'

'Has the pendulum come back to centre?'

He shrugged and was silent.

'You tell me nothing!' she exclaimed.

'I can't. Anyway, it's of no interest——'

'Not even if it would help me?'

'It couldn't help you. Not in any way.'

§

'Your father,' he said, after a silence, 'couldn't he help you?'

'No . . . hardly. He'd lived up here so long that not much of the real world with all that coming and going and people being able to tear other people up into strips made much sense to him.'

'It's a point of view.'

'Oh, sure. It was restful to be with him; even for yourself, things dwindled a little, and you began to see them almost as he did. He was kind to you if you were unhappy, but he couldn't for the life of him understand why you were.'

'What did that to him?'

'Climbing, I think. He was quite a climber when he was young —there wasn't anything he couldn't climb. I don't think he thought about much else; it was a kind of religion: the only one he had, I guess. Know anything about climbing problems?'

'A little.'

'Well, all that kind of "What's the best way to make the last pitch on Bracken Crag?" cuts you off a bit from life. It's all complex but ultimately soluble, like higher mathematics. It makes ordinary human problems look messy and tiresome. As I suppose they are.'

'So he couldn't help you?'

She shrugged. 'I wrote to him and told him I'd like to come here and stay for a bit. He got the letter two days before he died. I found it when I came up here, in a coat pocket somewhere. It was opened, so I suppose he'd read it. Hope he did; I only said nice things, like wanting to see him and be with him and play around up here in clothes that didn't mean anything. The sort of thing he understood.'

In some way, Mark thought, the image of the dead man was beginning to take shape within the walls of his house: the climber whose ropes lay coiled in the hall. 'And then?' he asked.

'I got a phone call. From the local doctor. Father'd called him in——'

'There's a telephone here?'

'Yes. In the hall.' She checked herself, looking at him. 'That worry you?'

'No.' (All the same, it's a chink on the armour; a feeling of someone listening.)

'It hardly ever rings. I made Father have it; he didn't want to, but his heart wasn't all it ought to be, and I said either a telephone or a liver-in, and he settled for the phone. All the same, he had the laugh on me in the end; he always said it wouldn't be any use; he telephoned the doctor, but when he got here, Father was dead.' Her face looked paler and paler, belying the rough words. 'So I came up here. All pretty tidy, in its way. Everything finished.' She flung a look at him. 'I said I wasn't complaining, and I'm not. I'm not. I'm just telling you.'

'All right,' he said. 'Go on telling me.'

'You're listening, aren't you?'

'Yes.'

'I don't understand why, but you are. As no one has ever listened to me before.'

'Didn't he listen to you?'

'He? Lionel? Good lord, do lovers ever listen to you, they only listen to themselves. . . .' She bent her head suddenly. 'Oh, I'd rather he'd died! I'd a hundred million times rather he'd died!'

'That's not loving him, that's loving you.'

'Oh, those are words. I've tried saying them. But I've nothing left of that kind of feeling. I thought I had at first. I thought I'd solve it by loving everybody—*everybody*, no holds barred. But it only worked in the beginning, when I was crying and it hurt very much; things are easier then; you have something to keep the engines turning, even if it's only pain; a few sparks get given off, like wishing to be good and loving. But all that goes, and then there's nothing at all, a kind of dry desert, where there's no grief nor goodness, nor desire of any kind.'

'All right,' he said. 'On that you can build. On the dry desert.'

'I don't know how.'

'You've got a place that's unspoiled—nothing there. Nothing to stop you doing whatever you want. Like a bare room. Easier to work on than a room full of ugly furniture——'

'Yes but—do *what*? Men talk so grand—women deal with facts, large lumps of things as they are. What d'you suggest I

should do? Take to good works? Grow vegetables? Wheel
out orphan children?'

'Well, possibly. But you have to make a start by going back
to life, and hearing what people say to you. You have to learn
that nothing anyone does to *you* can harm you. Only you can
harm yourself——'

She rose suddenly. 'Oh, if only you'd *tell* me! What happened
to you, and what you did!'

'Why?'

'Because it's the part that's missing. Without that, you don't
give me enough. You begin to help, but you stop too soon.
You only give me the promise of help.'

'I've no more to give you.'

'But if you make me feel that I can talk to you—say everything
to you—in a way no one else has made me feel, no one, not from
the beginning——'

'You don't understand.'

She stood motionless in the rough clothes, the lamp making
shadows on her face. 'No, well—how can I?'

'I'd help you if I could,' she said. 'If things had been different,
I'd've helped you.'

§

And now, into the quiet morning air; into the wide, mountain-
shielded silence. Into the quiet, at whose edges the danger waited.

He moved quickly on to the road. No sign from the house;
she still slept. Remembering her he felt sharply lonely, as if he
walked away from someone known and loved. His loneliness
seemed composed of the naked air about his shoulders, and the
unbroken silence.

He had fed, rested, shaved, slept under cover. Now, his brain
cleared, his body little trouble, he had questions to answer.

'What now?'

'I'm going on. As far as I can.'

'What d'you hope to gain?'

'Some kind of freedom——'

'Freedom! Within days—perhaps hours—you'll be back there,
at Scarside. The shutting of the gates, the shutting of the door,
the high walls and the cell.'

He persisted: 'I don't quite mean that kind of freedom——'
'What then?'
'I suppose . . . some sort of peace in the mind.'
'Achieved how? Running and hiding from certain capture?'
'Having a time to be silent——'
'Didn't you get enough of that in Scarside?'
'It was no good there. Nothing came of that silence but the same endless record of bitterness, remorse and fear.'
'And out of this? What d'you expect to get out of this?'
'I don't know yet. But there's a promise, a kind of hope in my head that I can't account for or explain.'
'Fine position you're in, to hope. They may be close—barely a mile away. Perhaps they have you in sight, even now.'

The thought made him glance quickly round; the rough road was empty, nevertheless he felt driven to leave it, and begin climbing amongst the boulders and bracken on the sloping fellside. The morning air touched his lips like a cold moist sponge. As he climbed further, he began to feel in some way revived and confident, alone in his kingdom of rock and cloud; he was comforted by the immediacy of moss and grass and stones under his hand. He stared at the rough strawy grass, and at a stone covered with the scribbling movement of ants. I can see how a man could be a hermit, he thought; bounded by a nutshell, and a king of infinite space.

He climbed on. A little of his confidence ebbed from him; for, after all, what was he to do? In the ordinary terms of finding shelter and food? He couldn't get far; he was like an animal in a trap—a large trap, in which for a time he could wander, but which in the end allowed no escape.

All right, he said, I know all that; something still says, Hell to all that; just give me a little time, a little more time. I don't know why. One more doomed, clumsy foolish thing? One more gesture of absurdity that no man in his right mind would make, that would lead to nothing? He supposed so. But while he could, he had to go on.

It was not until he paused to rest that he heard the noise. A plane? A car? He dropped to his knees amongst the bracken, his heart lively; he didn't want to be taken yet——

Yes, a car. It was coming along the rough road with a furious noisy slowness, near to his hiding-place. When he recognized the car, he smothered the impulse to jump up from his hiding-place and run towards her. That was done now and finished; he must let her go by.

He was surprised how difficult it was. His hands trembled with the effort not to run towards her. He watched her drive on. The sweat broke on his forehead and he felt not far from childish tears: he recognized a weakness of mind and body, only now showing itself truly.

When he saw the car stop, perhaps a hundred yards ahead of him, he had to draw his hand across his eyes, in case he had imagined it. No, the car was still, and after a moment or two he saw Gillian climb out and stand with her hands on her hips, looking about her.

He waited. If she got back into the car and drove on, he'd probably never see her again. Oh, make her go on, he said, yes, make her go on, for that'd be best; that's how it's got to be. Sooner or later, she'll guess who I am; someone's bound to tell her of the 'escaped prisoner', how can she help knowing? Make her go on, because I haven't much more strength.

Slowly, looking from side to side, she was walking back along the road towards him. Every now and again she stopped, as if wondering whether to go on. The mist was clearing; weak sunlight showed the valley and the hills in whitened, diminished colour; the only brilliance lay in the fox-red of bracken and the bronze mist of clustered bare trees; she walked beside a long, morning shadow.

Sometimes, when he remembered it later, he tried to tell himself that she'd seen him before he made any movement; that the whole thing was an accident, no fault of his. But, of course, he knew at heart that wasn't true; he'd lifted his head, made a movement with his arm, and that had caught her attention.

She came towards him, lifting her arm against the low morning sun; he stood up and came clumsily down the rough slope.

When he reached her, she stood silent, smoothing her hair against the light morning wind. Her eyes were on him, and for a moment he could not read them—wondering? hurt? Without knowing why, he began to feel afraid.

She said, 'I found your note. As for absconding husband. It didn't tell me very much.'

'No. I'm sorry. There wasn't much I could say.'

Again her eyes showed something he could not read. 'Suppose not. Didn't you believe me when I told you I needed help?'

'Yes. But I'm not the person to help you.'

She was looking towards the ground. 'Isn't that for me to say?'

'No.'

She put her hands in the pockets of her trousers and wandered to a cluster of boulders. She made a small gesture with one hand, a curtailed movement of invitation, and he sat beside her. She seemed to be shivering in spite of her thick sweater; the morning air was still cold. 'If I'm being a bloody nuisance,' she said, 'you must tell me, and that'll be that. Woman in trouble, obsessed with it, talking too much, boring the pants off you . . . if you see it like that, then I'll go. Right now.'

'Oh, don't be an ass,' he said, rather tiredly; 'of course I don't see you like that. You may be in trouble, and you may want to talk about it, but the wall hasn't closed in; you can still see the other person opposite you. When *that* goes . . .' He smiled and shrugged, leaving it there.

'You sound as if you'd had plenty of that sort.'

He said evasively, 'Most of us do, at one time or another.'

'Not me; when I used to meet up with that sort, I ran, faster than light——'

'And would you still run?'

She glanced quickly at him. 'Yes, sure; what makes you think I wouldn't?'

'Just an idea I had.'

'About me?'

'Of course.'

She shook her head. 'You know you really are a very remarkable guy. You sit there on that rock, having ideas about another person——'

'Why not?'

She started to speak; checked herself, shrugged and said, 'Oh, well, I don't know why not. It's just surprising.' She shuffled her feet on the ground. 'I've got an offer to make to you.' She paused, put her hands on her knees and stared across at the sunlit fellside, screwing up her eyes against the light. 'If you think I'm absolutely crazy, you can just say so; no hard feelings. I daresay

I am—but here's the idea. You seem to be . . . are, I suppose . . . in some kind of trouble.' He thought she was choosing her words carefully. 'Stay with me a little longer, and I'll do all I can to help *you*. That's fair, isn't it? It's crazy, but *reasonable*, after all?'

He frowned; his heart was beating heavily; his thoughts seemed confused by a mist of excitement. 'How could you help me?'

'In whatever way you want.' She was turned towards him, concentrated with hope. 'I'll do anything. I've got the car; if you've had . . . some sort of trouble at home and you want to stay away from it, I've got cash, and there are clothes of my father's. . . .'

He was silent, staring at the road. The excited beating of his heart still confused him; somewhere, quite lost to him, was the rational man who would say no instantly to this impossible plan. He said, 'How far north would you go?'

'How far north? Look. I'll go anywhere. Do anything. I've come to an end. You're my only hope. I told you. This isn't a line, or every woman's dream palace of emotional crisis. Or well—maybe it is a bit of that; after all, how does one know what's behind things, all one knows for sure is what one feels, and this I do know. I've cut loose from all the strings; no one's waiting for me, or hoping for me, or getting hurt because of me——' She broke off.

'What made you stop there?'

'I—something you said last night. About the worst thing being to hurt someone else—beyond repair, you said.'

'Well?'

'For a moment I caught a glimpse. . . . I saw that it might be. Never mind that now. I tell you, I've nothing to lose. I can't be worse off than I am, inside *me*. D'you get it? People are worse off than me, plenty worse off, but they're still holding on. I've lost grip. Nothing to be proud of, but I don't even mind that, because I don't want to be proud.'

'But you want,' he said, 'to hold on to life, else why do you ask for help?'

She was silent; then said at last, 'Yes, I guess that's right. I suppose I do want—to want life. Yes, I do. I don't know why.'

The increasing light was enlarging the distance; prospects were opening in great silent sweeps as the mist cleared away to show the riding, continual summits of the hills. 'And you think I can help you?' he asked.

'Oh, sure. Like nobody before.'

He wanted to say something about the escaped prisoner, casually, to find out how much she knew, but the words wouldn't come. Like walking a tight-rope, he thought, being careful to say nothing dangerous. ... And she? Is she walking the same tight-rope? She knew nothing last night, that I'll swear. I still think she knows nothing, though there's a difference about her this morning, and I don't know what it is.

The excited humming quickened in his head; here it was again, the gambler's move, the diver's plunge. He said, 'Would you go as far as Scotland?'

She shrugged. 'I told you. Places are all one to me.'

'We may not get there. That's only a kind of hope——'

'It's all the same to me.'

He stood up. Sheep were complaining on the hillside; voices, perhaps of shepherds or hill-climbers, carried towards him on the morning wind. The day was alive, the many sounds springing up like small flames.

'All right,' he said.

Her face relaxed. 'Well, blow me. The first good thing that's come my way these many moons.'

'You may not think so——'

'Headed for trouble, are we? Oh, fine, fine. ... Come on, back into the car, and then the house, and then ... north, you said?'

'Yes.' He stood overwhelmed by doubt, misgiving, fear, a longing to tear all this up and say no. 'But——'

Her face changed, pleading for the first time. He stared at her in the morning light, and touched some stony limit of certainty: he couldn't leave her yet. 'No, all right,' he said. 'I'm coming.'

'For a moment you had me worried ... so we're off, are we? And you're still worried? Let it go, boy; put it all out of your mind, and we'll make our way, for as far as we can.'

§

The small room was close and smelled of dust, ink and stale ash. The Superintendent, a heavy man whose grey hair ruffled easily, rose and opened a window. A calendar on the wall, black and white, month by month, everyone's office calendar, flapped in a slight wind. The Superintendent gave it a tired, surly glance, as if it had offered him a guarded impertinence. The harsh black figures spelled out his problem: three days and no capture.

He turned the papers over on his desk. The draught from the window blew them back over his hand; he swore and shut the window. The calendar flapped again.

Oh, blast it, he thought, what's gone wrong? Chaps out hunting, with every modern convenience, and not so much as a footprint in good condition to show for it. He suddenly felt very angry; wanted to shout and bang his fist on the table and *make* him be found. . . .

He rubbed one eye with his knuckle; the trouble was, he didn't sleep. Not more than three hours in a night, sometimes. All those bastards out there slept, all those fools dashing about over the fells came up bright as paint every morning, while he had to drag himself to work from the grey hours of lying awake. He wanted to say peevishly, Oh, look, of course you can find him, he's sitting there waiting for you to find him, a smile of welcome on his simple face . . . sitting where? Oh, Lord, I don't know, somewhere on this ruddy map; he can't be far off; he's been sighted in six different places at once: there's something for you to go on. All you chaps sleep, anything's possible to chaps who sleep.

Look, he *can't* be difficult to find. That sort never are. All higher education and the right kind of voice—gets them nowhere. You've got to be tough as heather roots and twisty as an eel—and even then the curtain comes down sooner or later. He won't have friends, the kind who'll hide him and slip him on to the next stop; all his friends are dining at the Athenæum or walking in the park or sleeping, I daresay; yes sleeping . . . hell, I hate everybody who sleeps——

A light tap on the door. He looked up with a kind of dull hope as a Sergeant entered.

'Well? Got him?'

'No, sir.'

'Didn't think so. Asking altogether too much. Difficult to find a chap; after all you've only got the entire force, with dogs, planes, walkie-talkie and——'

'We found his prison clothes, sir.' The Sergeant, whose sandy hair was thinning before its time, had a stoical, unhappy look.

'Wonderful. Where?'

'At the bottom of Heron's Tarn, tied with a stone.'

'Been there how long?'

'Two days, sir. Perhaps a little more.'

'Not, then, a great deal of use.'

'Except that it pretty well proves that he's wearing the clothes that went from the guest house near Leader's Fell. And that if he goes far out of this district, he'll be conspicuous in climber's clothes.'

'Unless he's changed again, into a lounge suit, perhaps, this time, or a dinner jacket. In which case he'd be conspicuous *here*, wouldn't he?'

'Our theory is that he's been hiding——'

'Oh, *hiding*? Oh, clever, yes; hiding, I didn't think of that.'

The Sergeant seemed to make an effort, '—in some disused hut or byre, moving from one to another by night, and lying low by day——'

'Not too difficult to go and look inside them, I suppose?'

'We've searched hundreds, sir.'

'Well, tell them to search some more. I'd tell them myself, but this damn wireless contraption makes noises like a sheep in a blizzard every time I switch on; nothing like mountain districts for giving you reception with all the clarity of Scotch broth. . . . Yes, tell them to search some more——'

'Right, sir.'

'No . . . wait a minute. I've got a hunch. One thing about not sleeping, it gives you hunches. He may have been hiding. I don't think he is any more.'

The Sergeant lifted his eyebrows to show interest, and succeeded only in looking mildly sceptical.

'I don't think so,' the Superintendent repeated. 'Not only a hunch; there are reasons, like a natural hitting batsman being tied down by the bowling; in the end he has to hit out.'

'Yes, sir.'

'He does, you know. . . . Here come and look at this map.' The Sergeant came and stood behind him; the Superintendent leaned over his desk and drove his thumb at the centre of the map. 'Here we are: Fastness. The hub of the wheel. Come to sunny

Fastness, fell-walking, rock climbing, chasing chaps out of gaol, all within easy reach. . . . And here's Scarside, at anchor by itself on Allen Moor, south of the main fleet of mountains, as you might say. Now I daresay all these reports of his having been sighted on the fells are moonshine, but we can't take any risks. We've got a ring round the central hills, right round them——' He made a circle with a plump hand—'and if he's outside he'll have the devil of a job to get in, and if he's *inside* he'll have the devil of a job to get *out*—or he ought to have the devil of a job, if all you chaps can spare the time from your knitting or whatever it is you do.' He brooded for a moment or two over the neat brown patches, the web of tracks and roads. 'If he *does*, there are two main exits. Bordens Pass, by way of Stile Pass, to the north; Lengaller Pass to the south. Where's he most likely to go?'

'Back home.'

'Precisely. Down south.' The Superintendent stared at the map, as if he might find Harvist on it. 'Know of any friends he had elsewhere?'

'No, sir.'

'No.' The Superintendent frowned, and measured distances on the map with his pencil. 'All the same . . . yes, I'd say he'd try to go south. But he might *just* not. . . .'

'Men go back to places they know, sir. That's been my experience.'

'Yes, perhaps. But there's something buzzing about at the back of my mind . . . can't quite get at it.' He frowned, drawing absently with his pencil on a corner of the map. 'No, I can't remember. But it was something about the north. Keep an eye that way. If he's on the move, it should be easier to pick him up.' He sighed, suddenly seeing the end of the game, and the routine days dull again, divided only by the patchy, sleepless nights. 'And then what? Damn-all he's gained by this fool running off.'

'Sudden impulse, I expect, sir. Mist and the open country; once started he had to go on.'

'I suppose so.'

But when the door had closed behind the Sergeant, the Superintendent sat frowning, making an unfamiliar effort of the imagination, trying to put himself in the skin of Mark Harvist.

Out there, hiding and hunted, fearing capture . . . wonder what life looks like from there? Without comfort or friendship? No putting his feet up or leaning on the pub counter with a pint; couldn't sleep much, either; such sleep as came his way must be full of alarms and dangers; brief dozes, waking abruptly to fear and bruised limbs. . . .

He sighed. Odd, but he felt a kind of sympathy. Harvist was an outcast, and in some way his own long wakeful nights made him an outcast too; he didn't belong to the large company of those who slept. For a brief moment he was sorry he'd said that about the north; he felt on the same side as Mark Harvist; he wanted him to get away.

Or at least, he thought, to have a little more time. 'Time to do what, for goodness sake?' he asked himself, and found he had no idea.

He drew his palm across his eyes, and returned to the map. Silly, trying to get in the skin of another man. Led you up all sorts of paths; no good came of it. They'd find Harvist soon; and the job'd be done. Better so. He looked at the pale light of the window; the still air seemed to throb silently with the hunt that went on out there; it strung his nerves up. Yes, he'd be glad when it was done, and Harvist captured again. After all, the poor chap couldn't get anything out of being at large; nothing but hunger and fear and hard sleeping on rough ground.

§

With afternoon the day changed; cloud suffused the sky, though now and then coin-silver light slid down like a blade, touching an edge of rock, grass or water. They were climbing with a raging noise of gears to the summit of Leader's Pass; once over the Pass they were within the central mass of mountains. On either side the hills rose in steep enclosed melancholy; huge boulders, thunder-grey, lay where some ancient disaster had thrown them.

'I sort of feel,' she said, as they came to the summit, 'that we might take a rest here.'

'Why?'

'You look as if you'd had about enough. I'm tired too. I could pull in here at the top and we could rest on the grass. There's a rug in the back of the car.'

It all sounded very ordinary, he thought; any day's drive in the hill country. 'Well, why not?' he said, trying to make it sound light, but his knees and hands trembled; there was a pressure in his head, and for the last hour in the car some sort of sickness had been gaining on him.

'Here,' she said, when they were out of the car, 'put this jacket on. It's my father's, it's going to be a bit big, but never mind. You look cold.'

He took the jacket gratefully, turning its collar up and wrapping himself in it. He still shivered slightly. When they were sitting amongst the grass and boulders at the side of the road he said, 'I hope I'm not going to be a bloody nuisance.'

She sat casually beside him, drawing out cigarettes, keeping an eye on him. 'Nothing to that. I've got some drink here if it'd help you.'

He shook his head; nausea jarred him like a rough journey; they might have still been in the car. His head spun as if he were being carried fast along some strong running sea. Mixed with all this was the embarrassment of feeling ill in front of a stranger. Oh hell, I'm going to be sick, he thought, and moved away from her, but the need passed, and he returned and sat beside her again.

'Better now?'

He nodded.

'What did it to you? The car?'

'I don't know.' He recalled vaguely the long cold nights, the sparse food, the months on prison diet. 'I'm a bit scared in cars. I had a crash once.'

'Bad one?'

'Yes.'

'Were you alone?'

He shook his head, but said nothing more. After a moment or two she accepted his silence. 'Ready for a drink now?'

'Yes, I think so.' He drank from the flask, and strength began to return. Comforted by the jacket, by the drink, he glanced at her, sitting on the rug beside him. He said, 'You're very kind to me.'

She shrugged. 'Because I want you to help me. That's not being kind.'

'It feels like it, to me.'

She gave him a slight smile; it conveyed an unexpected gentleness which touched him. 'Does it? Honest? Oh well, that's something; sunk without trace in one's own concerns, one can still be useful, here and there.'

He went on looking at her; this odd relationship seemed to consist of moments of recognition, each a little deeper than the last, each following rapidly, as if the normal processes of friendship had been speeded up, to be contained within days or hours. For the first time in many months something hard and frozen within him seemed to melt and change.

'Yes,' he said, 'you can be useful, all right.'

'Fine. Have some more drink.'

'No thanks.' He pulled the jacket closer about him. 'Perhaps we ought to be——'

He broke off, as a car, coming up towards them, from the direction in which they must go, drew level with them and stopped. A broad North Country face looked out towards them, a pipe in its mouth; beyond it a woman, wearing a tweed jacket over a flowered frock, wore also an expression of prim interest.

'Had a bit of bother?' the man asked.

'No,' said Gillian. 'Thanks.'

'Thought you might've stuck.'

'No——'

'Plenty do, on a slope like this. Done it myself, once. Sure y're all right?'

'Yes, thank you.'

The man looked vaguely disappointed. 'Oh, aye.' He sucked at his pipe. 'Got your driving licence?'

'Yes, of course,' said Gillian. 'Why?'

'You're going to get asked for it down there.' He gestured to the foot of the Pass. 'Little reception committee. Asking questions.'

'Questions?'

'Aye. About this chap. Chap on t'run. Harvist. Heard about him, haven't ye?'

After a moment Gillian said, 'Yes.' Mark was silent.

'Aye.' Again the man looked disappointed. 'Well, you'll find a couple of cops down at the bottom of t'road. Nosey as maiden aunts. Fair daft I call it; anyone can see I'm on holiday and not straight out of gaol; what would I be doing with Emily here in gaol——'

'It's not daft at all, Joe; it's the law and good luck to it.' The woman spoke from her tweed and flowered cotton. 'The sooner they catch him the better I'll be pleased.'

'Go back and tell them, I should——'

'Now you be quiet, Joe Marchant. He's a man who's done wrong, and being rightly punished, and that's——'

'Oh, aye, we've heard all that before.' The man looked bored. 'All the same you can't help wanting him to get away with it; the odds are all against him, aren't they? It's a sporting effort; they tell you not to give him a lift, but *I'd* give him a lift all right if he asked me; I'd say "Hop in, chum——"'

'Not with me here you wouldn't, Joe Marchant.'

'Oh, aye; I forgot that.' The man grinned. 'Well, cheerio. I wish him luck, all the same.'

When the car had gone Gillian and Mark were silent. Mark could feel the heavy beats of his heart. The Pass was silent and empty; the grey boulders seemed to come a little closer with the silence. Gillian had a cigarette in one hand and matches in the other; she swung the match-box round between her fingers as if she were debating whether to use it.

Mark tried to frame some sort of question, but the words wouldn't come. Well, I suppose this is it, he thought; we've got to go on down the hill, and I suppose there she'll turn me in; she can't have much doubt . . . surely she can't? He glanced at her; her eyes were still on the match-box and he could read nothing from her face. Would she, perhaps, refuse to go further? He thought of putting his cards on the table; of telling her the whole story and making his own way back, away from the road block; but this was so final a step that he recoiled from it: once she knew for certain, they'd have to part; as things were, he could still hope . . . for what? He shook his head, defeated, waiting for her to speak.

She said at last, 'We'd better go on now. Feeling all right?'

'Yes, thanks.' His heart was suddenly empty with lack of hope: some promise which had seemed to be coming closer, now appeared to be lost for ever.

She nodded, saying nothing more, and got into the car. Before he followed her, he looked down the snaking road to the foot of the Pass.   Trees, traces of light down there, and movement: the little sinister insect movement of cars grown small.   And beyond them the hills again: the taller hills, lifting high shoulders against the sky.

He sat beside her in the car.   Her face looked set and firm, though that might just be the strain of driving down the steep hill. She still gave him comfort, sitting there beside him; but, he told himself, there at the bottom of the hill, this brief history of escape, which was already beginning to have the absurd shape of all finished things, would be ended.

Now, as they took a bend in the road, he could see the figures down there plainly.   The sunlight defined them with pointed accuracy; they had the significance of people in an arena.   By the side of the road a beck ran down over stones, clear water coming briskly with arched sinewy vigour, falling over the rocks into the busy icy confusion of shining foam.   It seemed in some way the essence of his brief mountain freedom.

They were down now.   The road was blocked by a wooden pole placed on two trestles; a police sergeant and three constables were ranged on either side, their blue uniforms giving the whole thing an air of prospective excitement.   A police car was parked a little way off.

'Good afternoon.'   The Police Sergeant who approached them, notebook in hand, was young, suntanned, with a slight North Country accent; put him in shorts, sweater and sou'wester, thought Mark, and you'd meet him a dozen times in the hills, trudging earnestly and giving you good morning.   'May I see your driving licence, please, miss?'

Mark waited.   Gillian said, 'Why, sure.'   She handed it to him. 'It's all yours.'

The Sergeant looked at it and handed it back.   'Which way've you come?'

'From Bleadale.'

'Aye.'   The Sergeant was writing down the number of the car. 'Not seen anything suspicious—chap trying to hide, asking for food, a lift, summat like that?'

Scarcely a moment's pause before Gillian said, '*Quite* my favourite sort of thing; no, unfortunately we haven't.'

'Aye. If you don't mind, I'll have to look in the back of your car. . . .'

'Go ahead,' said Gillian. 'Old clothes, mostly. A sandwich or two, I daresay.'

The Sergeant gave a slight smile, turned the clothes over, withdrew himself from the car. He stood with pencil poised. 'Your name?' he said to Gillian.

'Fairfax. Gillian Fairfax.'

Another car had drawn up behind them; a small boy was leaning out of the window, calling, 'I say, look, Daddy, cops!' The Sergeant did not glance their way. He made a small gesture with his pencil to Mark. 'And this gentleman——?'

'Fairfax, too,' said Gillian, before Mark could speak.

'Your husband?'

'My—brother.' The hesitation was brief.

'Aye. Have you any means of identification?'

He seemed to be addressing Gillian again and she pulled a letter from the space under the windscreen of the car. 'This help you?'

The Sergeant looked at it, nodded and handed it back. He turned to Mark, ducking his head lower. 'And you, sir?'

Mark hesitated; there was a spinning noise in his head; he knew how much he'd hoped to get through this; how little chance there was. He said, 'I'm,—on holiday. I doubt if——' His brain froze; no further words came; they were all silent. In the silence he could feel his chances ripping away——

'Isn't there a letter in your pocket? Have a look.' Gillian's voice: perhaps only to his ears a little breathless.

Bewildered, obeying her automatically, without much hope, he put his hand in the pocket of the strange jacket. His fingers closed on an envelope; he drew it out, looked at it through the blur of silence and apprehension, with the Sergeant's shadow falling across it: 'Graham Fairfax, Esq.'

'Here,' he said.

The Sergeant glanced at it, was about to hand it back, then glanced at it again. Mark waited, the sound in his head growing louder.

'I see, sir.' The Sergeant made no explanation of his second glance, handing the letter back. But he did not seem quite ready to let them go. 'And ye're heading for——'

'Well, that isn't quite decided.' Gillian sounded friendly and conversational. 'We're taking it easy, motoring round, staying where we please; sleeping in the car sometimes.'

The Sergeant nodded, took a step back from the car. Gillian's hands rose to the wheel, but the Sergeant stepped forward again. The small boy behind gave a cheer.

'You do the driving, miss?'

'Yes. My brother's been ill; that's why we're taking it easy.'

'Aye.' He stepped back, with a little final movement of his hand that might have been defeat. 'Very well. Good day.'

§

The questions raged in his head; he remained silent. His heart thudded heavily with relief, but his mind was already going ahead, meeting the hurdles that waited. Gillian first, he thought: how much does she know? She can't have much doubt left, yet she's saying nothing. Is that the drill? If so, my dear, it won't do; who'll believe that you didn't know who I was? I should never have let this start; it's turned into my kind of trouble: I should leave you, and it's damned hard to do. Here we go, deeper into the mountains, but there's no safety there; we can lose ourselves in them for a time, but we can't get beyond them into the open country again. We had luck at the road block; you don't have luck twice. So what now? A pause, somewhere, perhaps; time to think. . . .

They were climbing slowly. The country was rough and deserted; a whitish sun sent pools of shadow sliding down the mountain-sides; over streams and rocks was a radiance like the reflection from snow. He said, 'I'd like to stop here.'

'For the usual reasons?'

'No; I'd like some food. And a longer rest than we had last time.'

She stopped the car, it seemed a little unhappily. 'You don't think . . . it'd be better to go on?'

He shook his head.

'Very well.' But she still did not seem happy; as she fetched the rug and food from the car she was silent. He followed her on to a grass patch under the foothills of High Skeld. The evening sun was warm; as he lay and looked up he could see the crags of High Skeld, half in shadow, but draped with fallen flags of light. She brought cold meat, rolls and fruit, and two flasks of coffee, but she did not at once sit beside him. With her hands in her pockets, she moved a little restlessly, looking into the distance. After some moments, seeing nothing, she came and sat beside him. The silence between them was filled with the complaining of sheep.

He said at last, 'Why did you lie to the police?'

She hesitated, but when she spoke, her voice was casual. 'To save time and trouble. If I'd told them the truth, they'd have had to ask a lot more questions. Tedious; I wasn't in the mood for it.'

He said, 'The truth?'

She shrugged. 'That I'd met you, climbing, on a day when you'd forgotten your food and given you a lift.'

He pulled at the grass beside him. It wouldn't do; he should get clear of her quickly, yet he was held both by weakness and a thread of anticipation, the hope of an answer to an unformed question. Before he could speak, she went on, 'The police aren't my kind of chaps. I don't like people who've got it clear between right and wrong. I'm outside all that now—way outside it. More coffee?'

'But you can't make yourself an outlaw—not obey any of the rules—live at odds——'

'Can't you? Why not? Look, I'm like a person whose needle doesn't swing to the north any more. I walk to my own tune, my own pace; I have my own rules. I don't go along with any-one—except you.'

'Why me?'

'Because you know what it's like—I think you know what it's like—to feel forsaken.'

'Yes,' he said at last. 'Yes, I know that.'

After a few moments she asked, 'D'you know what day this is? What day of the month?'

He could see the last date on the calendar in the cell; he tried to think. 'The end of April . . . the thirtieth.'

'Yes, that's what I make it. Round about the thirtieth. I tried not to know the date, but where does that get you? Better to let yourself know things. Lionel's getting married on the thirtieth. He didn't tell me, it came my way by accident—or rather a kind friend, you know how kind—why do people do things like that? Telling me, I mean? Sometimes I think we all behave to each other as if we were going to live for ever.'

He glanced at her; she was looking towards the distance, with the light of the evening sun defining her cheek. He felt in himself the heavy ache of responsibility misused, of a weight that he hadn't the energy to carry. The unmusical insistent wail of a sheep seemed to thrust the unwelcome thought home. He said, 'To-day?'

'Yes, I think so. But of course, that doesn't matter, really, does it. Though it seems to. But the moment in time when a thing happens isn't really important, it's the climate that made the thing possible.'

He said with sympathy, 'But the moment hurts.'

'Oh, sure. It gives the imagination plenty to work on: you think, now they're dining, now they're in bed together, now it's all as it was with me.' She shrugged. 'So what.'

The noise of the sheep grew louder; he frowned with irritation and said, 'When you say we all behave to each other as if we're going to live for ever——'

'Well?'

'That sounds like . . .' He frowned against the continuing noise of the sheep.

'Pity? Kindness to others? No, boy, I meant *me*; what had been done to me. I'm inside a space-helmet; I don't see other people. Not pretty; just the way it is.'

He nodded. He wanted to say more, but the noise of the isolated sheep distracted him and he glanced upward. On a ledge some thirty feet up the sheep stood complaining insistently. The small apron of grass on the ledge had been entirely eaten away. Now and again the sheep made nervous scrambling movements to the limits of its ground, but the rocks were too steep below it, and the ledge above, from which it must have jumped, was too far for it to climb back.

Gillian's eyes followed his. 'What will it do?' she asked.

'I don't know.' The animal's frenzied scramblings jarred his nerves; its bleats grew louder, more pitiful. 'It's cragfast. Unless it'll jump to that other ledge, lower down, it'll starve. Go *on*,' he said to the sheep, 'you can do it—oh, go on, don't be such a fool.' The animal made its unlovely movements, its hooves slipping painfully on the edge of the rock. It scrambled back on to the safety of its ledge, made efforts to gnaw at the stripped and fouled soil at its feet, bleated again. 'Oh Lord,' he said, 'the blasted silly thing.'

They sat looking at the sheep with fixed, unhappy attention. It was an ugly thing, dirty and frenzied. Its patient silly face belied the frantic movements of its legs and the painful and desperate bleat.

'It isn't going to jump,' said Gillian.

'No.'

'We ought to be going on.'

'Yes . . . perhaps.'

The far hills were drowning in a mist of milk and amber; here mild blue shadow gained on the fellside. He got to his feet and went over to the base of the rocks. They rose steeply, but here and there he could trace the little flare of white, the scratches of climbers' boots. He felt the rocks with his hands. They were dry and warm. His fingers moved over the smooth surface.

'This is a rock climb,' he said. 'Not a very difficult one, by the look of it. Not unlike many I've done, in the past.'

He paused, tentatively reaching for the first handholds. Gillian stood up. 'We should go on. Besides you're in no condition to——'

He was frowning and looking upwards, feeling for the holds. 'Food and drink's pulled me round.'

'All the same——'

'It isn't far.'

'What could you do?'

'Chivvy the silly thing off, so that it jumps to the lower ledge.'

'Let me try.'

'Done any rock climbing?'

'No, but——'

He shook his head. 'Not the time to start now.' He bent to untie his shoes.

'What are you doing?'

'Can't climb in these. Socks are better.'

'What can I do?'

He grinned a little feebly. 'Stand at the bottom and cheer.'

'If you fall——'

'I shan't fall.'

The first move was a difficult one; he had to make a high stretch with his right leg, find the small foothold, and get himself up with only the thinnest help for his hands. He tried once, twice; his foot scraped off; his knee ached and he panted a little.

'Let me try,' said Gillian. 'Please let me try.'

He shook his head. The sheep scrambled and cried; the harsh, unvaried note made him impatient; he swung his leg high, felt the small edge firm, scrabbled with his hands and got the handholds and was started on the climb.

Odd how familiar it seemed; his knees and hands trembled; he was climbing badly, but the tang of it all came strongly back to him: the challenge of the thin, scraped footholds; the concentration that narrowed your world down to the rock before you, the ledge for your feet, the hold for your hand.

The next two moves were fairly easy; he paused when he'd done them, surprised at the height he'd gained. The distance made his head swim a little; he shook it free. From below Gillian said, 'Are you sure you're all right?'

He nodded briefly. For a moment he could not see his next move; the rock seemed to rise unmarked straight above his head, smooth and ungenerous. He stretched upwards, feeling with his hands, finding nothing. Then he caught sight of the buttress of rock at his side. The rock swelled out, overhanging the rocks below; on its face was the unmistakable scratched foothold.

The handhold was above it, a good one; at another time he wouldn't have hesitated. But the footholds were mere ridges in the rock, not a toe's width. For a few moments he would be dependent entirely on his hands. If they failed him, he would fall.

The noise of the sheep grew louder. 'Oh, be quiet,' he said. 'Be quiet, you fool, be quiet.' He swung one foot out and reached with his hand.

His foot skidded off, his courage misgave him, and he drew back and rested. Then tried again. This time he had the hand-hold firmly ('Don't climb with your hands'—but this was climbing as best he could, not according to the rules); his right foot—then his left—was on the fraction-wide ledge; he was out on the buttress of rock. There was a moment when fear came right up and broke over him, a different fear from the fear of capture; sharp, sweating, immediate: the fear of pain. He could remember the fear from other climbs long past: cursing his foolishness in starting the thing; nothing in his mind but the ugly insufficient rock and the space below.

He swallowed, shut his eyes. The noise of the sheep went on, just above his head now. 'Oh Lord,' he thought, 'let me get to it.'

His head cleared; he opened his eyes, swung his right leg almost blindly and found a ledge. His foot was firm; he found a true place for his hand, and with a merciful levering of good holds, he was round the buttress, on the easier rocks. He rested, while the trembling of his knees stilled. He looked down at Gillian and grinned. 'So far,' he said, 'so good.'

'Are you all right?'

'Climbing like a bird.'

Liar, he thought. The sheep had seen him and made clumsy efforts to escape, turning from one side of its ledge to the other.

'Oh, keep calm, you idiot,' he said. 'I'm not going to hurt you. Why d'you think I've come all this way, you fool?' It seemed to help him, to abuse the sheep.

When he drew level with it, it grew frantic.

'Now,' he said. With one foot firmly on a good hold, he put the other across on to the sheep's ledge. The animal sprang and bleated wildly. 'Pipe down, pipe down. I'm a friend, you ass, don't you know a friend when you see one?' He had both feet on the ledge now; there was scarcely room for him and the sheep; he had good handholds, but the animal twisted and scrabbled with a desperate sinewy toughness, and he was afraid it might push him off.

To make it jump on to the other ledge, he must use his hands. He tried with one, but the rough woolly haunches of the sheep buffeted and eluded him. Bracing himself, he let go. The distance from the ground was no more than thirty feet, but the ground below him seemed to swim past like running water. With his back against the rock face he thrust with both hands at the sheep.

'Go on,' he said, 'jump. You can do it. It's your last chance; I can't stay here for ever. If you won't move, you'll stay here and starve; I've got to get on. I've troubles of my own.'

The animal kicked and resisted; for one moment he thought it would push him clear of the ledge; but a savage unreasoning impatience drove out his fear, and he set his teeth and pushed with desperate strength.

The sheep pressed back, slipped with his front hooves, bleated in fear, then seemed to quiver, freeze for a moment in indecision, then spring with bent forelegs and land on the lower grassy ledge.

'Well, that's that,' he said. 'Good hunting. Don't try climbing back, because you've had it if you do.'

Now that the task was done, he felt very weak; all his limbs trembled. He lifted a hand to Gillian.

'Well done,' she called, 'well done.'

He looked down to the sheep, gnawing with frenzied hunger at the grass. 'Yes, perhaps.'

The way down was oddly easy; it was like dreaming he did it. When he reached the ground again he slumped on to a rock.

Gillian put a hand on his shoulder. 'All right?'

'Yes.'

'I thought you were going to fall.'

He glanced back at the rocks. They looked harmless in evening shadow; not, after all, very high. 'It wasn't much of a climb, but then I'm out of practice.'

'It was well done,' said Gillian. 'Now we have to go on. Are you ready?'

He stood up slowly, with some reluctance. 'I'm afraid I've muddied these clothes——'

'Cut your hand too.'

He was surprised to see the blood on his fingers; he had felt no pain. Now the small wound smarted.

'I'll bind it up—but not now. Now we must get on.'

For the first time he felt a spasm of irritation with her, inspired perhaps by weariness: he didn't want to be taken by the arm like this and driven on; to go on could only lead ultimately to his capture. 'Why?'

'We stayed too long there.'

'What d'you mean?'

'I don't know. I just feel we did.' She bent abruptly to gather their belongings from the ground, as if regretting her words.

At the door of the car she paused. 'Well—are you coming?'

He felt an extreme reluctance to move, yet at the same time he had no energy to protest; weariness had soaked him like a heavy shower. He said, 'Yes; very well,' and in silence sat beside her, to begin the journey again.

§

It was some twenty minutes later, at the summit of Stile Pass, that they saw the man running. He was coming down a rough traverse that led from the tall buttresses of rock, between boulders and coarse blond grass to the road; and his figure, small in the distance, was discernible because of his red woollen cap. This small blob of red leaped and danced downward against the shadowed hillside, now and again touched by a shaft of sun.

'Only a fool,' said Mark, 'comes off a mountain like that.'

Gillian drove on, considering the rapidly moving figure with its lively cap. 'Yes, he's travelling all right. Wants to get home to dinner.'

'Or showing off.' Mark found that his irritation had now turned against the youth whose leaps and runs seemed full of an arrogant cocksureness. 'All alone, too; if he sprained an ankle or broke an arm he might lie there a long time. Hardly anyone on this road in the evening.'

'But in fact,' said Gillian, 'we shall meet him almost certainly at the bottom of his path.'

'Yes.' But he found himself hoping that somehow they'd get ahead and miss him.

The red cap dipped and swung, never losing pace——

'Hullo,' said Gillian. 'He's waving.'

Mark frowned. Unmistakably the figure had halted in its break-neck run and was waving with both arms.

'We shall have to stop,' said Gillian. Her voice was tentative; for the last half-hour constraint had lain on them.

'Yes.'

He felt cold and defeated; somehow he had no heart for this. The young man still came on, pausing every now and then to wave. Now that they were closer to him, they saw that he was calling to them.

'Wants a lift, I suppose,' said Mark. 'Running down to catch us.' He thought, but did not say, If you'd not hurried me on, we'd've missed him.

Closer still, and they could see the young man's face. Under the gay cap it was incongruously white.

Gillian drove level with him and stopped. He plunged at the

car, as if it were a flung rope in a heavy sea. He was not more than nineteen; he wore neither sweater nor jacket, and shivered in the evening wind.

'I saw you—from the top of the—of the path——' He was breathing hard, and his words came out unevenly. He swallowed; his mouth was trembling. 'I need help—someone to get help——'

'What's happened?' said Mark. For the first time he saw blood on the boy's shirt. 'Are you——'

The boy looked at the blood too. 'No, no, not me. It's my friend. We were climbing on Heel's Tor. He was leading.' He drew his hand over his face. 'He fell. I couldn't do anything; he fell past me. It's a hard climb, a Severe; I said all along it was too ... He's badly hurt.'

'How bad?' Gillian's voice was brief; the boy wetted his lips; his full-mouthed indecisive face looked bruised, shaken out of order by shock.

'I think ... I don't know ... I think maybe he's had it.' He looked as though his own words had scared him; he swallowed again. '*He* thinks he's had it.'

'How d'you know?' Mark was leaning forward in the car. A trace of the late sun touched the boy's face, colourless beneath the red cap.

'Oh, because he kept saying things. ... Kept on saying ...' The boy drew his hand across his mouth.

'What things?' Mark heard his own voice, sharp and edgy; the boy blinked at it.

'He said there was something on his mind. ... Half the time he doesn't seem to make sense; maybe he's a bit delirious. He keeps moaning that he's going to die and he wants a priest.'

Mark was silent. His eyes slipped from the boy to the curtailed view through the windscreen of the car. Steep rough ground on either side, one in shadow, one in light; no one anywhere on the road or the fellside; a dry, warm silence on the summit of the Pass.

'A priest?' said Gillian.

'Aye, he kept on and on about it; but what good's a priest to him?—it's a doctor he wants. Can you take me quick to get help? To a telephone? They'll send the Rescue boys from Fastness——'

'Right away——' Gillian began.

Mark touched her arm with his hand. 'Just a minute.'

'What is it?'

He hesitated, frowning at the light that for a moment dazzled the windscreen. Then, a little clumsily, he thrust at the door, got out, and stood in the road. The soft wind touched his face, a reminder of different and easy things, now far off. 'I'd better go up to him,' he said. He was buttoning his jacket; he saw that his hands trembled a little. 'I'll see if I can do anything ... help him in any way. I've met things like this once or twice before; I've some idea what to do.... Can I find him easily?'

'Aye: he's at the very foot of the climb. You know the Traverse? ... O.K., follow it to the bottom of the rocks, and he's—he's there. You're bound to see him. I did what I could, I put all my clothes on him, and put a stone against his leg; he broke his leg, you see. But——'

'Yes, I'll go,' said Mark. He saw Gillian's eyes raised to his face; he avoided them; he was anxious for her to be gone.

'But his friend here can go back to him,' she said; her voice was puzzled, uncertain. 'We can get help——'

'No ... no ... it's best that I should go.' Mark could feel his throat drying; he hoped she wasn't going to be difficult; his nerves were pulled out like wires.

'But you and I could get——'

'Oh, leave me alone! Let me go to him!'

When he saw the rush of tears over her eyes he knew how sharply he had spoken, but there was no time to regret it or take it back. She said, 'Very well,' so quietly that he could scarcely hear.

The boy hesitated. 'He's awfully bad. Supposing while we're gone——'

With the perception of weariness and urgency Mark saw that the boy thought he should stay with his friend and was afraid to stay.

'I'll see to him,' said Mark. He was surprised how much authority his voice had.

When they had gone, he turned and began the ascent. It was rough and stony, fairly steep; the crags about him were built in a difference of quiet light and shadow; in a fall of ground to his left a tarn gave back the placid blue-white of the evening sky. Perfection hung in the air.

He went on over the clumsy stones, breathing harder, and feeling, in spite of the colder wind, the sweat on his forehead. More of this rough traverse than he'd expected; the path rose to avoid large out-crops of rock, fell as it crossed the reddish slopes of scree. He followed it mechanically, his mind elsewhere, only now and again recalled to the present by a skidding of his foot, or by some tall dark profile of rock high above him, staring out towards the sky. No one anywhere; no one in any part of the Pass below him, on this rough traverse or the higher rocks. The climbers—if there'd been any here to-day—had all gone home. All except the boy who lay waiting there.

The lulling, rhythmic effort of making his way upwards set his thoughts free: they swung out over the past, touching odd, trivial things: words he'd spoken, lines of poetry learned long ago; three lines, spoken in some schoolroom, now returning sharply to mind: 'The hills, like giants at a hunting, lay, Chin upon hand, to see the game at bay—Now stab and end the creature!' ... Gaining height, he seemed to be climbing out of his own past, into new and strange air.

He breasted a sharp rise in the ground. For a moment it was the triumph of making the height, of commanding the rocks below you and the fallen, haze-drowned distance and the far streams.

And then he saw the boy. Below the steep-shadowed rocks; still with a stillness different from sleep. He saw the blood splashed on the rocks; the rope, useless now, coiled haphazardly about the stones. He went closer, the sound of his feet on the stones loud in the clear mountain silence.

A rough bandage had slipped aside to show a savage wound on the boy's head, matting his hair with blood. More than this Mark could not see, for the boy was covered with sweaters and a climbing jacket, but the round young face was sharpened and shadowed, the eyes dark with pain.

'Tom....' the boy said. His breathing was quick and shallow.

'He's gone to get help.' Gently Mark lifted aside the sweaters and the jacket; in spite of himself his hands shivered; the bone of the thigh was through the flesh. The boy moaned. 'Pain,' he said. 'Such pain.'

'We'll stop that, when they come.' Mark was taking off his own jacket; he added it to the clothes on the boy; there seemed

little else he could do.   The evening wind drove at him in strength;
no shelter on this high ground from the white open distances of
sky.

'How long . . .?'

'Soon.   As soon as they can.'   Mark crouched down beside the
boy.   He could imagine the little beginnings of alarm down there
in the valley: the first telephone call—to the police, wasn't it?—
and then the summons multiplying to six, seven, eight of them:
they'd need that amount at least to get the stretcher down over the
traverse: young ordinary men, their minds on other things, suddenly cut off from the ordinary day, brought together for the high
adventure of rescue.   How long before they came?   He looked
down below him; the Pass was all in shadow now.   It would soon
be dark.

The boy moved his head a little; he whispered, 'Doctor?'

'No—not yet.   They'll come.   The Rescue boys . . . they have
morphia with them.'   Years ago, in the bar of a mountain hotel
someone had brought out the first-aid kit, and they'd all stood
round over drinks, looking at the bandages and splints and the
typewriter-ribbon tin labelled MORPHIA; stood and looked, making
occasional jokes; men at their ease, looking at something far off.
'They'll bring it soon,' he said.

The boy wetted his lips; the rucksack beneath his head was sewn
with gaudy badges; a garish magazine was thrust into one pocket
of the pack.   In the normal way of things, thought Mark, perhaps
we wouldn't have had much to say to each other.   As it was, he
seemed to share with the boy a sharp intimacy, as if they'd both,
at great cost, come to some meeting place.   'It hurts,' said the boy,
'hurts so much that I——'

'I'd do anything I could!   Until they come——'

'Makes me think . . . wonder if . . .'

The boy closed his eyes.   Mark leaned closer to him.   'Yes?'

'Makes me think . . . this is my packet.'

'You're all right.'

'Think so?   Honest? . . .   I dunno.   If not . . . I wanted . . . I
told Tom . . .'

Silence again.   Odd, thought Mark, how he wanted the boy to
say nothing more, how he would be glad if the difficult effort of
speech tired him, so that he gave it up: and yet, how something

93

within him drove him to question. 'Yes?' said Mark. 'You told Tom? . . .'

At first Mark thought the boy wasn't going to answer, then he gave a little sigh and said, 'I'd've liked . . . a priest.'

The wind strengthened; Mark pulled the jacket over the boy's shoulder. 'A priest?'

'Yes. Something I'd like to say . . . to be forgiven. Just in case . . .' The pain went over his face. 'I'm scared, you see.'

Mark was staring at the flung, useless rope. 'Yes, I understand.'

'Tom thought I was talking nonsense . . . but it isn't, not if you believe it, and I've believed it, all my life. Haven't been back, the last year or so . . . but I used to go, regular. I used to serve Father Langdon at St. Christopher's, Menon Street; so you see . . .'

Mark stared to the far ground of the valley where it was all evening now, but saw instead the large, ugly Anglican church, dominating the shabby North London street. He said, 'Father Langdon . . . yes, I've heard of him.'

Silence again from the boy. Mark looked down at his face; the eyes were closed. Perhaps nothing more? Perhaps after all——

Slowly the boy's eyes opened again; he gave a faint smile. 'Funny, but . . . even with it hurting like this . . . I wanted a priest more than anything. Tom thought I was crazy . . . you think I'm crazy?'

'No . . . no. I understand.'

'I remember how it used to be, after confession. I want it to be like that, now. . . . Just in case . . .'

'Tell me what it is.'

The boy's eyes, drooping with pain, went over Mark's face. 'Yes, but . . . a priest. It has to be a priest.'

Light was falling away everywhere; their faces were beginning to be indistinct to each other; with the increasing shadow the rocks seemed to become featureless and immense, black headlands rearing to the sky. The wind thrust hard and Mark shivered, pulling the jackets closer about the boy. 'Yes,' he said.

Bewildered, the boy kept his eyes on Mark's face. Mark said, more firmly, 'You can tell me. I am a priest.'

Silence all about them; only the sliding of the wind. The boy said, 'You . . .?'

'Yes.'

94

'*You?*'

'Yes.   That's why I came.'

'But . . . you must have been . . . where did he find you?'

'I was below, on Stile Pass.   He told me you were asking for a priest.'

Like some cold, dark dream, Mark thought; like the dreams he had so often had, of performing the rites of his church with desperation in absurd and strange places.

'On the Pass?'   The boy seemed to repeat the words without understanding.   'And you'll hear . . . what I've got to say?'

'Yes.'   With an effort he recalled the gentle phrases.   'Yes, my son.'

Breathless, in pain, fumbling for his words, the boy began. 'Father, it was a girl. . . .'   Mark sat listening in the increasing cold while the boy brought out his story.   An old story, but here, under the rocks, spoken in pain, it was sharp and new.   He'd betrayed her, got her with child, left her. . . .   Every now and again he paused.   Once blood slipped down his cheek, and Mark wiped it away.   'She must have been frightened, Father, left alone.   I can't forget it. . . .   Lying here . . . I keep thinking of her.   She was a nice girl, not the wrong sort, and I just left her. . . .'   The boy fell silent.   Mark waited, drawing one thumb up and down against the other, but it seemed the boy had no more to say.

Mark looked once round at the darkening theatre of rocks, then bent his head and spoke.   'Our Lord Jesus Christ, Who hath left power to His Church to absolve all sinners who truly repent and believe in him, of His great mercy forgive thee thine offences. . . .' The boy's eyes were closed; there was more blood on his cheek; Mark wiped it away.   '. . . And by His authority committed unto me, I absolve thee from all thy sins, in the Name of the Father, and of the Son, and of the Holy Ghost.   Amen.'

Silence came after the words.   The boy's eyes were still closed, but after a moment or two he opened them, gave again his slight smile.   'Thank you, Father.'

'Rest now.   They'll come soon.'

'Yes, Father.'

§

'They'll come soon.'   But how soon?   The boy was silent now . . . asleep?   Unconscious?   I did what I could, Mark thought.

Isn't that enough? Need they know—the others—when they come?

He looked more closely at the boy. He was breathing, fast shallow breaths, but . . . when they came, the men from Fastness, would he still be breathing? Able to talk, to tell them what he'd learned? The men from Fastness, who'd know of the parson who broke away from Scarside.

He looked again at the boy. Before they came . . . would he have slipped into unconsciousness? Or death? I want him to live, said Mark; surely I want him to live. I *must* want him to live; but fear nudged his mind with the thought; if he's going to die, better if he dies before they come.

He put his head in his hands and tried to thrust the thought away. He prayed, 'Oh, let him live.' He thought he heard the boy murmur a word, and he leant close to him, saying, 'Yes? D'you want something, old chap?' But the boy didn't answer, and Mark was left in silence to fight with himself, and wait and listen amongst the darkening stones for the men from Fastness.

§

He was very cold, his hands numb. Dark possessed the rocks and stones and the rough grass. A place where you waited in fear, he thought, had the wearisome familiarity of a page read a hundred times. He began to feel that nothing would change; he was set here forever in this cold watch beside the boy, with no other company but the wind. But suddenly he lifted his head.

Yes, voices. Very strange after the long silence, carrying clearly through the mountain dark, so that they seemed closer than they were.

Voices; and the sound of boots on the stony path. So they were coming now; bringing help for the boy. And for himself? He leaned towards the boy, as if to escape the thought, as if to force himself to think of nothing but the boy's good. 'Listen!' he said. 'Listen, they're coming!'

The boy gave no sign of having heard. Mark said again, 'They're coming now. They'll be able to stop your pain.' A Very light went up, swimming smoothly into the dark air, painting the traverse and the rocks and the boy lying there in the colour of some unnatural and menacing day. Mark got to his feet; bent to rub a cramped knee. Now he could see the men, a small company, moving in single file over the traverse; in the strange light they threw complex and ungainly shadows; they came steadily on.

Mark stood waiting, straining his eyes as the light dissolved and it was dark again. He called to them, and a voice answered. 'They're here,' he said to the boy. 'They're almost here.'

Another Very light. This patch of earth under the rocks flood-lit for a brief drama of pain and rescue. The men were close now; seven of them; in their rough similar clothes they were scarcely distinguishable from each other; only one stood out because of his good looks and the light abundant brilliance of his hair. Gillian and the boy were with them; in this sharp acid light the red wool cap was darkly brilliant, like a warning.

Blankets, vacuum flasks, splints, bandages, ropes, the stretcher lying waiting. Mark stood watching the young men as they went quickly to work. He would have liked to offer help, but they seemed busy and withdrawn from him, knowing what to do, throwing each other only brief and casual words. Gillian came and stood beside him, but he felt divided from her; when she murmured a few words to him he answered mechanically, his eyes on the boy, and she fell silent.

So far the boy had said no word, had not opened his eyes. Mark stood waiting. The air seemed to grow rapidly colder; he could feel himself shivering.

They had taken the sweaters off the boy's broken leg; a young man with tousled dark hair knelt beside him with an ampoule-syringe in his hand. Mark stood watching, grateful for the darkness and his own obscurity. Perhaps this was how it was going to be; the quiet work on the stones; the boy eased of his pain, himself unquestioned, an anonymous watcher, someone who——

But slowly the boy moved his head, opened his eyes. He looked bewildered by the movement and the men close to him. His eyes came to rest on the young man beside him.

'Morphia?' said the boy.

'Just about,' said the young man. 'Something that has the same effect.' He tore off the metal cap.

'Will it . . . will it put me out?'

'No, just put the pain out, chum. Make you a bit sleepy. Hurting, is it? Soon see to that.'

'Before you give it me . . . I wanted to say . . . to the Father . . .'

'Yes, yes, don't worry.' The young man was busy with the syringe. 'You say all you want, in good time. Just now we've got to make you into a tidy parcel for posting down the hillside. . . . Give him a swig from that flask, Jim, put some warmth into him——'

The boy made a feeble effort to push the flask aside. 'I wanted to say . . . to ask the Father . . .'

'Yes, you say all you want; just for now——'

The boy's eyes searched for Mark, he said 'Father? . . .'

Mark hesitated for a moment; his knees trembling with a longing to turn and run. Then he came and knelt beside the boy again. Someone held a torch, which carved the boy's face in sharp shadow. Mark waited.

'It's true, isn't it, Father? You were able to . . . You are a priest, aren't you?'

The men did not cease in their work, but to Mark there seemed to be a pause; he saw Gillian's eyes raised to him; he saw the young man with fair hair give him a long glance, startled, alert and curious. The torch poured its light steadily on; the young men who were strapping the broken leg to the splint had blood on their hands; the scene had the isolated savagery and pity of some primitive crucifixion.

'Yes,' said Mark, 'it's true.'

CHAPTER SEVEN

THE needle went in; the boy winced and moaned. Slowly, with great care he was tied to the stretcher; at last all the first-aid equipment was packed away; as, with six of them carrying the stretcher, they began to move on, Mark looked back at the place where the boy had lain under the rocks. Nothing remained there; when the rain had washed the blood off the rocks, it would look like any other part of the mountain-side.

Marvellously skilful, with help from Gillian, Mark and Tom, they brought the stretcher over the traverse. Like a strange procession, Mark thought; mourners, perhaps, following a great man. The moon was up, and showed boulders, scree and grass as if reflected in dull steel. The tarn was white melted metal within its dark rocks.

When at last they reached the road, the evening with the boy's pain and the cold dark and this place under the rocks seemed to Mark familiar and exhausting like a long journey through strange and unlovely country.

With brief farewells, the young men put the stretcher into the waiting jeep. Mark could just see the words on its side: FASTNESS MOUNTAIN RESCUE. Before he jumped aboard, the young man with fair hair turned once more to stare at Mark.

Slowly the jeep moved away, dwarfed by the tall rocks. When it had gone the Pass was a haunted place, the steep fellsides cracked with light where the moon caught the streams.

Gillian stared after the way the jeep had gone. Then she moved, as if coming out of a dream. 'Will he die?'

'I don't know. I'm afraid so.'

She sighed heavily, kicking at the ground with one foot. He waited for her next question; he wanted to say, Soon enough I'll tell you it all, tell you the whole story. But for the moment he was lost in his own weariness, and the sharp, sad silence of the end of the boy's climb; a silence like that other silence of his darkest memory, with death at the heart of it.

CHAPTER EIGHT

MISS LETTICE WRAYBURN hurried across the upper end of the street. Colour in the shop windows, frilly flowers in window boxes, the calm glory of lighted stone built this London prospect in terms of spring. 'Somehow French,' thought Miss Wrayburn, though she had not in fact been to France, and probably would not now go, since she was hard up and over sixty.

She turned into a side-street, pretty with tree shadow and new paint. The street broadened to a square: on the other side of the square the grey spire of the church rose to receive the mild unclouded light of this spring day. 'Pretty,' said Miss Wrayburn, 'nice,' looking to see if she had her umbrella, her handbag, and her coloured raffia basket; sometimes, now, she left things behind, in the tea-shops and on the buses where she seemed to spend so large a part of her life.

She walked quickly beneath the large trees in the square, making for the church. Twice before she'd come this way; perhaps this time (she had an instinctive trust in clichés) she would be lucky. Twice before she'd knocked at the door of the vicarage close by, been answered by a housekeeper, stern but not unfriendly (even so, Miss Wrayburn was frightened of housekeepers) who'd said that the Vicar wasn't there; that he was a very busy man; any message?

No, there wasn't a message; it wasn't exactly the kind of thing that made sense as a message; few of the things Miss Wrayburn thought of did.

It was as she hesitated at the edge of the pavement, looking for a long time carefully, to right and left, for she didn't trust an empty road; she had a feeling that large lorries might hurtle from nowhere and run her down—it was as she stood there that she saw the black-skirted figure walking quickly along on the opposite side of the road. His head was bent, but from this distance he looked serious, rather young. He was not alone: at his side walked a small, gesticulating man who seemed to be in full flood of indignation.

Miss Wrayburn stood waiting. When at last the small man moved away, the priest stood for a moment, staring at the pavement as if hoping to find the solution to some problem there. Miss Wrayburn gave a small gasp, prayed that she wouldn't say anything silly, plunged towards him and said, 'Excuse me, but are you the Vicar?'

Now that she stood face to face with him she saw that he was not quite as young as all that: the jaw-line was firm, but there was a deep little line between his brows like a scar; grey lay thickly amongst the heavy dark hair.

'Yes, I am.' A polite, rather formal smile; behind the smile—fatigue? A wish to be left alone? Miss Wrayburn grew breathless.

'The—the Reverend Mark Harvist?'

'Yes.'

'Then . . . oh, I'm so awfully sorry if I seem impertinent—or if I've made a mistake . . . or something, but are you by any chance —the name, you see—the son of Anthony Harvist?'

Her words had got tangled up as they always did; perhaps that was why a small shadow went across Mark Harvist's face; she felt abject, bursting with apology. 'I'm sorry if ... but the name, you see——'

'Yes, he was—is my father.'

'Oh! Oh, how *interesting*.'

'You knew him?'

The brief words were not unfriendly, but some edge on them disconcerted her. 'Well ... yes. Oh, yes! When he was at All Hallow's, Wrenfield. I admired him so much.'

'Many people did.'

'Oh! Yes, of course. . . .'

'Perhaps you'd like to come in here?'

He was pointing to the door of the vicarage; Miss Wrayburn went with him, in pleasure and fear; once a door was closed behind her, she was shut in with the increasing uncertainty: how—and when—to go? Too soon could be rude, too late a tedium. Perhaps Mark Harvist would rise, or, if standing, make some final gesture like pushing a chair out of her path on the way to the door, and then she would know.

The room was small; the desk crowded with papers; an open diary lay, scored with names and the times of meetings, lending conviction to the housekeeper's term, 'a busy man'. Miss Wrayburn had seen men who kept their desks covered with papers to make a show; this wasn't like that. This was the authentic muddled accumulation of the fatigued and busy man. *Not* married, Miss Wrayburn thought; alone herself, she knew when other people lived alone.

He sat before the desk; the full spring light fell on his face, which seemed to her to convey some sort of struggle. He said nothing, and Miss Wrayburn felt compelled nervously to speak.

'Yes, I lived in Wrenfield for many years, and in all that time I don't think I ever missed—d'you mind if I smoke? No, no, I have plenty of my own, thank you; I'm afraid I smoke rather a lot. . . . What was I saying? Oh yes, I never missed a Sunday. I remember you, quite often, as a boy.'

A gentle, remote smile; rather less than she'd expected; a little disappointed, she went on, knocking ash nervously towards the ashtray. 'And when I passed the church the other day I saw the name—it isn't a very common one, and I thought perhaps . . .'

Mark Harvist was making abstracted efforts to push the papers on his desk into order. His brow was furrowed. Nothing here, Miss Wrayburn thought, of the smooth parson's manner that she knew so well and which imposed a curtain of unreality between the priest and the one who talked to him. Had she been able to surmount her shyness, talk between herself and Mark Harvist could have been a real thing, live and striking sparks.

He gave her an upward little glance of enquiry as she was silent; he was faintly smiling, as if perhaps to say, Look, I'm doing my best, but there isn't all the time in the world, not time just to sit——

'How delighted,' she exclaimed, 'your father must have been, that you should follow . . . that you should have decided——'

'Yes. Though I'm a late-comer to the church.'

Miss Wrayburn prevented herself from saying 'Better late than never.'

'I was ordained only five years ago.'

'They say, don't they, that the childhood influence makes itself felt in the end——'

'Yes, perhaps.'

'What did you do—before?' she asked.

'Oh . . . a number of things.' He looked rueful, as if he could give himself marks for none of them. 'An unsuccessful publisher, for one. Never really settled—never really felt at home.'

'Until now,' said Miss Wrayburn, eager for the happy ending.

Mark Harvist gave a faint sigh, as if at some defeat, but said nothing. Between them, she thought, was the large question: what made him do it? But of course I can't ask. Though if I did he would be truthful with me; he's a man who is truthful with himself, and that, no doubt, causes him some unhappiness.

Silence had fallen again; she said nervously, 'I expect your father's so pleased, so awfully——'

'He's been ill, you know.'

'Oh! I'm *so* sorry. Oh . . . if I could . . . perhaps see him? Take him something—very ill?'

A slight shake of the head, that might have been at his own thoughts. She went on, 'I was always a little afraid of approach-

ing him, but you stop being afraid of people if they're in any sort
of need, don't you?'

'Yes——'

'I'm—I'm rather a lonely person—that is, I've not a great deal to
do with my time, and if I could go and see——'

'No, you can't do that, I'm afraid.'

'Oh. Really? Really not?'

'No.'

'He's not allowed visitors? Then he *is* very ill—gravely ill?'

'No; it isn't quite that.'

Odd, the thought that crossed her mind: that Mark Harvist was
pleading with her. For what? She had no idea. To go, perhaps.
She made fluttering movements, crushing out the cigarette which
was not finished. 'Yes, I see.' She'd made a fool of herself in
some way, as she might have known she would. She took out
another cigarette, saw his eyes travel over the movement. 'Expect,'
she said, breathless now, not really thinking what she was saying,
'expect you think I smoke too much. Seems—I expect it seems
odd in an old spinster like me, but I . . .' She rose awkwardly to
her feet.

Mark Harvist rose too, and was leaning now towards her, across
the desk. 'I'll tell my father that you remembered him. He'll be
so glad to know.'

She was surprised at the warmth in his voice; perhaps it sprang
from relief that she was going.

'Thank you. Yes, please tell him.'

On the step she took his hand, dropped her basket, thanked him
for retrieving it. His eyes seemed full of something too strong to
be merely thankfulness at her going; she was quite lost. Before
she turned away, she searched his face.

'You're not like your father!' she said.

'They say not.'

Some wild courage enabled her to say, 'Yet I think I can see what
made you go into the Church.'

'Yes?'

The word was gentle; nevertheless she was appalled, smiled
foolishly at him and fled down the bright London street. She said
aloud to herself, when she had gone some distance, 'Because you
have the kind of pity that hurts.' A man passing her stared in

some surprise; she shook her head vaguely, walking on. Before she crossed the road she looked back; the spire still caught the light, but the pavement beneath was in shadow, and Mark Harvist still stood on his step. She had an impulse to wave, but controlled it, being unsure that she could convey by the gesture what she wanted to, which was to reassure and comfort him, and tell him she was all right.

§

'Lot of ash,' said Mrs. Shell, the housekeeper, as she put a tray of tea down on the desk. She was middle-aged, unmade-up, but had, rather surprisingly, bright auburn hair. Her expression looked as though she disapproved of it. She gave off a faint whiff of disinfectant.

'Yes,' said Mark absently, standing and frowning at his diary.

'Man, I suppose.'

'No, a woman.'

'Messy.'

'She was nervous,' said Mark. Her voice still echoed in his mind: a lifetime of lonely teas in tea-shops, of petty economies and despair on Saturday afternoons sounded in that voice.

'Ah.' Mrs. Shell blew from different angles at the ash. 'Poor soul.' The words were comfortable, formal, not suggesting any particular pity. 'Suppose she wanted to talk?'

'About my father.'

Mrs. Shell was silent, as if she didn't know the right answer to this. Mark went on, seeing the tea tray, 'I shan't have time for that, I'm afraid. I've got to put in an extra visit.'

'Your extra visit can wait three minutes while you drink a cup of tea.'

'I'm late as it is.' Absently Mark took the cup she poured for him, drank half and put it down. 'I have to go.'

Mrs. Shell sighed with the mingled concern and pleasure of a woman indulging in solicitude. 'Make yourself ill. You don't get enough rest. I couldn't help noticing, you've looked off-colour lately. Pale, sort-of.'

'Spring weather,' said Mark, rubbing his eyes with his hands. 'I'm all right.'

'Mrs. Hendron's been ringing up. She says she's coming round at five o'clock.'

Mark nodded. 'I'll be back.'

'She's a waste of time,' said Mrs. Shell. 'I've seen plenty of her kind: talking to her's like pouring water down the sink. You might as well give up.'

'Oh . . . I don't know. People can be very surprising. Endlessly, endlessly surprising. I've learned that.'

'There aren't no surprises in Mrs. Hendron. Put your hand anywhere you like in the bran tub, you'll pull out the same package.'

'Yes, but . . . you have to go on. There isn't anything else to do. It's the only hope; the question is, of course, how long——' He broke off, aware that Mrs. Shell had given him a glance of surprised curiosity; it had happened before, that when he was talking to her his mind slipped away and he used the wrong idiom. Yes, I suppose I am tired, he thought. 'If I'm late,' he said firmly, regaining ground, 'you must be kind to her. Give her a cup of tea. Tell her I won't be long.'

Once out of doors he walked quickly through the streets of grave Victorian houses; placid spring light gave them an unusual cheerfulness; he felt proud of them, like a parent whose plain child is looking its best. The spire of the church dwindled, was lost behind the Pimlico roof-tops. He strode on rapidly, lost in an argument with a part of his mind which told him that Mrs. Hendron was a fraud, who wanted no kind of spiritual help, but five bob or ten if she could get it. All right, all right, he said to this part of his mind, I know it. Even so, there's still hope for her. There must be. To deny that——

He found that he'd walked on too far; he retraced his steps and stood before the large pillars and steps of a terraced house.

Two women passed him; one glanced at him as he stood there; he saw how he must look to her, a man dressed in authority. Unlikely that she could conceive that he paused here because for the moment his nerve had failed him.

He mastered himself; went up the steps and rang the bell. Familiar maid-servant; familiar hall; familiar smell. Miss Challon coming to meet him with a prim smile and sharply waved blue hair; her voice, which could cut unpleasantly, changed when she spoke to him, took on a manufactured reverence for his cloth; he was sorry to notice that, and sorry, also, that he could not help noticing it. He wondered, not for the first time, in what part of his mind the saint kept that sharp insistent sight which perceives unfailingly the hypocricies of others, as well as his own.

'He's not been quite his old self to-day,' she said in answer to his question. 'Well, we all have our good and bad days, don't we? Oh yes, no reason at all why you shouldn't see him. You know your way, don't you? Should do by this time.'

He climbed the stairs slowly. On the first landing was a recess with a plum-coloured plush sofa. It was a familiar landmark, part of his apprehension; he could not imagine that anyone ever sat on it. He went on to the next floor.

When he came to the door, he knocked. A faint sound which might have been anything came from the room; he went in.

The old man with the untidy white hair who sat bowed in the chair had the light behind him. He might have been lost in deep thought. His clothes had a slight oddness, as if half-way through putting them on he'd grown tired of the whole thing.

'Hullo, Father,' said Mark.

'Oh ... Mark.' He frowned a little pettishly, as if he'd hoped to see someone else. 'I don't know ... I suppose ... no one told me you were coming.'

'No one knew.'

'They keep things from me here, they never——'

'Father, no one——'

'It gets on my nerves sometimes; I suppose you're too young to realize it, but it's particularly irritating—oh, so terribly irritating—not to be *told* things, when you ...'

The voice trembled on. Mark sighed, and went to the window. In a pause he said, 'I've had a visit from an old parishioner of yours.'

'What? What? I wish you wouldn't say things when I can't see you; people are always doing that; walking about the room and talking to the walls and windows——'

'An old parishioner of yours. She came to see me.'

'Oh, I don't want to hear things like that. How silly of you to come and tell me. ... People never seem to tell me the sort of things I want to hear. What I want——'

'She remembered you with great affection. She suggested that you'd been an inspiration to her——'

'Oh, I don't suppose she meant it. I expect she was a bit touched;

women do go like that. Especially . . . spinster, I expect, wasn't she? . . . Sex, starved of it, it gets them in the end.'

'She showed no special——'

'Oh, you don't see things straight. She was a spinster, wasn't she? Yes, of course she was, you don't have to tell me—— Oh, you needn't look so . . . down your nose about the whole thing, just because you've got this absurd idea of staying celibate; you'll never keep it up. . . .'

(Oh, look; do stop. Because we have this every time: an old man's senile preoccupation.)

'She was a spinster, wasn't she?'

(Oh, never mind. It isn't the hardest thing—to do without sex. It seems it must be, but it isn't. There are other things, harder to do.)

'Celibacy's all very well for some men, I daresay, but not for a man like you.'

Mark was silent, making no protest.

'In fact, I've always felt there was something a bit . . . rather absurd, about your going into the Church at all. Not that you made much success of anything else, but you're not the type. You're too emotional—all over the place. *That's* no good. Plunging into the Church as if it were a set at tennis——

'No, that's not fair!' Mark walked back and forth, making an effort: no good being angry. He said more quietly, 'I talked with Father Elliot for hours, evening after evening. As far as I could, I tried to be certain——'

'Oh, old Jim Elliot; he's one of the soft ones. A sentimentalist, if ever there was one. Always has been, ever since he was a young man: wanted to forgive everybody, when he was at Oxford, a hundred years ago——'

'Not a bad thing, perhaps——'

'Oh, you never agree with me now; you don't know how irritating it is not to be agreed with——'

Mark bent down suddenly, arrested in his pacing about the room. An empty bottle, put discreetly in a corner. He touched it with his foot. 'This?' he enquired gently.

'What? What are you . . .? Oh . . . that. A bottle, is it? Yes . . . I . . . it's just something I had in for . . . for Christmas.'

Mark found that he could not say, 'Christmas was four months ago.' He said quietly, with a certain hopelessness, 'You've been told not to, you know.'

'Oh, don't go on about it. It's old. Old. Let's discuss something else.'

'How did you get it?'

'Oh, I don't know. . . . forget . . .'

'I must know how.'

'One of the girls—maids who works here—got it for me. Oh, heavens, you needn't look like that. It's good for me to have a little drink; that's where doctors are so stupid; they don't understand. . . .' He looked at Mark from under his brows, cautious, doubtful. Mark stood frowning, saying nothing. 'A little for Christmas,' his father said.

Mark sighed, leaving it. A difficult interview with Miss Challon (not to-day, but soon); she could be touchy if accused of negligence: 'Everything possible is done, at the present high cost of wages, the staff may possibly . . . If, of course, you'd prefer to remove your father . . .' Difficult, because he didn't want that said, was afraid of hearing her elaborate, continue: 'As a matter of fact, I've been thinking that it might be better if you did . . .'

Mark glanced at the clock. 'I must go, Father. I've a lot of other people to see.'

'Oh, you're going, are you? Going? You never stay long, do you. Never seem to have anything interesting to say. . . . Other people? What other people?'

Mark shrugged. 'People who need help, I suppose.'

'Oh, you're a fool to do that sort of thing. You'll get every professional hard luck story and every crazy, neurotic woman, all sucking your vitality like snakes sucking eggs. Waste of time and trouble. I kept out of the way of them myself.'

'I'll come again. And then I'll try to——'

'Yes, yes; well, never mind that now. If you're going you'd better go; there's nothing irritates me more than somebody hanging about half in and half out of the door.'

'Good-bye, then, Father.'

§

Some five hours later Mark stood in the living-room, looking out at the spring dusk. About half the things he'd hoped to do had been done; each visit had taken that much longer than he'd intended, but they always did; you went on talking, knowing you were getting nowhere; yet the small doubt, the hope that sooner or later you'd chance on the word that would prove of help or comfort kept you sitting there while the minutes ran past, and some part of your mind took tucks in the programme, saying, You can see Mrs. Jenkins to-morrow, one day won't make any difference. . . . He'd said Evensong in the empty church. Now he stood waiting for Father Elliot.

Mrs. Shell had prepared her usual dinner; Mark could smell it approaching like a noise that grew louder, pork with apple sauce, followed by pears. 'Father Elliot's an old man,' he had said not long ago, 'I honestly don't think pork . . .' Mrs. Shell had appeared to listen and agree; but here they were having pork again.

For a moment he felt angry, wanted to go down and say something to Mrs. Shell. Half-way to the door he checked himself; he knew what this was, the irritation of frustration and fatigue, because, for all the effort he'd put into the day, he'd seemed to get nowhere. And because that picture of his father, sitting bowed in the chair, was printed in the colour of challenge.

Mark crossed to the sideboard and poured himself a drink. Seems unfair to drink when you've just told him not to. 'A little I had in for Christmas.' I wish he hadn't said that. Like father, like son: I can't get through a really bad worry without taking a drink.

He stood by the window, the drink in one hand. He entered again on the familiar argument.

'He's alone, you know. A sad, defeated, lonely old man. That proud, self-confident, self-sufficient person, who moved through your childhood with such remote authority, now undermined and lost. That makes it worse, somehow: if he'd been gentler and more humble, approachable and loving, you could hope that he'd accept this kind of defeat. But you can't help feeling that somewhere there's the old Anthony Harvist, looking on, terribly humiliated, hating it all so, hating being an old man who drinks and talks sex.'

'Well, but . . . don't you do your best? You go and see him, talk to him, help to support him. What more can you do?'

'Have him here to live.'

'That doesn't make sense. Your work'd suffer; as it is you

haven't energy enough. It's wrong to sap the young for the sake of the old——'

'Oh, yes, one can argue. Good arguments, but not good enough. Sooner or later it always comes: the thing you have to force yourself to do, to go through with and come out the other side, stronger and assured. Have him here. . . .'

His imagination showed him the whole thing in sharp detail: the endless, senile voice pursuing him, the reproaches, the arguments about the drink; trouble—all kinds of trouble—with Mrs. Shell; the task, which now seemed heavy, made heavy beyond endurance.

He took some of his drink. 'Well, nothing to say but—here I fail, O Lord. This is my defeat. One of many, after all.'

By half past seven the smell of dinner was overpowering; difficult to talk against it, Mark thought. He said as much to Father Elliot as he sat, drinking sherry; a small, tired old man; as old as my father, Mark thought, but so strangely different. Elliot said he didn't mind the smell; didn't really notice it. He sat there, amiably still, while Mark moved restlessly about the room.

'I'm afraid it's pork,' he said. 'Can you eat pork? I do hope——'

'My dear boy, don't be so concerned. Of course I can eat pork. Or if I can't, it doesn't matter.' He watched Mark for some moments. 'What worries you?' he asked evenly.

'Oh, I don't know . . . yes, I do . . . everything.'

'As much as that?'

Mark paused, rueful, hesitant. 'I must try not to talk about it——'

'Really? Why?'

'One can't ask people to dinner and then give them nothing but a history of one's despair——'

Elliot brought his glass of sherry slowly in the faintly trembling hand from the table beside him. 'Despair?'

'I don't really mean that. I wasn't thinking.'

Elliot looked up with enquiring eyebrows, but made no comment.

'Dinner is served,' said Mrs. Shell, with the faint mistrust of someone who has been taught to say this, but doesn't feel it's right.

'Yes,' said Mark, 'I thought as much.'

The dining room was spare and dark brown, and smelled of sharp polish; 'Like an old leathery library book that's been disinfected,' Mark said.

'I've got a bottle of wine,' he added, 'I hope it's going to be all right.' (A little I had in for Christmas.) His hand shook and he spilled the wine. 'Sorry.'

Elliot moved his head vaguely as if to say he didn't mind about things being spilt. He took occasional mouthfuls of his food, but for the greater part of the time sat, leaning back in his chair, slightly smiling, placidly content.

'You don't like pork,' said Mark, 'I can see you don't——'

'You must try not to get so excited about the pork,' said Elliot. 'Or indeed about anything.'

'Yes, all right.' Mark put down his knife and fork and sat silent for a few moments. Elliot said nothing either; the room trembled slightly with the passing of heavy traffic outside.

Mark stared away towards the drawn curtains. 'It was all a mistake, you know,' he said.

'What was?'

'My going into the Church.'

Elliot was silent for a few seconds more, then said, 'Oh, really? You think so? Mistake?'

'Yes, certainly. I ought to get out of it now, right away, but—well, that's difficult.'

'Get out of it? D'you really think so? I shouldn't have thought that was necessary. Why?'

'Because I've failed. Because some part of me, some nerve of conviction and belief and hope isn't alive any more. No, wait, listen. When I first went into the Church, after that year in the theological college, I was shocked at some of the things I found—shocked and disappointed and hurt.'

'Well, naturally.'

'I saw—I couldn't help seeing—that my vicar was a kindly, self-interested, rather lazy man; I had to learn, at clerical meetings—that many parsons are professional men like other professional men; I've heard a vicar from a neighbouring parish called "a bloody coffin nail sucker" because he was making a corner in funerals, getting ten bob a time, and making in all something like ten pounds a week.'

'Good gracious, what a large sum.'

'I wasn't discouraged at first—or only seldom, as everyone is in whatever they do. I remembered what you'd told me—oh, look, please go on eating—that my early blaze of—of, oh, conviction, extreme happiness, all that—couldn't last. When it began to go I thought, This is all right, I know about this. I just have to keep going and in the end I come to a place of calm and certainty, as they tell you marriage does, illusions gone but something set for ever. That was all right. But now . . .' Absently he pushed the salt towards Elliot, then took it back. 'I suppose I found in the end that nothing other people do matters very much; there's only one failure, and that's inside oneself. . . . I really can't help this sounding like one of my poorer sermons: it just seems to be coming out like that. Anyway, that's where I've failed.'

Elliot, sitting unmoving with his chin sunk, said, 'I hear good things of you. Of the work you do.'

'Oh, I go on doing the job; I go and talk to men and women whose lives, for some reason or other, no longer seem endurable. I talk to them. But I get nowhere. I'm not advancing the Kingdom of God, I'm a social worker whose heart isn't really in it, and who's tired of cups of tea. I don't feel like a priest any more, I feel like a man dressed up as a priest. When I say those tremendous words in that church there, some part of my mind doubts them all. In short, dressed like this, I'm a fraud.'

Elliot moved slightly in his chair. 'Oh, well, everyone's a fraud. More or less. As for doubts . . . we're all blown through by doubts; I've been in the Church for fifty years, said Mass I don't know how many hundred times, yet I can still feel suddenly that my prayers are sterile heaps of words and that this world's cut off neatly at earth and sky, and there's nothing beyond. How else can it be? How can one not sometimes doubt, when there can be no solid certainty; when I can't bring God in and sit Him down at your table? You'd say, I suppose, that you've lost faith.'

Mark played with the mustard pot. 'Lost faith in my power to do any good, perhaps. Or that any good can be done through me.'

Elliot sighed. 'You're still quite a young man, that's the trouble——'

'I'm forty-five.'

'That's still young. You expect certainties, full marks, people who live up to what they say they are, people who mean what they say all the way through. When you get to my age you stop expecting that; everything moves in a kind of shifting shadow, the hard edges vanish. Or let's put it another way: the mountains and valleys of good and bad, truth and untruth, even out; wonderful how the ground evens out with age.'

'You make it sound good to be old.'

'Oh, well, you don't want to be as old as I am; I'm awfully old, dreadfully old, and a little mad; oh yes, quite a little mad; I've thought so for a long time. But then who isn't? ... I wonder what I can say to you—no, I don't want any more to eat, thank you; I'm talking now. ...' He changed his position in the chair with slow purposefulness. 'Can you not accept yourself—your failures, doubts and disappointments—for what they are? Can't you just do your best, and let the rest go, hoping all things?'

'Sometimes I think I can, but then I catch myself out in some gross piece of hypocrisy; or I have to go and see my father—I did to-day——'

'Does it still eat you—the idea that he should come and live here?'

'Yes.'

'You know what I've told you about that.'

'Yes.'

'What's more I know where he could go. A home for old people run by nuns. They'd be good to him.'

'He wouldn't go.'

'I could persuade him.'

'He wouldn't be really happy.'

'You're a difficult man to help,' said Elliot.

'I know. I'm sorry.'

'And you're greatly distressed. Now what to do for you?' He drew one hand slowly across his chin. 'That I don't know.'

'You musn't worry about me.'

'Naturally I worry about you. I'm the one with the key to it all: it was to me you came when you first thought of going into the Church: I knew your father, and Gerald and Lorraine and Daphne: I believed in the end that you'd much to give, that you were a man, whatever your past sins, who had the heart of the matter in him. Of course I worry about you.' He drew one finger slowly across the table-cloth. 'What would you say if I told you your duty was to go on, saying Mass, visiting the sick and the troubled, preaching your sermons, living each day as it comes, and asking nothing more?'

'Yes, I suppose that's what I've been trying to do.'

'Well?'

'Somehow—I'm afraid. As I go on, I seem to be waiting for some kind of punishment.'

'You have to learn to forgive yourself.'

'I know. It's not easy.'

Elliot sat in silence. He said at last, 'Would it be possible for you to get away—just for a short time . . . a few weeks, something like that?'

'No, not at the moment.'

'Not even if you were ill?'

'I'm not ill.'

'Are you sure?'

'Mean that I could get a doctor to say I'm half-nuts—something like that?'

'Well . . .'

'Do you think I am?'

'No, you're as sane as anyone is. And saner than some. But I'd say . . . oh, goodness, I don't know what the modern language is . . . they talk about stress and conflict, don't they? . . . Whatever troubles you, whether I and my kind are right and it's your soul, or a mass of things with names like *id* and *animus* and *persona* . . . whatever it is, I would suggest a little time of quiet . . . to be alone and untroubled, to let yourself float uncommitted, make no effort to *live up* to anything, to believe anything——'

'I can't do that yet.'

'It would be a good thing.'

'Perhaps in a little while——'

'I should be interested to know when you last had a holiday.'

Mark shrugged. 'Holidays are expensive. There's my father——'

'When did you last get away?'

'I suppose . . . three years ago.'

'Time you went again.'

'Yes. Perhaps later——'

'Why not now?'

Mark rubbed his forehead with his hand. 'I don't feel free to go. There are people in various complex bits of trouble whom I see fairly regularly. In a way they depend on me; if I went——'

'There'll always be that kind of person in that kind of

trouble. Sometimes you've got to leave them, for your own good.'

Mark leaned forward, frowning at his clasped hands. 'Perhaps. I can't do it yet.'

'Will you make me a promise and do it soon?'

'I'll try. Although I don't really know that a holiday——'

'What I'm suggesting,' Elliot said, lightly stroking his forehead with the tips of his fingers, 'isn't exactly a holiday. Well, not in the accepted sense. I'm retiring, you know, from St. Anselm's. ... Retirement ... I suppose you'd call it that. Yes, retirement. Necessary, I'm afraid, because, as I told you, my mind wanders now. I'm quite sensible sometimes—I was just now, when I was talking to you. But every now and again, the blank patches come ... so you see, I have to retire. And I'm going away——'

'How you'll be missed!'

'Not for long. No one is ever missed for long. My idea is that you should come and stay with me.'

'Stay with you?'

'Well—stay with us, perhaps I should say. I'm joining a Community. For the rest of my days. It seemed the best way to end them. Visitors are allowed.'

'Where are you going?'

'Where—oh, didn't I tell you that? It's in Kilbrennan in the Western Isles. The S.C.C.—The Society of Christ's Compassion. A good place, I feel, for a man to go who's done with the world.'

§

On the third day after Elliot's visit, Mark answered the telephone. It was ten o'clock in the morning; the house had its morning smell, of floor polish and the fading remnants of fried bacon. He still held in his hand the torn envelopes and the letters of his morning post. Amongst them was a card in Elliot's old craggy hand: 'I do beg you to remember my advice. Get away soon.'

'Hullo,' Mark said to the telephone.

'Mark?'

For a moment he was puzzled. The voice was sharply familiar, yet he could give it no name.

'Yes ... who's that?'

'Thought you'd know.'

'Yes, I do, but . . .'

'Disappointed. Thought I had a voice different from all the other girls.'

'Of course! *Daphne.*'

'Daphne for sure.'

Something that he could not account for was lodged in the heart of his pleasure: a little core of disquiet. She said after a small silence, 'Pleased to hear from me?'

'Of course. As always.'

'Then can I ask you something?'

'Of course.' (Let it be simple, let it not be anything difficult; anything that involves——)

'You haven't got to pack at once and take a plane. I only want to come and see you.'

He reflected ruefully that he had forgotten her acute second sight—or in this case, perhaps, second hearing. 'How splendid. When?'

'When are you free to talk?'

'I could be free—in the evening.'

'To-night?'

'Yes—yes, I think so.'

'Any reason why I shouldn't come?'

'No.'

'Why do you sound——?'

'Look, Daphne, I shall be delighted to see you. What more can I say?'

'Uh-huh.' She sounded a little further off, her exuberance quietened. 'Have I made you angry? I don't see why.'

'Daphne, I've told you——'

'Yes, you have. Sorry. Expect you're busy. I'll come to-night, then. Some women'd flounce off and be hurt and say not on your life, *never* am I going anywhere where I'm not wanted—but not me. I'm coming. What time?'

'Nine—say, nine o'clock.'

'Yes. Fine. Good-bye, Mark.'

When his day's business gave him a few moments of blank thought, the small conversation nagged at him; he played it over in his head, trying this time to say the right things. He recalled the last time he'd seen Daphne. More than eighteen months—nearly two years ago. She had come to say good-bye before going north to act in repertory; had stood in a scarlet frock, aware of herself, yet not quite assured, saying, 'I play an unhappy wife for the first week, a betrayed girl for the second and a tart for the third; am I shocking you, can't I say things like that to you any more?... You shouldn't mind; Catholics don't, and you're as near as makes no difference; wish me luck, Mark, I shall need it, playing to six yobs in the pit, all the best people back home watching television. Why do I always come to you at moments of crisis, decision, or what have you? I used to try to hate you, you were my great hate—even now, you're a kind of friend and enemy, I don't know why.'

Moments of crisis, decision. As the clock moved a little way past nine, he began to rehearse the conversation again, wondering if he'd finally put her off.

At twenty past nine the door bell rang; he could feel the draught from the open front door; it always blew in like that, a small cold touch, vigorous, alert, saying, Come on, now, you've got to face this. When Daphne came into the room he found himself searching for the word that would define the difference he saw in her. Gentler? No, not quite. She still had about her an air of challenge, as if each entrance into a room were the prelude to an argument, perhaps a quarrel. But he still sought for the word—tolerant, perhaps? Ready, with a glint of mockery, to accept that there were other sides to the questions she'd been so certain of?

She greeted him a little guardedly. 'Mark? Greyer, aren't you, and isn't it becoming. ... Sit down, shall I? Yes, all right. Mind if I smoke? You're to watch me and not let me have more than six.'

He tried to put warmth and certainty into his welcome; but as on that evening in her room, many years ago, some part of him seemed to be pulling back, saying, I'm not in the right mood for this; I don't want it.

'We're going to have some coffee,' he said, 'Mrs. Shell will bring it any moment, on a trolley that sounds like a tumbril.' He found he would be glad of the coffee; something to do, to ease the early moments. He looked steadily at her, trying to fit this newer Daphne into the one he had last seen nearly two years ago.

Her glance caught his; the light mockery shone in her eyes. 'Think I've changed? Grown plainer? Not so nice?'

'No. You look well and handsome. Thinner, perhaps.'

'Time I got thinner. I'm twenty-four.'

'It sounds very young to me.'

'Oh, yes, it's young enough. I don't try to shoot that kind of "But I'm so terribly old" stuff. But, all the same, I haven't got as far as I ought to have done. Girls younger than me in this theatre racket have got further.'

'Is that what's worrying you?'

'Oh—no. Not really. I know all about work, my kind of work, I mean; that moment of luck comes—if it comes at all—at any hour of the day or night, early for some and late for others. Anyway, I may have got my big chance. Moment for holding the breath: maybe Daphne's coming bursting out as the white hope of the British stage. . . . Maybe not, at that.'

'What's the play?'

She waited while Mrs. Shell wheeled in the coffee. Mark saw the quick look which Mrs. Shell flung at Daphne, not hostile, but containing the acute, restrained envy of a middle-aged woman for one with the twin edges to her sword of youth and beauty.

When Mrs. Shell had gone Daphne stood up and walked towards the trolley. 'Shall I pour this? Black or white? Black for me; I drink lots of black coffee; not because I like it, but because I like to see myself drinking it: it makes a good picture in my mind. See how much I've learned about myself? . . . Sugar? Not for me, keeping thin. . . . What were we on? Oh, yes, my big chance.' She moved with light grace to her chair, sat and stirred her coffee. 'It's quite a thing, at that. Daddy's got a new play in rehearsal. And there's a girl who has hysterics in the second act who's been handed to me.' She frowned and made a small impatient movement with her head. 'I talk about myself all the time, don't I? Don't ask about you, or anything?'

'Let's hear about the play.'

'Well—it isn't all jam. I'm afraid Pop's going to be disappointed.'

'Why?'

'Because—first of all I have to tell you that Pop is a playwright who sticks around at rehearsals: has ideas—doesn't interrupt, I don't mean that, but he sits there radiating critical listening. And when I'm on stage the temperature revs up; he doesn't move an eyelash, but *I* know he's tuned up to the top note, and the whole atmosphere's so tense that I can't bear it, and of course I fluff everything. I don't think he knows he's doing this to me—in fact I'm sure he doesn't. But if only he wasn't there, I'd be all right. I'm pretty good. I've got an awful lot to learn, but what I do on the stage gets over the footlights—I suppose it's something to do with being noisy and assertive. But with Pop in the stalls all I've got to give staggers just about as far as the orchestra pit and then falls flat on its face.'

She smiled a little wryly at him. 'Still listening, Mark? Still with me? Or is your mind digging away at a lot of old-age pensioners?'

He grinned. 'No, you have the stage to yourself.'

'Seriously? Honestly? Of course I can see, if you've just come from something really fiendish, like hard-worked mums dying of cancer, and husbands who drink, all this must seem pretty . . . well, a bit on the trivial side, to say the least.'

'Oh, I hear each case on its merits.' He grinned at her again. 'Why don't you ask your father to stay away?'

'Oh, well, no can do. He is, after all, a Big Man of the Theatre; they may all grumble behind his back, but when he's there it's gangway for Gerald Minestaff and let's hear what he says, chairs pulled out of his way and touselled young men in pullovers standing on the bare stage listening . . . you know the sort. Not for me to reason why: I may be his daughter, and he may have helped soap my ears when he was young and struggling, but as far as the theatre is concerned I'm a very low form of life, and he's the tops.'

'But afterwards? When you're out of the theatre?'

'No good either. He doesn't say anything, and, heavens, nor can I. I try out sentences in my head first, but I can't say them. And the hell of it is that there's something else I want to tell him, and I can't because this not talking about my part in the play fills all the space between us. If you see what I mean.' She put down her cup. Of a sudden Mark saw that she was nervous. After a moment or two of hesitation she said, 'That's why I've come to you.'

Mark nodded. Mrs. Shell had her wireless on in the kitchen;

some sort of noisy modern wail was going on, with the background of an insistent jazzy beat; the whole thing too loud; it rasped his nerves. He tried to let nothing show, but Daphne's eye was on him. 'Worry you, listening to me? Make you nervous?'

'No.'

'I don't really see why it should.' She looked thoughtfully aside. 'After all, I'm not tied up with you in any way; never was——' She broke off abruptly, as if she, too, at that moment had remembered Lorraine.

'You tell me anything you want.' (But you bring a kind of danger with you, the cold wind of unrest. I don't know why.)

She stood up. 'Thing is, Mark, I want to get married. I have —as they say, or used to say—met my fate.'

He was surprised and somehow relieved. He had expected something more difficult.

He grinned with relief. 'A lucky man,' he said.

'D'you think so? Oh, Lord, no . . . on the whole, I think not. I can be a bitch when I'm angry, and I like my own way. But this is it, so far as I'm concerned. Him too, I think.'

He put his cup back on the trolley. 'Well?'

'It isn't quite as easy as all that. I suppose nothing is.'

'Very seldom.'

She made a small grimace, moved with the slightest suggestion of a swagger across the room; he tried to gauge where acting ended and reality began.

'Trouble is, it means taking him away from someone else——'

'He's married?'

'No—no. Even I obey the rules to that extent; in my church that's out.'

'So you still——'

'Oh, sure; I go along with my religion; that's part of the pattern that's me, sticking to things, hammering on; it's no great credit, mostly pride, I think, proving myself to myself.' Very slightly he saw her move one foot in time to the sound of Mrs. Shell's wireless; how serious is all this, he wondered.

'Well?' he asked again.

'He isn't married. But for some time he's been living with a woman. And it means taking him away from her. A woman a good bit older than me. Thirty, I'd say—perhaps more.'

He smiled slightly. 'Her life isn't over, you know.'

She answered seriously. 'I don't think thirty's old. I just mean it's older than me, and that makes it a bit . . . oh, surely you can see.'

'So—what are you asking me?'

She stood frowning a little unhappily. 'I don't know. I suppose I want to be told that it's all right to go ahead.'

'D'you know this woman?'

'Well—yes. Sort of.'

'Will she mind very much?'

Daphne frowned at the carpet. Her face looked suddenly lean. 'Yes, I think she will.'

'You haven't put a question to me yet.'

'No.'

'Are you afraid to?'

'Yes, perhaps.' She gave a quick, unhappy glance at him. 'You can't condemn it completely; you can't say I mustn't; no one can do that, not even my Church. It doesn't come under the heading of any of the sins.'

He said tentatively, 'Cruelty? That thing inside your head that tells you beyond all shadow of doubt that you're wrong?'

'Oh, I might have known you'd say that! Cruelty . . . and what about cruelty to me? Doesn't that count? This matters to me more than anything on earth. I can't lose him. I can't bear to lose him.'

He sat for a moment, turning the handle of his coffee spoon. 'What sort of man is he?'

'What sort? Oh Lord, I don't know, what sort is any man.'

He persisted gently, 'Loving? Honourable?'

'Oh, heavens, nobody is that; they're words. He loves me and wants me and I love him and want him: that's all there is to it, that's all there ever is.'

'Will he make you happy?'

'Oh, heavens; no, I shouldn't think so—oh, yes perhaps . . . in a way. He makes my hand shake just by being there; he turns me inside out, brain and body——'

She caught his glance. 'No, I haven't slept with him. Surprising as it may sound for a girl of twenty-four, I haven't slept with anyone. Haven't really wanted to, not enough, anyway. But this time it's different. I ache for him all the time.'

He could feel the force of her longing, there in the room. He closed his eyes for a moment, making an effort. I'm not giving this enough, he thought; falling short of concentration and sympathy; perhaps she was right, and somehow at heart I feel it's trivial beside other things. He said, 'Gerald and Lorraine? What's their view?'

'They don't like him. Or at least—Lorraine doesn't. Pop doesn't see people clearly who don't bump into his work, and Philip only bumps into the fringe of his work: he's a journalist who came to write Daddy up; that's how I met him. But Lorraine took one of those instinctive, feminine, scalp-prickling dislikes: she practically gives off sparks every time Philip comes in view.'

'Does she know you want to marry him?'

'No. Well, I haven't told her. She may have a kind of smudgy cloud of an idea, the way women do about other women, daughters or not. But she doesn't *know*; if she did she'd hate it and there'd be one almighty scene with tears and foot-stampings and "I'm your mother, Daphne——" the lot.'

'Doesn't that hold you up?'

'Should it? No, I don't think so.'

'If she wants you to be happy——'

'Wants me to be a success, rather. Wants me to get my life right. For her sake, not mine.'

'That is unkind. And unfair.'

She looked at him levelly for some moments. 'You sound angry for the first time.' He did not answer, and she shrugged. 'All right, I'll give you that. I'm unfair to her—always have been. But you can take it from me, if I marry him, there'll be fireworks from Lorraine.' She was looking doubtfully towards him. She said, 'Don't go against me, Mark. I need people on my side.'

He sat, saying nothing, his head down, and she answered for him, 'So does she, you'd say? Oh, I know, I know—let's leave that—just now it's me. Me, oh Lord, standing in the need of prayer.' She grinned at him, but her face was a little strained and shadowed, as if she'd been on a long journey.

His pity spoke to his irritation, his inadequate sympathy: She can't help it, that blazing egotism of the young; she's genuinely perplexed, and she doesn't want to cause pain. That should be enough.'

But still some inertia, some preoccupation weighted his mind and obscured his sympathy. He said, 'It'd be easier if I knew a bit more about the other people concerned. Both the man and the woman.'

'Yes. . . .' She moved slowly towards the window and back. Her head was bent; she looked disconsolate. 'I can see that, but I don't know how to do it. How can one explain people to someone who hasn't met them? *Really* explain them, I mean?' She lifted her head and looked unseeingly at a picture on the wall. 'It's no good trying to describe Philip; one can't describe people one's in love with; they're just a haze of joy and despair, they're not really people at all, they're like weather, making you hot or cold, happy or unhappy. As for her—' she frowned more deeply. 'I—I think she's tough. I mean—she's grown-up and smart and good-looking, it isn't as if . . .' She let her words trail, as if something in her disliked them. She gave him a sideways, apologetic glance. 'Well, you see . . . I can't explain. Not properly.'

'No.' He tried to black everything else out, to concentrate only on Daphne. 'I can't help feeling, you see, that whatever I say, you'll do what you want to do.' (Oh, the easiest of all ways out; you're not even trying.)

'All the same . . . be nice if you'd say something.' She paused, looking in front of her, and then made a sudden movement, as if she'd come to the end of a trail of thought and found certainty. 'No, it's not true, that I'd go ahead . . . that I wouldn't take any notice of advice. If someone—if you—came and put up a sword and said Positively Forbidden: *no one* to go beyond this point, not even Daphne—I'd obey. I'd do what I was told.'

A silence then. He said at last, 'I can't do that—I can't go so far as that, knowing so little. How can I? I can only say that if *you* have so much doubt, then you should wait longer . . . think more. . . .' The words were useless; he knew it as he said them. He looked up at her; she was standing with her head down, frowning, one hand running absently along the edge of a chair. She looked in some way abandoned. His heart misgave him. 'Look, Daphne. I admire you enough to say this: go by what you *know*. You'll be right, your judgment will be right——' He broke off.

She stayed silent and her silence seemed in some way to rebuke him. 'I've said all I can—the best I can!' he pleaded.

'Oh, yes—sure. I asked too much, anyway, I can see that; one's got to go it alone when it comes to the important things; no one can help you.' She seemed resigned, gentle now. She smiled at him across a new polite gulf. 'Sorry to come and bring trouble. . . . Not to worry, Mark. I shall work it out.' Her eye rested on him. 'You look as if things had been a bit tough for you, too.'

'Problems come and go.'

'Meaning I'm not the person to discuss them with?—oh, well, daresay that's right: I can't go far enough outside me; I'm fenced round with me; it's a whale of a job to be much interested in anything or anyone else. But I'd *like* to be. I'd like to be un-selfish and deeply sympathetic. But I'm not. Too bad. Any hope for me, Mark?'

'Yes, plenty.'

'Is that priest's talk? The party line? Oh—don't look shocked, you know what I mean. I go along with the party line, I've told you I do. But when it comes to . . . to making it real, to tying it up with living, so much of what they tell me is words. Make God the centre of your life, forget about yourself, put your-self last—oh, fine, yes, it all sounds good—but *how*, in God's name?'

'In God's name,' he repeated. 'Precisely. That is how you're to do it. How it may be done.'

Her eyes, still on him, enlarged a little. She was unmoving. 'You said that as if you wished you believed it.'

He turned away. 'The hardest thing, after all, in the world to do. One can be forgiven for finding it difficult sometimes.'

She looked as if she might argue further, but then seemed to accept his protest of privacy. 'Yes . . . indeed. Sorry, again, that I worried you.'

These last few minutes had an uncomfortable urgency, as if there were some vital thing he could say before it was too late, some-thing that would solve her problem, twist the whole encounter round and make it the right shape. She thrust her arms into a loose scarlet coat; it seemed to hang gaily and incongruously on her; she was like an actor, at odds with the panache of bright clothes.

'Good-bye, then, Mark. Thank you for bearing with me.'

He stood at the door, watching her go. As she walked the scarlet coat billowed and blew, darkly brilliant, like a warning.

§

Saturday of that week came in to the sound of heavy rain. Mark lay in bed, hearing the shrill liquid clamour on sill and roof and pavement. The day that woke you to rain, he thought, was different from other days, it was like being woken to a voice crying your name.

In the grey light he turned his clock face towards him. Not yet half past five; always, these days, he woke early. The rain seemed to enclose him; he saw his room shut in by the liquid steel-coloured bars of the rain. Warmth thickened the air and his head ached. The day before him seemed full of difficult prospects: a visit to the Police Court to speak for a woman charged with shop-lifting; a funeral at three; an argument with Raites, the manager, over the finances of the Boys' Club; a visit from his father.

He tried to prepare himself as best he could for saying Mass at seven, but his thoughts were muddied and confused. The image of Daphne's scarlet coat passed vividly across his mind; he tried to brush it away, saying, I did my best; I did all I could. She's in the kind of dilemma that needs a jolt from outside to solve it. Sooner or later—for me, too, perhaps—the unexpected thing will happen, to change and make an end.

He pushed aside his bed-clothes, got up and drew the curtains, and prepared to meet this day.

§

The rain continued all the morning, but at midday it drew off and gradually the drenched trees and the watery pavements threw back a blinding painful light. Drops splashed with hollow heaviness from the trees, gratings swallowed noisily, even the shadows were brilliant, blue as the sky.

Though the rain had stopped, the air was muffled, moist and heavy with sun. In the blinding light, Mark noticed that his headache seemed worse, his nerves irritably exposed. Someone had said that sunlight illumines the scars and rents of the heart; well, that's about it, he thought; I'd like to skip this day and get on to

the next, I don't know why. The scene at the Police Court had
left him frustrated and angry; he'd gone on talking, trying to
explain that Mrs. Blenskop, with three children under six beyond
her control and a husband living with another woman two streets
away, wasn't going to gain anything from punishment, but the
words had seemed to die on the air in the drab court. 'We have
to deal with facts,' the magistrate had said, and it had seemed useless
to protest that the whole desperate unavailing effort of Mrs.
Blenskop's life was a fact, and the only one of real importance.
Nevertheless he'd gone on talking, making, as far as the court was
concerned, a nuisance of himself, protesting from the body of the
room until a policeman put a hand on his arm to make him
sit down. Mrs. Blenskop stood and shivered in the dock, saying
nothing until she heard her sentence of three months' imprisonment,
when she gave a muffled yelp of protest and cried, 'But the Father
said——' She was taken away.

Back home at five o'clock Mark looked for the first time at his
post; amongst the letters a post card in Elliot's old wavering hand,
repeating the phrase, 'I do beg you to go soon.' For a moment
he saw Elliot as a forgetful old man who wrote the same thing
twice and whose advice could mean little. He tossed the card
down and went back to his desk.

Two sermons to-morrow; the notes on his pad swam a little
before his eyes; he remembered for the first time that he'd had no
lunch. He'd had to hurry to the funeral, and it'd been a tough one:
an only son dead and a mother far lost in the harsh barren country
of grief; he couldn't get her out of his mind. He thought, not for
the first time, that he would never be a professional parson; never
entirely think and feel in the context of the Church. He forced
himself back to his sermons. How quickly each Sunday came by;
as you grew older a week was nothing, a blink of the eye.

He glanced at his watch. Time for half an hour's work, perhaps,
before his father came. Each part of this day seemed oddly divided
from the rest; no trace now of that morning rain. He pulled his
notes towards him; his headache still went on.

§

'I want to have a serious talk with you, Mark. I hope you're
going to listen.'

'Yes, Father. D'you want some tea?'

'No, certainly I don't want tea. I get enough tea at that silly place—someone's always bringing me tea. Any hour of the day or night.'

'What did you want to say to me?'

'You'll be able to give me a drink before I go, won't you, Mark? You've got some somewhere, haven't you?'

'Yes.'

'Thought you would have. Don't know how you can afford it.'

'Simple. I can't.'

'Then why?'

Mark shrugged. 'I don't seem able to get through the job without it.'

'Not surprised to hear *that*. About this place I'm staying in. You won't know anything about it, you hardly ever come there——'

'I was there only a few days ago.'

'Oh, well, they didn't tell me; they never tell me anything; I don't expect at your age you know how irritating it is not to be——'

'About this place.' Mark leaned on his desk; he felt sick and his headache seemed worse; he wondered vaguely if he was going to be ill. His thoughts seemed to fly in odd directions; some part of his mind was making a note of the address of the mother who'd lost her son; if she wasn't in church to-morrow he must go and see her on Monday; try to talk to her and tell her that——

'You're not listening, Mark.'

'I'm sorry. Go on.'

'I don't like this place I'm in. I want to leave.'

'Yes. Why exactly?'

'It's not the right place for me. Oh, not at all. Not my kind of place. There's a silly old woman on the floor below—did you say something about a drink? Said you had some?'

'Yes. Before you go.'

'Oh, very well. Yes, I want to leave it. This place, I mean. You'll . . . find something better, won't you, Mark? Something more . . . well, quite frankly, my *class* of place. The man in the room across the landing has the most dreadful accent. . . . I think I'd like that drink now, Mark.'

'A little later——'

'What have you got? Whisky?'

With a sigh Mark rose and poured the drink.

'Oh, thank you.   Thank you.   Aren't you going to have one?
'Later, perhaps.'

'I should have thought you'd find it too stimulating; stimulating
to the wrong——'

'Where d'you want to go?'

'Yes, funny thing about drink: Shakespeare said that it increased
desire and took away the performance, but of course——'

'Father, where?'

The old man shrugged and fiddled with his glass. 'Oh, I don't
know. I don't know. Old Jim Elliot's been talking to me about
a place run by nuns, but I don't really want that. I suppose if the
worst came to the worst I could go there, but, well, as a matter of
fact, Mark, I've been thinking . . . adding things up. And it really
did seem to me it'd be so much better—better for everyone—if I
came and stayed here with you.'   The old blue eyes rested on Mark.
They were watchful, hopeful, wary, and in some way afraid.
'Perhaps just for a little while.'

Mark got to his feet. 'Yes, I will have a drink. I'll have a
couple of aspirin, too, I've got a bit of a headache.' His father
made no response to this, and Mark wondered if he'd said it aloud
or only thought it. When he'd poured the drink he walked to
the window and stood frowning at the sharp light.

His father was making brief, ruffled noises, moving about in his
chair. 'I can see,' he began with wavering dignity, 'I can see you
don't like the idea. Don't want——'

'It's what *you* want,' said Mark. 'You'd be happy with me?'

'Oh, well, I don't know about being happy; at my time of life
one doesn't expect to be happy; it merely seemed to me the best——'

'But you'd like it?'

'Oh . . . well, yes. I suppose so. After all, you are my son.
I get lonely sometimes.'

Mark stared out at the street. He said at last, 'Very well, Father.
I'll give Miss Challon a week's notice, and you can come here.'

'Oh, really? Really? Oh, well, yes. . . . I think you're right.
I think it'd be best.'

'And when you're here, you won't . . .'   He let it go; all he was
saying was, 'You'll try to be different from what you are,' and that
wasn't any good, was never any good.

'Well, I'm glad that's settled. Yes, very glad.' The old man shifted in his chair. 'I'd like another drink, Mark.'

'I mustn't give it you. I really mustn't.'

'Words. Doctor's nonsense. Oh, well, if you're going to be difficult about it; I don't want anything like that, arguments, having to ask, *plead* for things. Not going to do that.' He rose clumsily from the chair. His hands quivered; he looked impatient of them.

'I'll come back with you,' said Mark.

For a moment his father looked as though he would protest; then a shadow of resignation went over his face, a recognition of feebleness. 'Oh, well, if you'd like to. . . . Perhaps that'd be best.'

§

Nine o'clock. Somehow the aspirin and two more drinks hadn't removed the headache. He'd left most of his dinner; Mrs. Shell had taken it away with protests and advice about going to bed.

'Yes, all right; I'll go early. Catch up on some sleep.'

Mrs. Shell looked mildly astonished. 'That's the first time I've heard you say that.'

He grinned at her. 'I'm growing in wisdom.'

'About time too.'

'I'll do half an hour's work and be in bed by ten.'

'Gracious,' said Mrs. Shell, going out.

He sat at his desk, frowning at the unfinished notes for his sermons. His brain felt clumsy; the words slipped from its grasp like weights. Oh, come on, he told himself; half an hour's solid effort and the thing'll be done. Then bed, bed by ten; bed, sleep, darkness, softness, silence——

His nerves jumped. The door-bell. Loud in the quiet house, cracking the silence. Oh, no, he wanted to say; oh, go away and leave me alone; I've earned some peace, haven't I; I'm going to bed.

Mrs. Shell looked in, heavily conspiratorial. 'What shall I say?'

'Say I've gone to bed.'

'That's right. So you have in spirit.'

'Yes.'

'It'll be someone most likely who'll talk till midnight, and to-morrow's Sunday. You can't keep going day *and* night, you know. Something cracks in the end.'

He made a movement with his shoulders; his skin prickled with irritation; he wanted to say to Mrs. Shell, Oh, look; just stop all that; just leave it that I'm tired and I'm going to bed and I'm not going to see anyone——

The bell sounded again. Long and rather desperate: perhaps someone in great distress, someone who, if help were not forth-coming ...

He sighed heavily and flung down his pencil. 'Oh, it's no good; I'll have to see them. If it's just a talker I'll cut it short.'

'But——'

'No, no, go and answer it. If it's for me, say I'm here. Hurry up. The sooner we get started, the sooner it'll be done.'

The scuffle of arrival in the hall, the draught, a trace of a woman's voice that somehow he knew for certain was not Daphne's but was also terribly familiar. ...

'Oh, heavens,' he said, as he got to his feet. 'Lorraine.'

'Hullo, Mark.' She stood just inside the door, making short nervous pulls at the fingers of her gloves.

'*Lorraine.*'

He had no composure or readiness to meet this; he felt jarred and incapable of finding any words that would suit her. 'What an astonishing thing.'

'You sound ... angry?'

'No ... no. Surprised. I haven't seen you for three years.'

'Four.'

'Four,' he repeated, looking at her. Older, perhaps, but the age did not seem to be part of her; it was as if she had said, I'll put this on to show you what I'll look like when I begin to be old. 'Good heavens,' he said.

'Am I a nuisance! Are you busy? The good body who opened the door growled at me and said you were going to bed early.'

He smiled a little wryly. 'I was.'

'Really?' She looked round the room, her eyes faintly puzzled. 'Is this a hard job, Mark? The Church, I mean?'

'Fairly hard.'

'Is it? I never thought parsons worked; I always saw them blessing people and sitting back giving holy and unacceptable advice. ...'

He started to speak; checked himself; he'd learnt years ago that it was never any good being angry with Lorraine. He moved a chair for her and she sat in it, as beautifully as she had always sat in chairs; Lorraine, he thought, will move beautifully on her death-bed.

She went on, glancing at him as he lit her cigarette, 'Sorry, didn't mean to be rude. Don't look so worried; I know you're not glad to see me; I didn't expect you to be.'

He looked steadily at her. Glad? No, I don't think so; I don't know what I feel; impatience, even a kind of anger; even, when I look at her, a trace of the old pain.

She was looking at him a little anxiously. 'I've kept away, haven't I? It seemed the only thing to do. Though sometimes I used to think ... Oh, I don't know, I used to think how wonderful it would be to come and talk to you, pour it all out, everything, and for you to listen and understand and make it all right——'

'Make what all right?'

'Oh, I don't know ... how one feels as one gets older; how one's set inside a kind of loneliness and can't get out. Talking to parsons never attracted me much; I always saw them somehow bloodless and less than human, like fish—but if the man were *you*——' She raised her head as if some third person had tapped her on the shoulder to remind her that time was running out. 'Anyhow, I didn't come. But now—Mark, I need your help. Badly. And there's no one else I can ask.'

He nodded and sat down a little heavily in the desk chair. He could see the pencilled notes on the desk; they looked oddly far off, as if written many months ago.

'Don't say no, please.'

'I'll try not to.'

'It really is terribly important—oh, well, important to me, yes— but not only to me; it's something that's got to be done—has really got to be; you mustn't say no.' She was shivering and mild hysteria thinned her voice. He said, 'I think you'd better have a drink.'

She looked at him with the vague, not quite focusing glance of someone whose immediate problem walls her world. 'A drink ... I should never have thought ... do parsons have drink?'

'This one does.'

She glanced up at him, as if for a moment catching a glimpse of something outside her own distress. She took the glass; said in a tired, placid voice, 'I don't like whisky'; sipped it and grimaced like a child taking medicine.

'It'll do you good,' he said, taking one for himself. Her eye followed it, but she said nothing. He stood now, looking at her and waiting.

'It's Daphne,' she said.

'Yes.'

'I've been up north, in Edinburgh, with some friends of mine.' He caught a flash of the long-perished climate of jealousy; the man who would have thought, What friends? Lorraine went on. 'I wasn't due home until to-morrow, but I came a day earlier. I had a kind of hunch—I prickled with the need to be back.' She made a small irritated movement with her shoulders. 'Does that wireless go on all the time?'

'It's my housekeeper's. I'm sorry about it. It keeps her happy.'

'Oh, well.' She took a little more of the drink. 'Almost as soon as I got back, Gerald rang up in a blasting fury from the theatre. He said Daphne'd thrown up her part in his play and gone off—to-day—with this man. Of course the play business was the only thing that really worried him: he went on about how it was the one unforgivable sin, how she'd finished her career, how she'd never get another part . . . as if all that mattered.'

'Where's she gone?'

'To Dover. They're getting married by special licence to-morrow morning, and crossing to France the next day.'

'And you want to stop her.'

'I've got to stop her. Oh, please—you must help me. It's meant that I should stop her, else why did I come home a day early?'

'Meant by whom?'

She shrugged. 'Oh, I don't know; Providence, I suppose.'

'Well?'

'You must help me. You don't know this man. I do. He isn't any good, he'll make a mess of her life, I know the kind he is . . . oh, so well do I know. He's out for himself, all the way; everything he can get, and that includes plenty of women. Not only Daphne.'

He said to his glass, 'Perhaps she knows that. Perhaps she's ready to settle for it.'

'She *can't* be. She mustn't. She's—I don't know what it'll do to her. She thinks she's grown-up and tough and sophisticated, but she couldn't take that. She may be saying she could, but that's just a pretty idea. The thing is different. Like saying you're not afraid to die, and dying.'

Again, he got a flash-back: how Lorraine could suddenly, amidst a lot of talk, seem so wise. I don't like any of this, he thought; I should have gone to bed; I should have told Mrs. Shell. . . . He moved his head, trying to concentrate. 'Daphne always had courage.'

'Oh—courage, yes; that isn't enough. It helps, perhaps; I wouldn't know, I never had much. But you can't just let the child walk into a marriage like this, and say it's all right because she's brave——'

'She's scarcely a child. Old enough to take her own decisions.'

'Yes, but—oh, Mark, you must *see*. It isn't as if he were just some young man that I didn't awfully like—he's older than she is and he's going to make her damnably unhappy——'

'How can you be certain?'

'Oh, because I *know* about people; because I'm a woman and I see what goes on inside people, not just the outer layer of varnish as men do. This man's been living with another woman; he's walking out and leaving her flat because he's met someone younger and more attractive. He'll do the same to Daphne; can't you *see* that?'

'I don't know the man.'

'You can take my word——'

'Up to a point.' He seemed to have to make an effort all the time; to smother some part of his mind that wanted to play this over again and make Mrs. Shell go to the door and say, No, I'm sorry, he can't see anyone, he's gone to bed. . . . He went on. 'But you might be wrong. People change—even the worst of them fall in love, now and again; perhaps he really does love her——'

'I tell you, that kind of man——'

'Even so; even supposing he makes Daphne suffer—that could, in the end, be a good thing. She might be . . . let's say, a more worth while person, because of it.'

'Oh, what's the good of saying that? It's just another pretty idea. Can you honestly say that you'd want someone you loved to suffer? If you were me, could you? I haven't anyone but Daphne. We haven't always got on: mothers and daughters don't, but underneath she's all I've got, all that really matters. Oh, Gerald, yes, but work and God take up all his time; I'm a kind of well-known stranger. Daphne's my child, I produced her and brought her up and loved her; I'm not going to see her crash head-on before her life's even begun.'

Mark frowned, recognizing the woman whose time of love was past, making a final grasp at her child. He said, 'What is it you want me to do?'

'Talk to her. Persuade her.'

'How? You say she's left town——'

'I want you to come with me. To-night.'

'*To-night?*'

'Please, Mark, listen. I know where she is—she told Gerald the name of the hotel. I've got the car outside. Oh, please, listen. It isn't a long drive. We could be down there in two hours——'

'But, my dear girl, to-morrow's Sunday. I've got a service here at eight o'clock——'

'Yes, yes, I know, but you could be back. Once you'd talked to her, persuaded her, we could come straight back.'

'Giving both of us a restful night——'

'No, no, please don't be angry; please listen. She'll talk to you, believe what you tell her, I know she will——'

He was silent.

'She will, you can't deny it; she used to hate you, or tell herself she did, but now she respects you, she goes to you in trouble. Nothing I say'll make any difference, but you can. Oh, Mark, I do beg you to come.'

He stood, still silent. With evening the clouds had thickened and spread; the rain had started again. This day that had begun in rain, was, it seemed, ending in rain too. His thoughts were muddied: the headache, perhaps, or the drink, or the heavy, darkly-raining sky. 'I feel somehow that her life's her own. That she isn't a child of seventeen being kidnapped; that she's a woman with judgment and insight and——' (But do I feel all this? Or do I just want to get to bed early?)

'Oh, nonsense! She's a child who thinks she's in love. She's as much judgment and insight over this as a blind kitten——'

'No, you're wrong; she knows all about him; she's got it all clear——'

'Oh, *Mark*! What's the good of saying all those things? It's what I keep telling you, they're only words. She can't marry him. You must come. You said ... I daresay you've forgotten, but *I* haven't—you said, that day we parted, that if ever I wanted anything, I could ask you and you'd do it. Do you remember saying that?'

He stood frowning and looking down. 'Yes.'

'Can you go back on it? It was a promise.'

He looked to right and left, as if he sought some way of escape. Nothing presented itself. 'Suppose she won't listen to me—won't see me, even?'

'I'll make her. She must.'

'We can't force her——'

'She'll do what you say.'

'You can't be certain——'

'It's our only chance.'

He drew his hand across his forehead. He thought of saying, I don't feel very well; but it sounded feeble, like an excuse. He emptied his glass and put it down. He felt at a distance from his own fatigue; he thought, I suppose I'm held together by drink.

'You did promise, Mark. It means everything to me.'

He lifted his eyes to face her. She was pleading, sad, at his mercy. Some part of the old love shifted like a load inside him. He'd failed Daphne; perhaps he'd got to pay for that now.

'All right,' he said, 'I'll come. I'll do what I can.'

§

He sat beside Lorraine in the car, a passenger being taken on a dubious journey. The rain drummed on the roof, light from the street lamps went sliding away down the full gutters. He felt absolved from responsibility, driven on, fast and fluid, like the rainwater. 'It was a promise,' she had said. Later, perhaps, he would discover the flaw, the thing he should have said in answer; now he could only agree, but with a deep mistrust, as if he stepped on to a plank whose end grew slippery and sloped downwards.

The night went past them with the sound of wet and heavy wings. He felt cold and cramped, but the touch of fear, of doom waiting, began to leave him; he was just tired and uncomfortable, doing a silly thing because Lorraine had asked him to, and the pattern of doing what Lorraine wanted still held. He glanced at her; her face looked pale in the small dark cabin of the car, eyes turned away from him, hair vanishing into shadow; it was like dreaming of her; the frequent dreams down the years of absence.

'You didn't want to come, did you?' she said flatly.

'No.'

'It was the only thing to do.'

He was silent. It began to be like a dream; a half-waking dream where one part of his mind knew that he was dreaming, that reality was different, being made up of his desk and his room and Mrs. Shell moving about downstairs. The journey seemed to relax into long black rhythmic waves, each one growing from the other, swelling and forcing them on. . . . His eyes closed, and for a few moments the sound of the rain was the morning's rain, and he was lying in bed and all this day was still before him——

He sat up suddenly, sharply aware that she'd stopped the car. He swallowed, blinked and rubbed his eyes. They were at the side of a long featureless stretch of road; open fields lay to right and left, lonely in the dark. 'What's the matter?'

She was leaning on the driving wheel, her head on her arm. 'I don't know. Tired or something. A bit sick.'

'Rest here for a little.'

'No, we must get on.' She moved her head slowly; she looked drawn and pale. A lorry beat heavily past on the road; her hands trembled. 'Mark, do something for me?'

He tried to smile. 'What now?'

'Take over the driving.'

A motor-bicycle speeded past, grinding like a drill; he didn't like this place, with the deserted fields and the harsh unlovely stretch of road and Lorraine looking drawn and ill beside him. He was silent.

'*Please*, Mark. We've come so far——'

'Yes, I know, but——'

'You used to drive; you always enjoyed it——'

'Yes. But I've no licence now.'

'Oh, that doesn't matter. We shan't get into any trouble. . . .

The roads are almost empty. I'll be all right for driving home. Just for the rest of the way ... please, Mark.'

He was staring at the collection of things under the dashboard of the car: dusters and maps and a half-empty packet of cigarettes, a pair of Lorraine's gloves. They were small and intimate and ordinary and he hoped, by looking at them, that this moment would become ordinary too. It did not; he remained a little frightened, conscious of the night sky, the sound of the rain, the occasional assault of noisy wheels, the barren road.

I suppose I shall have to do it, he thought; I don't see any way out. More and more like a dream: doing things with an uncommitted ease, while some other part of his mind said, You *can't* be doing this.

'Yes,' he said at last. 'Very well.'

'Oh, fine. Oh, bless you.' He saw, as they changed places, that her cheek was marked with tears. He pulled a rug from the back of the car and put it round her. 'What can I do for you?'

'Nothing. Just drive on. Just get to her, then I shall be all right.'

'You don't want something? Medicine or something? Shall I stop and knock up a chemist?'

She gave a faint giggle which brought back a whole world of the Lorraine of the past. 'Sounds rather unkind. No. I'm all right. Just go on ... quickly. As quickly as you can.'

The road looked like black ice in the rain; she said, 'You'll go fast, won't you, Mark? As fast as you can?' He nodded, driving on. He had lost sight of an end to this journey; his thoughts went no further than the needs of the car; the drops of rain in the head-lamps, like splinters of light; the track of the windscreen wiper.

'Please go faster, Mark. A little faster.'

It was difficult not to try to please her. He felt the car move more quickly, the long black lake of the road plunged continually away; somewhere in his mind that third person revived, who spied on him and said, 'There goes Mark Harvist, he'd do anything for anyone he loves; and he loves her, he's always loved her.'

For that was true; slowly, wearing its way back through the anæsthetic of the years was the ache of loving. It was a placid, undemanding, undesiring love; he wanted only to be certain of her happiness and safety. This was the old haze of loving, the words singing in his head: I can do this, I've got it right. He went faster; this was the lordly speed of a man for whom luck has turned his way, with the sense that risks were being taken care of, that someone—God, perhaps, or St. Christopher, or just a golden margin of good fortune, was shielding him from any danger. In this fast and insulated ride perplexity and stress were lost; at the edge of his mind was a rim of promise: perhaps his own conflict was ending; perhaps in some way making this journey was going to solve it all. . . .

His glance flicked towards Lorraine and then back to the road. 'Are you asleep?'

'No.'

'Cold?'

'Yes, a little.'

'Afraid?'

She shook her head. 'No. It stops you being afraid if you know what to do.'

'Can you see the time?'

She held her wrist to catch the light. 'Just after eleven.'

'Soon be there.'

'We've done well.'

A lorry came in from a side road; its high, noisy shape rattled and swayed in front of them; he slowed down. He felt Lorraine move impatiently.

'All right,' he said. 'I'll get ahead as soon as I can.'

He drove on behind the heavy, harsh shape. The red tail light glowed at the corner of his field of vision. He began to dislike the lorry.

'Now, Mark? Surely now?'

The sense of luck was still with him as he pulled clear of the lorry. The shining road was empty; he began to go fast.

I say, look out.

The words didn't seem to come from anywhere; perhaps they were in his own head.

The luck broke; he jammed all the brakes on, but he was aware of clumsiness, a failure to grasp firmly and quickly enough; the wet road greased his tyres and sent the car in a swift and angry curve towards the motor-cycle that came from the hidden turning. He had time to pray for Lorraine, to say, 'Please God, save her, for it was my fault'; and then the moment came and towered over him like a high black wave, and then broke in the sound of falling glass, the cry of a voice, and then became silence; a silence like the end of things.

CHAPTER NINE

DENIS BRAND came into the bar of the Steel Crags Hotel in Fastness. He kept the rope round his shoulder just long enough for it to be noticed, then slung it off. Some part of him knew he did this; knew also that he stood squarely digging in his pockets for change, hoping to catch and hold a glance. He shrugged the charge of vanity away: young, sunburnt, coin-carved face, a mass of fair and shining hair; who wouldn't be vain?

'Pint of bitter, please, Maggie.'

Not many people in the bar: two pairs of hotel residents, filling in half an hour before dinner; old Sam Faskett from the post office, and two brick-red young men in corduroy shorts and enormous sweaters sitting in stupefied exhaustion over their beer. The wide window showed a metal-coloured, fast-vanishing light; tides of mist were diminishing the hills, and the fine, windy day was going down in evening rain.

Denis gave a sigh of mixed exhaustion and pleasure, and hoped someone would ask him what he'd been doing. If so, he'd pass quickly over to-day's climb (though it had been a Severe, and at any other time he'd have been glad to explain that there weren't half a dozen people who could lead it) and on to yesterday. The whole thing had been excitement from beginning to end, but part of the excitement had been that glow in his head at the prospect of standing in the middle of a breathlessly interested group, saying casually, 'Yes, I was there. I helped to bring him down.'

For want of anyone better, he leaned across the bar to Maggie. She was young, North Country and brisk; somehow impervious to the sun-god face and his prowess in the hills; he did not like her.

'That poor chap's still on the danger list, you know. The one we brought down from Heel's Tor.'

'Aye; so I heard.'

He had the attention of the couple nearest him; the woman, leaning with one elbow on the bar counter, had turned her head.

He kept his eyes on Maggie. 'Shouldn't think he stood much chance, myself. He looked like a goner the moment I saw him.'

Maggie only nodded, pausing very slightly in the act of polishing a glass to look at some point in front of her with a faint smile, as if she saw his vanity there. A small flame of anger lit somewhere in his head.

The woman on his right said, 'You were one of the rescue party?'

'Yes. We brought him down from the foot of Heel's Tor to the road. Poor chap.'

The woman made a sort of mooing noise of sympathy and admiration. 'I do think rescue work is such a splendid thing.'

He tried to keep his eyes on her, and to ignore Maggie who went on polishing the glasses and smiling.

'It was a hell of a job—getting the stretcher down. In the dark too. Of course we gave the chap a shot of om and scop—that's a kind of morphia—but it's a hell of a job to take him down smoothly.'

'Oh, it must be.'

She was rather a silly woman, but pretty in a vacant way; her husband had his head bent towards his glass. She went on, 'I suppose you have to be a terribly good climber yourself before you can go out and rescue other people.'

'Oh, well—' he still tried to keep Maggie's face out of his field of vision—'yes, I suppose you might say that.' He looked modestly down at his glass.

'Do you often get called out?'

'Well—quite often.' (And when was the last time? Never mind; it spoiled the show to say it was eighteen months ago.) 'Hardest time is in the winter, especially at night. You get ice then, and it's nasty.' (And when had he been out in winter at night? Oh, let it go; he was off now, drunk with the look of sheepish wonder the woman was giving him.) 'Best thing, of course, is when they're not hurt too badly, and you can get them down in time. Hope there's a chance for this chap, but I doubt it: he had multiple fractures of his leg, and head wounds; there was blood all over the rocks. When I saw——'

It was the little movement Maggie made, leaning over the

counter, that stopped him. She was looking just beyond his shoulder with an expression of pleased malice.

'Good evening, Mr. Holroyd!' she said. 'And Jim! I didn't see you waiting there; I was lost in Mr. Brand's story—what'll you have?'

Denis swung round; swallowed hard. A little spinning noise of shame and anger started up in his head: Holroyd and Jim Brooks, two of the most experienced climbers in the game, who'd been on harder climbs than he could ever do, who'd been there yesterday and been far more expert at handling the chap on Heel's Tor than Denis had.

They were grimy, coloured by the weather, slightly dashed by the rain. They came to the bar, gave him a nod, ordered their beer, then stood looking at their boots. The silence went on long enough for Maggie to draw two pints of bitter and slap the money into the till.

Denis finished his beer in nervous gulps; he wanted to say something to Jim or Holroyd, but the words wouldn't come. They stood murmuring together in the tired ashamed way of men who want to keep to themselves. He could have wept, cried angrily aloud, 'Oh don't be so po-faced about it! We all like to shoot a line sometimes, if the truth were told!' Gradually talk came back to the bar, leaving him isolated. He put down his glass and went quickly out, not saying good night.

He was humiliated and angry and hurt; but that wasn't the last word. Ever since they'd brought the chap down yesterday from Heel's Tor he'd had something on his mind. He'd done nothing about it, but now he was going ahead, because he'd made a fool of himself at a bar counter, and it seemed that to make this gesture would in some way restore his pride.

§

The Superintendent drew a square on a piece of blotting paper, put the figure '4' inside it, developed each side of the square into a triangle, then looked at it broodingly. After some moments he crossed it out, and threw down his pen.

Four days. Some people, he'd heard, were ready to bet that Harvist would hold out a week; others, even, that he'd get away with it altogether. . . .

Four days. He yawned and sighed; he'd slept badly, and the room was stale with evening and cigarette smoke and his pallid dead tea. Four days. Doesn't awfully worry me, just at the moment; funny thing, but that climbing accident put it out of my mind. Not much hope for him, they said; don't like it, young chaps like that, throwing their lives away. . . .

'Silly lad,' said the Superintendent aloud, and sat looking at the violent, unnecessary pain on Heel's Tor. Nineteen years old. His eyes smarted; he argued crossly, Sentimental be damned; I had a son of that age, blown to bits at Anzio—fighting for his country. Yes, well, I suppose that's different—dying *for* something, though for what exactly, just at this moment it'd be hard to say. Finished his mother; she died soon afterwards of a broken heart; yes, well, they say people don't die of a broken heart, but I don't know what else she died of.

'Yes, come in,' he said to the knock on the door; his voice sounded tired and sad; he was a long way from the police station.

The Sergeant with sandy hair kept one hand on the door handle. 'Friend of yours would like to see you——'

'I'm working.'

'Says he's got some news, sir.'

'Who is it?'

'Young Mr. Brand.'

'Oh,' said the Superintendent, not liking Denis Brand very much. 'Well, all right, I suppose he'd better come in.'

He thought when Denis stood before him that perhaps he'd heard that not very gracious sentence. Invited, Denis sat down in the chair opposite the desk; the Superintendent kept a brooding glance on him, wondering what it was he didn't like. Crazy for himself, I suppose that's it. Too good-looking and knowing it; you can see the knowledge going on all the time at the back of his eyes. 'Well?' he asked.

'You know I was on that rescue party yesterday? On Heel's Tor?'

The Superintendent moved his shoulders as if a draught blew round them. The point of the rescue was that the lad was badly hurt, not that Denis had been on it. Perhaps I'm being unfair, he thought. 'Yes—were you? Well?'

'And of course you know this chap, Harvist, the escaped prisoner
—was a parson?'

'Yes,' said the Superintendent dryly, 'I'd heard that.'

'*Well.* . . .' Denis leaned forward; a muscle clenched and un-
clenched in his cheek. Oh, cut this heavy stuff, thought the
Superintendent; nothing's as dramatic as all that, nor need it take
so long to tell. 'When we got to the foot of Heel's Tor,' Denis
was saying, 'there was a chap already there, sitting beside the boy.
Middle-aged, tired looking.'

'Like me.'

Denis shook his head slowly and solemnly; (Humourless too,
thought the Superintendent, that's another thing). 'Oh no, he
was lean this chap and rather good-looking——'

Well, hell, thought the Superintendent.

'And the thing *was*,' Denis went on, tapping the desk, 'that he
was a parson.'

'How d'you know?'

Denis's eyelids fluttered; the words had been a little sharp.
'This chap—the one who fell, I mean—had some idea about con-
fessing—being absolved, don't they call it?—and this other man,
the one I'm telling you about, had done the trick.'

'How d'you know that?'

'The boy said something—asked if the other chap really was a
parson. If he could really forgive his sins, and so on. And he
said Yes. Not my line, all that.'

'Nor mine,' said the Superintendent absently. He drew out a
photograph of Mark Harvist and tossed it across the desk. 'This
him, d'you think?'

'Why, *yes*. Oh, goodness yes, I'm sure it is.'

Funny, the Superintendent thought; I'd been hoping he'd say
no. The little leaden weight of disappointment went on pulling
at his heart. He took the photograph back, absently smoothed a
bent corner. 'Taken your time about coming, haven't you?'

Denis's eyelids fell. 'I didn't think of it at first.'

'What about the others? The rest of your party? Penny didn't
drop there, either?'

'No one said anything. You must admit the photos in the
papers haven't looked much like that.' He nodded towards the
photograph on the desk.

'No; curious thing about newspaper photographs; they never look like anybody.'

'And then of course there was this woman with him——'

'Woman?'

'She told me she was his sister——'

'Harvist hasn't got a sister.'

Denis shrugged. 'They were travelling together by car.'

'By *car*?' The Superintendent rang for his Sergeant; said when he came in, 'You'd better listen to this . . . by car, you say?'

'Yes,' said Denis, with a satisfied glance at the Sergeant; at last someone was taking notice. 'It all helped to put me off; somehow you don't think of these things. Or well—let's say you think of them, but you're afraid of making a fool of yourself.'

Yes, I can believe that, thought the Superintendent; that rings true.

'But I kept turning it over in my mind,' Denis went on, 'and it sort of—you know how things do?—became clearer. I got more sure.'

'Why?'

'Oh, I don't know, exactly. At the time it was all so strange—the chap badly hurt and the dark and the Very lights, and the woman there——'

For a moment the Superintendent saw it; the fallen body and the figures crowding round.

'There was so much to do one scarcely had time to think. I turned to look once or twice at this parson chap——'

'What did he do?'

'Sort of—well, I don't know exactly; he looked rather white and scared, but then, of course, the lad wasn't a pleasant sight, and it was dark; we all looked like ghosts——'

The Superintendent tapped the photograph. 'Yet you're sure this was him?'

'Oh, yes. Yes. I saw enough of him for that. The moon was up as we brought the lad down to the road, and we could see quite clearly then.'

The Superintendent sighed, and switched on the wireless speaker at his side. 'Superintendent calling Control. . . . Yes. . . . Got some news. Harvist may be travelling in a car with a woman . . . says she's his sister. . . . He was seen last night at the foot of Heel's Tor, above Stile Pass . . . you'd better seal off all the main roads to the north. . . . Yes. Yes. Where's the Inspector? . . . Oh, is he? Well, he won't find him there. Tell him to move further north fast, and keep in wireless contact with me. Right.'

The Sergeant leaned forward. 'Interesting about the car, sir. And the woman. Accounts for a lot.'

Denis looked more and more encouraged. 'You could have knocked me down with a feather when this chap said he was a parson. He didn't *look* like one—not one little bit——'

'Wasn't wearing his cassock, I suppose,' said the Superintendent.

'No, but—oh, I see, a joke. Don't know much about the clergy, but one has a sort of idea in one's mind—doesn't one?—of what they do look like——'

'Usually wrong—don't you agree, Briggs?'

The Sergeant grinned. 'In my experience, sir, once out of that collar your guess is as good as mine.'

'So I'd've thought.'

Denis leaned forward. 'Yes, but—I must say, I do find the whole Harvist story so odd. Beats me entirely how a man like that—goodness me, not only a gent but a *parson*—could get himself in this kind of fix. Getting roaring drunk and crashing about the Dover Road at night——'

'It wasn't quite like that.'

'The Judge seemed to think so.'

'Harvist struck unlucky. They'd found plenty of alcohol in his blood-stream; he elected to go for trial, and he got old Sir Hugh Lawton. Lawton isn't exactly renowned for leniency at any time, but when it comes to what he calls the-man-with-every-advantage, who has too much to drink——'

'So he *was* drunk?'

The Superintendent shrugged. 'Harvist said he'd eaten nothing all day and had several drinks in the course of the evening. But he swore he wasn't drunk. He swore he was able to drive. But then, of course, he was driving this woman's car and he had no licence. And he had an accident——'

'Accident! I'll say it was an accident. How many people killed?'

'Three. Harvist's woman passenger, and the father and child on the motor-bike.' The Superintendent brooded. 'When Harvist was told what had happened, he said he wished he'd died too.'

'Well—I'll bet. Having *that* on your mind. And a parson too. What did he get?'

'Three years.'

'And tried to cut it short by running away——'

'Don't think it was that.' The Superintendent's head was down and he was striking at the edge of his desk with the blunt side of his penknife. 'Don't think so—do you, Briggs?'

'Beyond me, sir. Suppose he wanted to try his luck.'

'No . . . seems to me he must have had too much time to think. To remember. A cell's not the best place if you can't bear to think.'

'Yes, but—' Denis ran a hand over his hair—'isn't that part of the punishment? I mean—other chaps stick it out.'

The Superintendent slightly shrugged, not wanting to argue. If he had to chose between Harvist and Denis Brand, he thought, he'd choose Harvist, and was not quite certain why. He'd felt he'd had enough of Denis Brand, and said, 'Briggs, you'd better go and get on to Control and find out how things are going. . . . Thank you, Denis. Useful information.'

Denis rose to go, looking a little disappointed, as if he'd expected more.

When they'd both gone, the Superintendent found that somewhere in his mind, distracting him, was a picture of Harvist (for he was certain it was he) sitting on the mountain-side in the growing dark beside the injured boy and absolving him of his sins. 'Well, it beats everything, doesn't it?' he said at last to some other part of himself. 'How can some words said in the dark on the stones by a chap on the run mean anything, one way or the other?' But the other part of himself went on looking at the picture, aware of unofficial and immeasurable things in this small ugly room.

He pulled the file on his desk towards him. He hadn't much doubt they'd get him now. Car or no car, they knew what to look for. Funny to think he'd never met Harvist; he seemed to know him with a peculiar intimacy. He looked down again at the photograph, but shook his head. This wasn't the man he knew; he'd learned that men were often unrecognizable from even the best photograph. Harvist wasn't this anonymous pattern of flesh: he was the car accident, the prison sentence, the dash into the mist, the vigil by the boy on the stones. . . .

He tried to imagine Harvist being brought to him. It'd be a

triumph of a kind, you couldn't deny that; but some faint misgiving stirred in his bowels. Perhaps it was nothing, only lack of
sleep. He'd take something to-night, else he thought he might
lie awake and see the mountain-side and the blood-splashed rocks
and the man crouching beside the boy who had fallen.

§

Carefully, Mark shifted his position in the front seat of the car.
The moon had died, and there was little light. Beside him Gillian
slept. It seemed the perfect moment; now was his chance.

He could just see the dial of Gillian's wrist-watch: nearly five
o'clock. He must have slept himself, though it did not seem like
sleep, only like strange vivid pictures going over his mind: of the
boy, of the rescue party, of the high rocks of Heel's Tor.

Very carefully he slipped down the handle of the car's door and
got out. He glanced back, but Gillian had not woken. He
stretched cramped limbs, glancing about him at the steep fellsides.
Yes, the darkness was thinning a little, the rough grasses stirring in
a dawn wind. There seemed a threat somewhere in the growth of
this grey light, as if the day came in to the sound of muffled drums.

'Where now?' Gillian had asked last night, when the rescue
party had taken the boy away. 'Back,' Mark had said, 'back the
way we've come.' She had not argued, obeying him in silence.
Why had she obeyed him? He shrugged; the question no longer
mattered; his plan was made. He stood now within a few miles
of Fastness. 'We've gone in a circle,' was all she'd said. 'We've
got nowhere.' He had not replied.

Now her words recurred to him. Nowhere. It rang bleakly
through the grey morning; he wandered to the beck whose water
wore a pale skin of light, and stood staring down at it, at the
continual, changing yet changeless water. Nowhere?

There came to his mind some words of Daphne's, spoken to him
not long after the accident: 'Won't you take any comfort? Is that
how it is? You'll kill yourself that way; anyone would. I could,
but I'm not going to. What good does it do? I may sound hard
and tough, but I'm being wise as well. I know I am, because
one's got to survive somehow.' When she paused, a new sadness
came down on her face; she wore it a little stiffly as if it were something to which she was not yet accustomed. 'I'm not getting

through to you, am I? But I'm talking sense. There'll be, from now on, plenty of people to rub it in and make it worse. Your only hope is to remember that there's something more important than the thing you've done; something inside you that must forgive yourself and go on and endure. That's true; it's something I've learnt.'

Nowhere? Perhaps a little way, he thought, as he turned from the beck; not far enough, but a little way.

He walked back to the car. Bird song clamoured; the dark was draining away. Gillian still slept.

She looked young and vulnerable in sleep. 'I'm sorry,' he said to her in his mind; 'hard to go without saying good-bye or thank you, or even telling you that I'll repay all you've given me. But there's nothing else for me to do now.'

He paused a moment longer, somehow reluctant to go, then turned away. His mind mapped clearly for him the road ahead. The day was coming in without sun; the clouds were close packed, and on the morning wind was a light trace of rain. But he had not far to go——

'Oh, please, no!'

She was standing beside the car. He turned back, and came towards her. His heart was beating heavily now; the day was coming up; he'd waited too long.

'I dreamt you were going. I dreamt you'd gone.' He saw there were smudged tears on her face. 'I must have heard something. I dreamt—please, don't go.'

'I thought you were asleep.'

'I hardly slept; I kept dreaming; about the boy; about you. Don't go. I'm frightened.'

'Why?'

'I don't know. Perhaps the boy, or just the dream I had. . . .'

'Why are you crying?'

'I don't know. I woke up crying.'

He stared at her in the dark grey clarity of this unlighted morning. Her tears seemed to make her a different person. Her face seemed colourless, a cast of flesh and light and shadow in unfamiliar form. She was shivering, and he put a hand on her shoulder. It was like going with great strides into some new and deeper intimacy; his heart misgave him. She said, 'You're surprised, aren't you? And

. . . disappointed; yes, I expect disappointed too. Thought I was tougher than this. . . . Well, I'm not. I cry with the rest of them, all those women who cry. . . . I don't know what this is; a kind of thaw, I guess.'

'You said you were frightened——'

'Yes.'

'Why?'

'Of being left alone.' She wiped her face; the wind ruffled her hair. 'Loneliness is the worst thing.'

'Only if you can't live with yourself.'

She shrugged. 'Well, maybe I can't.'

'But you're young; you've no reason to be alone. There are plenty of people——'

She sat down on the running-board of the car. 'I'm not tuned in to plenty of people. I don't hear what they say; maybe I ought to, but I don't. Only with you——'

'With me what?' He sat close to her, on the grass.

'I'm all right. I'm safe. You're the only person with whom I ever have been. Oh, this isn't the time for the early case-book stuff, how I was never loved; I daresay I've been loved, but I've never felt that kind of peace, of being *healed* with a person, that I felt with you. I never understood before how people throw everything aside and follow other people, as for the saints and Garibaldi, but I do now. Because I want to do that sort of thing for you—dash and get things you want, do impossible things, look after you—oh, selfishly, because it's for me in the long run that I want you looked after. But that's how it is.'

He pulled at the grasses beside him. 'What have I done to make you feel that?'

'It isn't exactly what you've done; it isn't what people do that's of help to you; it's whether something inside their heads connects up with you, and sparks off some kind of deep comfort. I daresay I don't talk sense; you mustn't worry about that; it *is* sense underneath the words; I know it is. Are you listening to me?'

She lifted her face; the childish words touched him, though some part of his mind still measured distance and time and the gaining light. 'Yes, of course I'm listening.'

'There were two things you did: the sheep, and going back to the boy. Those helped, but they aren't the most important thing. That's . . .' She wiped her face again, made an effort to smooth her hair. Touselled and tear-stained, she still had an odd, vulnerable dignity. 'That's . . . it's the way you really care what happens to me, have pity for me, want to help me. Not for yourself, because there's nothing I can do for you, nothing I've got that you want. You're not at all in love with me, though I suppose that is what I am with you, because that is how it is for women, isn't it; they make a whole gesture with their minds and hearts and bodies. But it's not like that for you, yet you mind what happens to me, I know you mind.'

'Who wouldn't?'

She shook her head. 'No. People say they mind, even behave sometimes as if they did. But it isn't really true, it doesn't go all the way through them. With you it does.' She had stopped crying, though her vulnerability seemed to sharpen with her control. 'I wish you'd tell me about yourself . . . about your going into the Church.'

He made a movement with his head, as if he were shaking this away. 'Oh, I'm not much of a priest. In some ways little more than a fraud.'

'Did you feel a fraud beside the boy?'

'That was different. It had to be done.'

'You haven't seemed a fraud to me.'

He couldn't help it, a sudden warmth entered him at the words. He said, looking down at his hands, 'If I've helped you—comforted you—then won't that stay with you, even if I go?'

'No. Not yet. Because when I'm without you there are spaces like cold empty rooms, and they get filled with all the painful things. Most of all they get full of the business of getting rid of the baby. I don't suppose you'd know much about anything like that, but it's cold and . . . I don't know quite what the word is, unloving, I think . . . harsh and ugly, like some intimate thing done in too brilliant a light. And after, when it's done, there's a feeling of loss wide as the sea.'

He looked about him in the growing light. No sun, but the increasing daylight washing the rocks and the steep fellsides clear. He saw again in his mind the rescue team, and the face of the young man with fair hair who had stared at him. He said, 'It can't be for long.'

She sat still, considering this. She looked touselled but calm, her eyes containing a trace of the growing light. 'Never mind. I want as much as I can—every drop squeezed out, and when it's done it's done. Nothing matters but that you should stay with me now.'

He was silent. She went on, 'You must, at any rate, be glad to have done what you've done—given me back hope, brought alive again some sort of desire for life and people and love. Isn't that what a man like you is meant to do, after all?'

He did not answer directly. He said, 'Very well. I'll stay with you as long as I can.'

§

At six in the evening those rooms where women were admitted to the Club had not yet come to life; the fires were unlit, and the large Morning Room seemed composed of sombre unoccupied shadows, folded newspapers and a clock that stitched the silence with small equal sounds.

Daphne stood alone in the room pulling off her gloves. She crossed to the table where the newspapers lay, and stood looking down at them as though, neatly folded as they were, they conveyed some troubling message. When her father entered the room she took a step or two away from the table.

Gerald nodded to her, removed his spectacles and rang the bell for a waiter. 'I expect you'd like a drink.'

'Yes, I would.'

'I should come and sit down over here. Presently a rather timorous young man in a white coat will come and light the fire.'

She remained standing, glancing round her. 'And perhaps turn on some lights?'

'Lights? Do you want lights? So early?'

'It seems . . . to need something. The room, I mean.'

'Oh, very possibly. This isn't, I suppose, a place built for the young.'

'I didn't mean I didn't like it.'

He went on as if he hadn't heard, 'No neon lighting or juke boxes or whatever they're called. I've never really known what a juke box is.'

She stood playing absently with the gloves in her hand as if she thought out an answer, but in the end she said nothing, moved rather tiredly to a chair and sat down. When their drinks had been ordered, she said, 'Does it have to be like this with us?'

Gerald was polishing his glasses. 'Like what?'

She made a gesture and a small grimace. 'You know quite well.'

'I should have said we were on the best of terms.'

She said, looking aside, 'It's a year since the accident.'

'Time, you think, to recover? To be Gerald-as-he-was?'

'Time at least to talk to me like a friend.'

'When have I talked to you as anything else?... Ah, thank you, Leslie, the drinks. Large whisky for me, the gin for my daughter: that's the pretty girl sitting opposite.'

The waiter smiled dutifully; Daphne had her head down. When the waiter had gone, she said, 'You're quite closed—fastened away from me like something locked in ice. It makes me very unhappy.'

'I think I'm surprised that it should.'

'What on earth did you imagine? ... Oh, goodness, don't men know anything about women at all? Not fathers or husbands or lovers? Look. I asked if I could come and see you to-day——'

'Because you've seen the notices of my play in this morning's press. And by now perhaps one or two of the evening ones as well——'

'It was cruel not to ask me to the first night——'

'Oh, cruel, no, I think cruel is exaggerated; I wouldn't have said cruel; according to the critics I did you a good turn—hullo, sir, good evening.'

Daphne glanced at the large man in a dinner jacket who passed sombrely across the room, like the ghost of Hamlet's father. She said, 'It wasn't my fault that the play ...' she hesitated.

'Flopped like a dozen millstones dropped from a great height? No, I never said it was. The play was ill-fated from the start. Collapsing on the road a year ago, being re-written, finding its feet and another management, opening at a theatre renowned for the number of people who stay away from it—not the right kind of start.'

She lifted her glass, as if by an effort she kept her hand steady. 'When I was rehearsing the part of the girl, a year ago—I was no good. I wanted to talk to you about it then, but somehow I couldn't.'

Gerald leaned away from her as if determined to keep this subject at a distance. 'No.' His voice carried a large mixture of unconcern. 'You could have been good. Your mind wasn't on it. It was—as we now know—on Philip Miles.'

'The girl who played it last night——'

'Would have been quite excellent in the annual school performance of *The Rivals* at Rottingdean.'

Daphne set her glass down on the table. 'Look. Oh, please listen. No one can really change as much as you seem to have. Underneath all this ice-cold unconcern there must be a part of you that can listen to me. All right: I walked out of your play, I made that wild dash with Philip. All that happened afterwards, you can say, was my fault. I don't expect to be forgiven: I can only say that's how it was for me; I was so crazily in love that nothing and nobody mattered on this earth, except that I should get to him. Is that so hard to understand?'

'Perhaps not. I don't know.' His voice was colourless.

'When you rang me up that night and told me about the accident, I left Philip. I only saw him once more, to say good-bye. He's quite recovered; he's having a roaring affair, so friends tell me, with his stenographer. I, on the other hand, still feel the same. Wouldn't you allow that as punishment, of a kind?'

Gerald was silent.

'Perhaps you think it's just words to say I still love Philip, kind of woman's big emotional thing; said for effect. It isn't; I've always stuck at things, stayed faithful to them; perhaps, if you think back, you'll remember that.'

'Indeed, yes; I used to think that was true. Until you threw up the part in my play; and when the play got on to its feet a second time, and I offered you the part again—you refused it.'

'Oh ... Listen. When you offered me the part a second time, after all that had happened, I was terribly grateful.'

Gerald carefully shed ash from his cigarette into the ashtray and said nothing.

'I found it difficult to tell you I was grateful, because, although you offered me the part, you still kept up this talking-with-the-gloves-on act, and there's nothing harder than saying emotional things to people who are walking around in ice——'

'There's no need to get angry.'

'But I *had* to turn it down. Oh, how can one explain to another person that absolute certainty—I *couldn't* play it. Couldn't pick it up again, that same part, saying the same words—after all that happened. I hadn't anything in me, not an ounce of anything that said "Yes", that could have made a movement or a gesture that would have been right. 'I——' She thrust one hand into her hair, setting it on end. 'I suppose it's no good. You don't want to see how it was for me.'

Gerald sat still in his chair. 'I must say it all sounds to me a little . . . exaggerated. Childish. Possibly I'm wrong. I don't see that it matters any more, one way or the other.'

'Oh, hell, of course it matters!'

'If you're going to make a scene you'll have to do it quietly.'

'*Please*. Please listen. You're a man; perhaps you find it easy to lose people, to do without them, not to forgive them for things. But I don't, and I can't bear it. Yes, I'm being quiet; I shan't cry; I seldom cry.'

Gerald lifted his glass; his face was unchanged, but his hand trembled a little. He said nothing.

'Oh, we'd do better if we came to the truth!'

'Being——?'

'It isn't the play that you're angry about; it isn't *that* you can't forgive me for. It's because, just before the accident, I went to Mark when I was in trouble and not to you!'

At the name Gerald had become still; the shadows seemed to deepen on his face. He stared at his glass, until he raised his eyes to Daphne. At last he said, 'You are looking at me as children do when they realize for the first time that their parents can grow old.'

'You've never forgiven him.'

'In your view I should?'

'Yes.'

'Difficult to see why?' The words were light, but the voice dragged.

'He didn't mean to do harm.'

'At the time, no. The harm came from the past. That very often happens.'

'You really hate him.'

'Hatred always seems to me . . . a word for the young. Let's say I just try not to let him come into my mind, because he does no good there.'

'Because of the accident?'

Gerald bowed gravely to, without apparently seeing, a man and woman in evening dress. 'Because of . . . shall we say, the past years.'

'They're over.'

'Over . . . yes, indeed. But their effect, as I say, endured long enough to bring about Lorraine's death.'

Her head was down; they might have been sitting in a circle of harsh cold light, while the conversation of other people in the room took place in a different and gentler climate. She said, 'I think he needs forgiveness.'

Gerald moved in his chair, took his glasses off, and drew a hand across his eyes. He looked suddenly defeated, as if some customary and essential weapon had been snatched from him. 'He asks too much.'

'If he came to you, what would you do?'

'How d'you mean—on the run? Not much chance of that; according to the paper he's somewhere up north in a car.'

'But if he did—you wouldn't tell him——'

'Tell him what?'

'That you forgive him?'

Gerald moved his bulk in the chair; looked unseeingly at his glass. 'No, never.' His glance, coming from a distance, focused on Daphne again. 'Why d'you look so sad?'

'Because I saw him after the accident. You didn't. He hadn't got anything left—he was right down on rock bottom.'

'I'd find that easier to believe if he'd stuck his punishment out, instead of running away from it——'

'Oh, but don't you see? He went because he was in despair——'

'How can you know? How can you possibly know?'

'I tell you, I saw him. He was a man . . . without a future. With nothing in front of him. . . .'

'I think you exaggerate.'

'That's your last word?'

'Yes.'

She sighed, looked round the room, glanced at the clock. 'I have to go——'

'Don't. Stay and have dinner.' He threw the invitation out, brushing ash off his trousers.

She looked at him with a slight smile. 'Is that a gesture of friendship? Olive branch, and all that?'

'Yes, if you like.'

'Well, thanks. Things beginning to look a little less bleak ... would you believe it. Encourages me to tell you something— why, in fact, I really can't stay to dinner, though I'd like to. I'm working again in the theatre.'

His head lifted slowly. 'You said you'd thrown it all up for good.'

'Yes. I said a lot of things. But, of course, one can't. I'm coming back. Slowly. To get as far as I can.'

There was a difference in the small encampment of their meeting. 'What are you doing? I haven't heard anything about it.'

'No. An awfully mixed-up girl in a theatre club near Gloucester Road. I'm not bad. I suppose you wouldn't come and see me?'

He played with his glass. 'Do you like it?'

She shrugged. 'It's work. The only work, really, I'm any good for. I do it with my heart and guts. I think I've grown older— I mean older than the time warrants—in the last year. I'm better than I was. I may even, in time, be good.' Her hand was trembling a little as if she had been saying difficult things.

Gerald pushed his glass into one or two different positions on the table. Then he said, 'Yes, very well. I'll come and see you. To-morrow night.'

Colour came into her face; she glanced quickly round the room as if pleasant words had come from some distant part of it. 'Then ... if you can forgive me, can't you forgive Mark?' but Gerald shook his head and said, 'I want to hear no more about Mark, except that they've caught up with him at last.'

§

The theatre was not much larger than a drawing-room; it gave you the feeling, Gerald thought, that if you didn't know everyone else in the audience, you soon would. He glanced round him without pleasure; he wasn't in the mood to find the audience of any interest. Just in front of him he could see Forrest Laird, stretching back in his chair, smiling slightly to no one, sitting insulated in the smooth golden skin of a man who can buy the whole place up if he wants to.

Gerald bent his head towards his programme; just at this moment he didn't want to meet Laird's bland sunniness; Laird, one of London's best-known theatrical producers, was a man to meet when you were on top of the world or not at all. But revolving his head slowly like some mechanical beam that must give equal light and warmth to all parts of the room, Laird finally turned it so that it brought Gerald within its scope.

'Ah! Gerald. I felt sure I should soon see someone I knew. The faces I looked at got more and more *like* someone I knew; that's always a sign. What are you doing in this *galère*?'

'Come to see my daughter.'

'Your—oh, how silly of me; of course you have.'

A woman who was not Laird's wife but was younger and prettier, came and sat a little breathlessly beside him and said, 'Darling, sorry to be late, but *honestly*—took me an hour to find this place, and now I've found it, I still don't know where I am.'

'You're in a quiet part of Kensington,' said Laird placidly, helping her off with her coat. 'It's good for you to see these remote places; travel broadens the mind. Know Gerald Minestaff, do you?'

Gerald bowed slightly and met the faint effort going on at the back of the young woman's eyes.

'Gerald . . . the . . . you mean, the playwright?'

'Let's say rather,' said Gerald, 'the late playwright.'

Laird's plentiful eyebrows made a civilized enquiry.

'My new play,' said Gerald, 'comes off at the end of the week.'

'Oh, there now, what a shame,' said the young woman.

'What bad luck,' said Laird, with the rich bland concern of a man not involved. 'Suppose it was the press.'

'More likely the play.'

'Oh, come now! Mustn't lose heart. The best writers have flops.'

'Feel that I'm . . . dropping behind a bit. Out of tune. This—'

he gestured to the closed curtains—'is the kind of thing that gets them now.'

Laird looked at him, keeping his bland benevolence on his face with a certain set steadiness, as if other thoughts went on behind it. 'Well, now! The last person—the very last—from whom I should have expected to hear words like that.'

Gerald's expression said, Well, you've heard them now.

'This—' Laird nodded at the curtained stage—'this, I gather, is about a lot of people who don't like anything very much and are very sorry for themselves because they don't.'

'Gosh, how jolly boring,' said the girl.

Laird was glancing round the ceiling, as if expecting to see cobwebs. 'The audiences, I'm told, haven't found it so.'

'Are you thinking of buying it?' asked Gerald.

Laird folded his arms. 'I've come to see. My spies tell me I should see.' He was turning back to face front again, and then checked himself. 'What a shame about your play!'

'Oh, yes, beastly,' said the girl, as if he'd shown her a rash.

'Thank you,' said Gerald, and the murmurs died, and, with a hesitation somewhere in the middle, the curtains came apart.

At first Gerald found it hard to concentrate; there was no sign of Daphne, and the dialogue, while sharp and unorthodox and sometimes funny, did not seem to him to be getting anywhere. Every now and again it lost itself in his mind, overcome by the nagging painful image of the notice pinned on the board backstage of Hayley's.

A week. Never had a flop like that: must mean something. Mind you, the press was bad, but it ought to have survived a bit longer. The play wasn't right; it had the patchiness, the curious unaliveness, of too much worked over things, but it wasn't all that bad. Good second act curtain, surely, when the chap came quietly back into the room, after telling everyone he would be away till the next morning. Good but—his ear caught again the fickle lively pungent words coming from the stage—if this was the kind of thing they wanted now, he could see it must look heavy and out-of-date, like a large wardrobe of good but Victorian workmanship. Moodily he went over the play as he had seen it on that disastrous first night; if you tried to cut out the poor performances and saw only the play, surely——

His wanderings ceased; he was back in the theatre again. At the edge of his vision was the smooth outline of Laird's profile, shining and catching the light, but in the centre was Daphne.

She wore a plain woollen blouse and skirt with a leather belt at the waist, little make-up, as far as he could see, and her dark, short-cropped hair was shining under the light as a child's does. She was very still; she had not, he thought, in the past had this quality of repose. In the small theatre she stood so near to him, and was so familiar, that for the first few minutes he found it difficult to believe in the character: this was Daphne, saying other words than those that would come naturally to her. But as the moments passed, he began to drift into the necessary illusion: this was Daphne; it was also the girl in the play, who was for some reason (he hadn't been attending) unhappy, fearful, perhaps, of losing her lover, hiding her unhappiness under a kind of nervous courage that now and again broke into wit salted with anger.

Almost unconsciously he uncrossed his legs, leaned a little way forward in his seat. Was it his imagination, or was the audience quieter now since her entrance? Did there blow over them that large, simple communal thought: This girl's good and we've got to watch her?

As if seeking an answer he let his glance slip to Laird's profile, for Laird might not have much interest in anyone but himself, but he knew good acting when he saw it.

Daphne was speaking, and Laird was watching her. His face was still and calm: a smooth interested mask, giving nothing away.

Oh, but surely she's good, thought Gerald. Very good; surely she is? She has the quality of grief, and in someone so young that is especially strange and moving. There was a feeling like a bruise in his chest: a mixture of joy, sadness and pride: Am I being a fool? he thought, and glanced at Laird again.

Daphne had taken the centre of the stage; she was speaking to the young man who stood a little way behind her. Laird was watching her, his face unchanged. The girl at his side leant close to him, as if about to whisper something. Before she could say anything, there flicked over Laird's face the swift imperative frown of a man determined that nothing should disturb him.

Yes, thought Gerald, relaxing a little and sitting back in his seat; yes, she is good. Perhaps not as good as it seems to me at this moment, but good enough; good enough to hold a man like Laird, good enough to be set for a career of some sort; good enough to light up the cloudy palaces of hope.

Daphne left the stage; a small spontaneous round of applause went with her. When it was done Gerald did not know if he'd joined it or not. Now that she had gone he found that his hands trembled, and that there was sweat on his forehead. With still unsteady fingers, he bent to pick up his programme which had slipped to the floor. As he lifted his head again the curtains slipped together for the end of the first act, and, within the sound of the applause, Laird leaned over towards him and said, 'I congratulate you!'

Gerald nodded, murmured, 'Thank you. . . . Yes, she is good, isn't she?' He was glad Laird had spoken, but he didn't want to talk about it; he rose clumsily to his feet in the narrow space and made his way out of the theatre. On the steps members of the audience stood smoking and talking; he wanted and did not want to hear what they said; he lit a cigarette himself and wandered a little way away. The street was dyed blue; lamps and lighted windows painted a Chinese brushwork of glowing amber.

He seemed to stand in a place of changing prospects, somewhere between his own failure and Daphne's success. He was, as yet, at home in neither, but the London evening, blue above dissolving structures, was run through with comfort; the notice on the board at Hayley's didn't seem to hurt so much; the shapeless voices not far off were voices speaking good news.

He returned to the theatre; his cramped seat had the pleasant outline of a place where one has been happy. But when she reappeared again after the interval, she seemed to be moving stiffly, to be doing with effort what before had been magically done with ease. He felt the sharp cold fall of disappointment: the thing, momentarily possessed, now gone. The audience, unheld, shifted and coughed. He sat, trying not to see Laird's face, which wore now an expression of prim, waiting surprise.

Nerves, of course, nerves, he said to himself. But she's got to throw them off. He began to dislike everything in the theatre: the audience, the stage, Laird, the play, his seat, his programme. His disappointment took the shape of being angry with Daphne: silly girl, he thought, silly, silly girl.

But then, just as he had decided that the whole solid sad lump of his own failure had returned, Daphne spoke a line, half-way between laughter and bitterness, and the old magic flashed back. Now *that's* it, he said to her, now you've got it; hold on to it, there's a good girl. You can do it. Like swimming or riding a bicycle: balance is all.

He leaned back in his chair, relaxed, the frozen disappointment thawing. It was all right. She was set now, there wasn't any question. He wondered vaguely what had thrown her in the interval; just trying too hard, he supposed. He glanced sideways; even Laird's face had come back to its right expression, like a film that for a few moments has lost focus.

Oh, bully for her, thought Gerald, as the play moved to its abrupt and inconclusive end; that's some kind of a triumph— surely it is? The applause was as solid as the four-by-two theatre could make it, though Gerald wished it could have been a thought more emphatic; he shouted 'Bravo!' thinking, To hell with it, daughter or no daughter, a man can show enthusiasm when he feels it.

'Very interesting,' said Laird, as he twitched his scarf into place with small civilized gestures.

'The play?' asked the young woman beside him, folding herself, like something expensive, into her coat.

'No, the girl. *Your* girl,' he said with a nod to Gerald.

Again, Gerald did not want to stay and talk about it. He acknowledged Laird's tribute, buttoned up his coat, and pushed his way out of the row of seats, conscious of his paunch. On the way out of the theatre he caught sight of himself in a glass: a fat elderly man, his grey hair blown about with enthusiasm: an extraordinary, rather distressing image; it didn't seem to matter.

He waited for her where they'd arranged to meet, wandering up and down on the pavement. He felt shy of her, and tried to work out what to say: it ought to be done on a tide of enthusiasm, a slap-on-the-back, kiss-on-the-cheek whirl; he didn't feel, with his bulk, and his untidy hair and the small pulsing ache of having been so much moved, that he could cope with that kind of whirl.

In a short time she came towards him, calling good night to someone behind her. He stood looking doubtfully at her, for she was in some way a new person, as he himself was.

'Hullo, Pop.'

'Hullo, Daphne.'

He took a breath and put a hand on her arm. 'Darling, you were terribly good.' It sounded exactly like the line spoken in his hearing with absolute insincerity a hundred times. He tried again. 'I do mean it.'

'Yes, perhaps I wasn't too bad. Something seemed to be connecting.'

'More than that. You had a triumph.'

'Think so?'

'I'm sure of it. So was Laird.'

'*Laird?* Was he? Didn't know he ever committed himself that far.'

'He did to-night.'

'Well, what d'you know.'

He tried to read her face, made half a gesture towards a cruising taxi, and then abandoned it. 'You're pleased, aren't you?'

'Oh—yes—I'm pleased. Sure I'm pleased. Success—what I've always wanted. Well, success of a kind. A piece of it. A beginning, perhaps. But——'

'But what?'

She shook her head, not answering, and it occurred to him suddenly that she wasn't far from tears. 'What, darling?'

'It's . . . oh, hell. I think it's Mark.'

'I don't understand.'

'No,' she said, ruefully, 'not sure that I do either. But it started in the interval. That was why I was so bad when I first came on again. It was all a bit much, I suppose—feeling that I'd done well, that perhaps I was getting somewhere at last. Knowing you were there, and hoping you'd be pleased. And wondering—I couldn't help it—if Lorraine would have been pleased too.'

He stood still; the street seemed to be emptying and darkening; the placard against the side of the theatre to be changed, seen from a greater distance.

'And so,' she went on, 'I came to Mark. I felt that . . . oh, I don't know exactly, that I wanted him not to suffer too much; to know that we cared about him still; that he isn't quite alone. I—oh, hell, don't look at me, I'll stop this in a minute; actress's hysteria; doing exactly the right thing, aren't I?—but I suppose it's part of having known I did well this evening. Of wanting, because of that, everything else—every*one* else—to be all right.'

He was still looking absently at the placard; he gave a small grunt of agreement, as if he understood, though he did not wholly understand.

He put a hand on her arm. 'Come along. You need food and drink and...' But he did not know what else. He hailed a taxi, still keeping hold of her arm.

§

When they were sitting at a table in the long Coffee Room, he thought she seemed more composed; but though her face was calm, her eyes were brimming with brilliance, with knowledge; with something more that he couldn't define, but which seemed to mark her for the first time as a woman rather than a child.

He lifted his glass to her. 'From here—who knows? you may be headed for the good things.'

'Perhaps. No one can say for sure, can they?'

'You have a grown-up kind of sadness, together with being young. That could do a lot for you. You can move people. You moved me.'

'Did I?' Her eyes seemed brighter and brighter; for a moment the abrupt young face was beautiful; he sat watching her, awed by her.

She was looking at the portraits of the actors and actresses, the scenes from the old comedies, on the wall. 'I was rude about them once, wasn't I? I wouldn't be rude now.'

'Perhaps one day you'll hang there with them.'

She smiled, looking steadily at them. 'They all had it, didn't they—fame, for a while. It seems to be everything I want—so it is, in a way—and yet—' her eyes were still on the pictures— 'they look, somehow, lonely. They achieved something—so shall I perhaps—but what good did it do anyone? Except themselves? A barren triumph—was it, perhaps? Am I making sense? I'm a bit drunk, I think.'

'No; only seeing into the distance because you've climbed a height.'

'Is that it? Well, maybe.' She still looked at the pictures; she seemed to be listening to the tumultuous clapping of hands that were now dust. 'But I feel—oh, divided in two; satisfied, yet hungry; I can't explain. Do you remember—years and years ago, when I was about fifteen—I went through a holier than the Pope stage, and wanted to be a nun?——Oh, don't worry; I shan't be; I want the things of this world too much; I want all *this* too much; I want to hear the applause for *me*; even though one day the theatre'll be empty and there won't be any applause—or if there is, I shan't be there to hear it. But to-night . . . I suppose that small part of me that wanted to be a nun is kind of lost because it knows it hasn't a hope.'

He smiled, groping in his mind towards the best thing to say to her. 'Perhaps it may help you if I tell you something. The play —my play—closes at the end of the week——'

'Oh, poor Pop! A *week*——'

'Well, let me tell you this. I felt like hell this evening in that theatre. I sat behind Laird, and he seemed to stand for all the things that were slipping away from me. And then you came on to that two-by-four stage. And it was all quite different.' (Was he exaggerating a little? Never mind, this was an evening for exaggeration.) 'I didn't mind about the flop—or at least, yes, I minded, but you were more important. You helped me over.'

She was looking at him gently; he caught again the strange youthful sadness that had been hers on the stage. 'Is that true?'

'Oh yes. I can—with content—watch you rise as I fall—though mind you, I'm not going to fall any further than I have to. I'm a playwright—shall be till the pen drops out of my hand . . . *what* a sad, bad line; perhaps we are a little drunk. . . . But you—you've got it all before you.'

Her eyes moved again over the long room, as if it were a king-dom being offered her. 'Perhaps this is the best time—hoping and wondering what may happen and not being certain. Not knowing for sure.'

'Yes, perhaps.'

She looked to the window and the warm empty London street. 'And Mark?' she said at last.

He supposed the name had to come back. He looked down the long lighted and civilized room; tried to imagine Mark Harvist in his context of fear and perhaps danger. 'What about him?'

She shrugged. 'As I said. He makes a shadow over it all. As I told you . . . I can't forget the last time I saw him.'

He sat over the table with his head bent. At last he said, 'If it's any comfort to you, I forgive him.'

'But truly? Not just to please me?'

'Oh yes,' he said on a sigh, 'truly.' He seemed by means of the confused emotions of this evening to have crossed some difficult track of country, to have travelled beyond the climate of anger and fear. Perhaps it's nothing to do with Daphne, he thought; perhaps it's just getting to be old, when mercy is all.

She took a drink from her glass, looked from the window as if she saw the distances of Allen Moor and Scarside. 'Can he be happy d'you think?' she asked, and as he did not answer, 'I want him to be happy; for my own sake, I suppose, most things are, but still . . . yes, I want him to be . . . to have some kind of peace.'

CHAPTER TEN

THE mist came down again. The day whose unlighted beginning they had watched together was soon muffled and smothered in dripping cloud. No more rocks or mountains or sky; only a grey melancholy silence and the close presence of the mist, like cold steam.

'Well, here we are,' said Gillian, 'and for as long as this lasts, here we stay. Good thing we've got food. Bananas and chocolate probably don't cover all the vitamins but they'll keep us from starving.'

Mark gave a half-smile, staring into the mist. The car was drawn in under the shelter of high rocks by the side of the rough road. They were, he reckoned, not more than four miles from Fastness, but the mist blunted his sense of distance, and created a private world, a place of safety.

Only the illusion of safety, of course, for all the roads leading out of this central mass of mountains must now, he was certain, be sealed off. But, like that other mist into which he had run, this enclosed and comforted him.

And something more. The man who had run into the mist

had been frightened, driven beyond himself, perhaps a little crazy. But now beside Gillian in the shabby car with the flocking mist about them, he was calm.

I suppose, he thought, I'm a man who's found himself.

The words sounded a little too grand and absurd, and he smiled and rubbed his ear. But all the same, he thought, looking into the mist whose colour seemed at times to change and lighten as if a lamp were carried through, then darkened again, all the same, it's true. I've come at last to certainty——

You? a voice said. And how many certainties have we known in all these years that were not certainties at all? How many large gestures and grand words and moments of vision that came to nothing in the end?

Yes; yes, I know all that, he said. Perhaps I shall fail again. But this seems to be a knowledge that I possess with my heart and guts and soul. I can't say more than that. After all, even a man like myself—wild and frightened and selfish, with his sins and his ignoble failures, his absurdities and his loves and his desire to be loved and his occasional shabby reverence to his God, can learn. Give him the car accident and Lorraine's death and prison and these last days—he can learn, can't he? Learn and change?

'Not talking very much,' said Gillian.

He smiled at her. 'No. I'm sorry. I've been thinking.'

'More than thinking, I'd say. Down deep below sea-level with communications cut. Sunk without trace.'

'Perhaps. Yes, it seemed a bit like that.'

She was sitting easily with her head tilted back, her eyes on the mist. 'What took you down so deep? Past or future?'

'Both, I suppose. Future mainly.'

She still looked lazily towards the mist. 'A few days ago I shouldn't have said I had one.'

'And now?'

She looked puzzled, hesitated, half-smiled. 'I don't know. It seems—different from what it was.'

'Even different from this morning?'

'Oh—sure. A little. This morning was a bit of bad behaviour —self-indulgence; crying and all that. I'm ashamed and I'm sorry. But I thought I was losing you.'

He began to speak; checked himself, and was silent. He waited for some further question from her, but she too was silent, as if she'd come to the edge of things that mustn't be spoken. After a few moments she said, 'When you talked about going to the north——'

He bent his head. 'Oh, that was just a wild idea.'

'But where?'

'A place called Kilbrennan, in the Western Isles.'

'What made you think of it?'

He hesitated. 'There's a Community there—a religious Community——'

'I don't know what a Community is—monks and things?'

'Yes. A friend of my father's, an old boy called Elliot, the vicar of a neighbouring church, went there about a year ago.'

'To stay? Finally?'

'Oh, yes. The whole hog. Solemn vows and all that.'

These few words brought a silence into the car; he did not look at her, but kept his head down. When she spoke again, her voice sounded careful, her words chosen. 'A friend of your father's . . . Where is your father?'

'In a home for old people run by nuns. He was going to come and live with me, but . . . something happened to prevent that. He's a little senile and makes passes at the pretty ones, but they seem to survive.'

She smiled. 'I like knowing things about you. Possessiveness, I suppose; a bad thing, but how does one help it, if that is how one is?' She stretched herself. 'Oh, Lord, to love, and just love and go on loving without asking anything, without wanting to know and to have and to be certain—just to love from rim to rim—now that would be something!'

'Yes. The only thing, perhaps.' He glanced at her, smiling. 'If you can say that, you can be happy.'

'Me? Well . . . yes; see what you mean. But I didn't say I could do it, I only said I'd like to.'

'That's a beginning.'

'Think so? Something new for me, anyway. Learnt, if I may say so, from being with you. In fact——' She broke off. For a few moments she sat still, her eyes on the blind windscreen. 'Well, it's as I said, I suppose. I was never one to go coyly behind a fern when I needed to say something, and I'm not going to do it now.

I could love you like that—have the beginnings of loving you like that—in me, here and now.' Her hands shook a little. 'It's all right. You don't have to answer. Men find it difficult, they tell me, to answer that. And you, I imagine, more than the rest.'

He made a sharp movement of his head, looking up and meeting the blank wall of the mist. His first thought was, What an extraordinary place to be happy. 'No,' he said, 'not difficult. Because I'm glad. No . . . listen.' He grasped her hand firmly, as if he pulled her back from danger. 'I can't love you. Oh, if I loved anyone again, it would be you. But I've got . . . a different kind of future; I can't explain; sometime it'll be clear to you. But for you I'm glad.'

'Don't quite get it. You must understand that when I say love, I mean love in all its aspects, including the wish to sleep with the person.'

'Yes,' he said gently, recognizing the sudden violence that had made her speak, and touched by the awkward, oddly dignified phrase. 'But someone else will love you——'

'And you're glad?'

'Because it means you're coming back to life.'

She made a small grimace. 'Not a very noble sign of life—just feeling the pricks of the body again.'

He was still gentle. 'Nevertheless, as I said, a beginning. And if you love like that I needn't have any fear for you.'

Her violence seemed to slip from her; she said, 'That sounds nice.' After a silence she added, 'But you loved someone once? Most people have, and . . . yes, I know by the way you talked to me that you know about loving.'

He said at last, 'Yes.'

'What happened to her? May I not ask?'

'She was killed.'

'Tough. And you still think of her?'

He saw the long wakeful nights in his cell. 'Often and often. Often and often.'

'And that was the end of loving for you?'

'Of one kind of loving, yes.'

She made one or two movements, rubbing her forehead with the palm of her hand. 'I feel shut out—jealous, I think. I meant to love better than that——'

He shook his head gently. 'You don't have to feel any of those things. It's just that now I have to—to learn how to want nothing more for myself.'

'That sounds very difficult.' Her voice was thin. 'Do you know how to do it?'

He said after a silence which, he feared, put a distance between them and frightened her, 'I think I begin to see.'

§

The mist did not lighten, but with evening seemed to press closer, filled with the gradual darkness, keeping the world away. Gillian got into the back of the car and slept. Mark stayed in his seat, sleeping only little. For most of the night he sat in his new found tranquillity, trying his foot as it were on his new knowledge and finding it firm; watching the time run out.

§

Morning. Mist and rain, and a throbbing challenge in his head, like the headache of a man who'd drunk too well the night before. Restive, impatient, he stared at the unchanging mist, but saw only a picture lit with curious menace in his mind, as the picture of another woman may be to a jealous wife. A picture of the young man from the Rescue Team. The young man with fair hair.

Vivid and sharp in memory, the face carried a threat. By now, he thought, what has he done? Talked to his friends? To the police? He could see the young too-handsome face eager and alight with suspicion, with the pleasure of bringing important news; it became a strangely potent focus of anxiety; he could not free himself of the boy. The boy who would say—it was almost certain—'He was a parson all right. And he was with a woman. In a car.'

The challenge beat harder in his mind.

The devil of it is, he told himself, that any large certainty and peace, such as I knew last night, has to be paid for. You can't just stride from shadow to light. The past drags behind you, and you have to settle with it. That's what I have to do now. And I'd give the earth not to.

Gillian's eye was on him. 'Trouble?' she said. 'Trouble that wasn't there yesterday?'

He smiled a little; he remembered that he had once said to her, 'Do all women know the thought in a man's mind?' and it hurt to remember it.

'Yes,' he said. 'Yes, perhaps.'

She said no more; he was grateful for the understanding of her silence.

Bewildering that anything so obvious, so necessary, should, at the last, prove so difficult to do. A shiver of panic touched his spine: would this be true also of his certainty: would he be in the end incapable of the final, perhaps terrible, step?

No, he said, I don't think so. That knowledge is rooted deep; I can't lose it. By some strength other than my own, I can't lose it. . . .

His thoughts were broken by the figure of a man in yellow oil-skins, who passed the car slowly.

'Filthy weather!' he called; he looked angrily towards them as if it were their fault before he went on, vanishing in the mist.

Not long afterwards three young men trudged by in capes and sou'westers; they too looked into the car, perhaps in envy of those who could shelter. The world seemed to be breaking through: even in the mist, there was no safety, and his moment was here, clear before him. But still he did nothing.

It was Gillian who spoke at last, as if she'd been travelling with him in thought.

'If I were you,' she said, 'I'd get it out. What's on your mind, I mean. Comes a time when you have to.'

He nodded, but still was silent. I've lived, he thought, these last days in a world that wasn't quite real, since it could have no future, and was kept in being only so long as we avoided the truth. I've been protected from the truth of things, like a grub or an un-hatched bird. I've grown used to my shelter, and now that the time has come to destroy it I don't seem to have the courage.

He looked up into the mist; even as he looked it began to dis-solve and lighten, to reveal torn patches of sky, though the rain streamed on: within these clearing depths, on the summit of the fell shadowy figures moved together. They moved silently and away, but they reminded him of the world outside, of the harsh truths that he couldn't escape.

I've no choice, he said, no choice at all. He stared again into the dissolving mist; the deadened nerve of courage leaped suddenly into life, and he said to Gillian, 'I've got to get this clear. I've got to ask you if you knew I——'

But before he could say more she thrust a hand through her hair. 'Oh, look—sure I knew.'

Odd the relief that went over him, like the ceasing of effort. 'I wondered all the time,' he said. 'I was never certain.'

'I didn't know at first—when I saw you, above Tower Crags. But the next morning, after you'd gone, the postmistress from Blencaller rang me up to know if I'd had my throat cut, if you see what I mean. She said there was a desperate criminal on the run, and living there alone as I was . . . all that. I asked her exactly what she meant by desperate criminal, and little by little, with enormous reluctance, she gave me the facts. Or some of the facts, anyway.'

'And you took me on?'

'Well, certainly. Seemed like my salvation—so it proved, it was.'

'Helping a criminal on the run?'

She shrugged. 'Helping *you*. It gives you a kick to do something for someone who hasn't much chance.'

There came into his mind the clergyman of Caudale Farm who'd said, 'How much help do you need?'

'I wondered if you knew,' he repeated. 'I didn't dare ask you——'

'Why not?'

'Because, if I was caught, I could swear you didn't know who I was. But now . . . you must see that I have to go. Then I can say that when I told you who I was, you realized you mustn't help me any more.'

'What a splendid epitaph!'

'That's the way the Law works.'

'So much the worse for the Law.'

'I had to ask you, I had to get it clear, and now I have to go. It's not easy.'

Her head was bent. 'Nor for me.'

Clumsily he sought for words. 'You helped to put my world on its feet again.'

'Oh, it can't suddenly end like this! Can't just stop like this, as if it meant nothing, as if . . .'

'What hope is there for anything else?' He spoke a little harshly, because his own heart was heavy at the thought of losing her, and he had to lose her.

'But where will you go? What will you do? Here, let me give you everything—money, a coat, a mackintosh——'

He shook his head. 'I shan't need them.'

'But——'

'I'm going back.'

'Where?'

'Where I came from: Scarside. What else?'

She stared at him, as if trying to see him as he would be, a prisoner. 'Are you afraid?'

'Yes, a little.'

'More than afraid?'

He paused a moment, stared at the prospect before him, then shook his head. 'No.'

'Is that true?'

He still looked at the shape of Scarside in his mind, the grim unwelcoming habitation that had almost overwhelmed his spirit. 'I think it's true. Five days ago I thought anything—even death—would be better than going back.'

'Now, then?'

'It isn't any longer so important, what they do with me.' He gave her a slight smile, fearing that the words sounded too large, making an absurd claim. 'All I want is to get back on my own—to give myself up, without being taken. I don't know why I should want that, but I do. With any luck I should bring it off; I shall keep clear of the roads.' A little nerve of apprehension had come alive in his stomach; the drenched fellsides, newly clear of the mist, looked unwelcoming; it seemed a lonely journey ahead.

'Well, this is it,' he said, and opened the door of the car. They faced each other; and he tried in the brief minute both to read her face, and to convey to her some kind of gratitude and strength and love. 'You will promise me——'

'I can't promise anything!' she said savagely. 'Why should I? Everything gets taken from me; even you go.'

'You must promise,' he said. 'You can't let me go, dreading all the time, remembering Tower Crags——'

'Would it be a dread?'

'Of course.   Of course.'

'Blow me,' she said, after looking at him, 'yes, I believe it would. O.K., I promise.'

'Truly?'

'Yes.'

Some of the rain bounced in through the open door of the car. It hurried down as if it washed all this away, as if it dissolved their encounter and his brief sanctuary.

'Goodbye, Gillian, my dear.'

'Goodbye, Mark.'

He tried to say more, but the rain splashed between them; he wiped it away from his eyes; there wasn't any more time.

§

He did not look back.   He stumbled over the sodden earth; now and again his foot sunk inches in the peaty ground; the rain beat on his shoulders.

Yes, it was lonely.

Now he had to get a grip on his new knowledge, make it close and alive; so real that nothing he endured was of importance; neither the rain nor the loss of Gillian nor the prospect ahead, nor any pain of any kind that might come to him. 'The hardest thing, after all, in the world to do.'   His own words, were they? They seemed to come across a great distance.

He paused and wiped his face.   Here the grey rain still fell, but away in the sky the hills were pallid, fraily shining, catching some trace of returning sun.   The clouds had all been pushed into one part of the sky where they hung, smoky and dark as slate.

He stood, looking about him.   Even as he watched, pale amber flame swept over the valley; the rain was charged with brilliance, and a whitewashed cottage, far distant, dazzled the jeweller's colour of its surrounding green.

I suppose you might say, he thought, that this is the last of freedom.

Yet it did not seem so.   Carrying his picture of the bright hills and the dripping shadows, holding on to his hope, he made his way down through the rain, towards Fastness.

§

Gillian drove along the shining mountain roads, watching the rain draw off.

All very pretty, she told herself; pretty as could be; we will, for the moment, shut off all parts of the mind except the one that can see how pretty it all is. Quite soon now we'll see the house again, my house, left how many days ago? Left three days ago, left a lifetime ago. It will be different, it must be different.

When she reached the house she got out of the car a little cautiously, as if her limbs were bruised.

So far, so good.

She went in. No sound but the full perpetual running of the becks and some answering sigh of leaves. Here the sunlight lay with the sad intrusive certainty of a torch that searches an empty place.

Now come on, she said, what now? for the emptiness and the water-edged silence and the quiet light seemed to be becoming too much for her. Don't like this, she thought, it's too much like the beginning, the afternoon before I climbed up to Tower Crags, and saw him for the first time. . . .

She went back into the hall, shutting the front door, and saw for the first time the letter on the mat.

She picked it up with a kind of detached wonder. Surprising to have a letter; I've felt so lost in myself, so unaware of everyone else in the world that I've felt they must be unaware of me too, as if I were invisible.

From Lionel. Now this is the oddest thing, because only a little while ago I couldn't have looked on his handwriting without . . . let's say, great disturbance of spirit. But this is like plugging in to something when the current's switched off. Would that be good or bad? Better to feel something?

She stood by the window as she read the letter.

'. . . I have rung the flat in town, and I have at last rung the house in Bleadale, which is where I'm sure you must be, but I can't get any answer, and I'm worried. This may seem an odd thing to write on the eve of one's marriage' (no, my dear lad; nothing seems odd to me any more) 'but you're still with me in a way, and it worries me not to know where you are. Laura, I may tell you, feels the same—' Well, blow me, if that doesn't beat everything: Laura feels the same—'so if—no, *when* you get this, I do beg you to let me know. . . .'

Gillian folded the letter, walked out of the house and stood on the stony path.

Possible, is it, to be sane again—in so short a time? To feel for Lionel—no, not indifference, but compassion; to see him as a man whose tangled past life has made a loop that might trip him up; to be so free of pain and bitterness that all one wants to do is to reassure him?

Well, what d'you know, she said. A picture came vividly to her mind of Mark, as she had left him, trudging away in the rain, outcast and pursued. It seemed an odd figure to free her mind from the dark cavern of self-enclosed pain, to stir again the warm impulses of living, of curiosity and interest and love.

I can't add him up yet, she thought; I don't yet quite believe in him: it takes time to believe in someone, longer than it does to love them; you have to get a little way away from them. All I know is that I miss him, miss him as if a whole piece of earth that I was used to had been broken away; I'm glad if I helped him; I wish I could be with him, to help him now.

That seemed to be all. It seemed to be enough.

She went back into the house. This is not quite like being alone, she thought; nor like an end; he has left me with a companionable silence.

She sat close to the window and began her letter to Lionel.

'. . . Yes, I'm here at the house, but for the last few days I've been'—now, what? In hell, what?—'driving around in search of peace and the good life, and that's why you couldn't get me. No cause for alarm; I am entirely whole and, in fact, on my way back to town and all of what waits there. . . .'

§

The Superintendent looked unhappily towards his tea. They'd brought it too early; it wasn't yet half past three: he had a conviction from childhood that tea shouldn't come before four o'clock. Half past three left too long a gap afterwards; there wasn't anything to look forward to.

He glanced at the window; the rain was clearing now; that depressed him too: if it was going to rain he liked it to rain all the afternoon, not to have to readjust all his ideas at half past three to let in the light.

He drank his tea; it wasn't hot, and he felt inclined to be angry with someone, and then thought better of it. What with Harvist and a solid bout of not sleeping, he'd been bad-tempered enough lately. I'll give them a rest from it, he thought, swallowing the near-tepid tea, and putting on to his face an expression of mild, fixed benevolence: after a moment or two his muscles felt stiff and he let it go.

As he did so, the door opened, and Sergeant Briggs came in, breathing fast and with a light in his eye. The Superintendent made a grab at his vanishing goodwill. 'Well?'

'News, sir. Harvist has been seen in the car with the woman. Telephone call's just come through from a man who passed the car and looked in, about an hour or so ago——'

'An hour?'

'Apparently he hadn't a clue at first; then it suddenly struck him and he stopped and thought about it——'

'You feel his thought was constructive?'

'The descriptions tally.'

'Most descriptions do.'

'I think we're on to it now, sir. It was only a short distance away—comparatively speaking; on the far side of Stile's Pass——'

'A car can go a long way in an hour.'

'There's a cordon round the whole district; we're in wireless contact with the cars. The odds have turned our way.'

'Yes ... well ...'

'You wait, sir. Our chaps'll be bringing him in.'

'Believe it when I see it.'

'You'll see it, sir.'

The Superintendent nodded; watched the door close and finished his near-cold tea. The afternoon was different now, it was like waiting for an election result: that pressure in the air, the bubble of silence, swelling to burst in the sound of news.

Well, perhaps there won't be any news, he told himself. Perhaps he'll slip through this time, as every time before. Lord, he must be damn' clever. Either that, or God's on his side. Perhaps he just has all the answers. Pitting his brains against the police and winning: that sort.

Well, perhaps; perhaps that's so: but then you've got to fit in somewhere that he stayed by the boy on Heel's Tor.

He could hear the noise of the office outside: telephones, typewriters, voices unsharpened by drama. Yes, I think he is going to get away with it, he said. He's going to be one of those lads who turn up in Buenos Aires or Montreal with a beard and a false passport. So much for Sergeant Know-All Briggs. So much for the man who looked into the car and had second thoughts. So much, I suppose you might say, for justice.

§

The day grew dark again; rain sketched a new design on the window. Harvist ... Harvist: don't believe there is such a man, thought the Superintendent; think he's a myth, something I dreamed up. He pulled a letter towards him, signed his name with a flourish which had, to his surprise, a trace of anger in it. Well, who am I angry with? he asked, and found he was angry as a host is angry when his promised guest doesn't arrive.

Four o'clock: half past four.

The door burst open. Sergeant Briggs, wearing the startled look of a man who has for the first time attended some rough natural function, like the birth of a calf.

He said, 'He's here, sir.'

'Who?'

'Harvist.'

'*Harvist?*'

'Yes, sir.'

'*Here?* You mean our mounties have actually got their man? At last?'

'Well ... no, sir.'

'*No?*'

'No, you see ... he came by himself. To give himself up, sir.'

The Superintendent heard a voice in his head say, Well that beats the lot: outwardly he stayed calm. 'I'd like to see him. And—Briggs. You'd better get through to Control and call the party off. Tell them they can take down the decorations and go home. .... You're quite sure it *is* Harvist, I suppose?'

'Oh yes, sir. Not a doubt.'

'Pretty done in, I suppose? Hungry?'

'Well ... yes, sir.   In a way.'

'What d'you mean, in a way?'

Briggs still looked mildly confounded.   'It's hard to explain, sir.
He doesn't seem exactly to be listening ... to be quite with us.'

'Mean he's bats?'

'Oh, no, I don't think so, sir ... just rather far off.   As if,'
Briggs added with faint bitterness, 'none of us out there were
capable of understanding his conversation.   He asked to see you, sir.'

'To see *me*?'

'Well, yes, sir——'

'How can he possibly want to see me; he doesn't know who I
am?'

'He said he'd like to see whoever was in authority.'

The Superintendent kept his face blank.   'You'd better bring
him in.'

'He's pretty wet, sir.'

'All right—change him and dry him first.'

He waited, turning a pencil between his fingers, not seeing it;
he could hear the clock tick.   It was raining hard again; the roof
of the house opposite glistened grey like fish-skin.   He didn't
know how long he waited; the time seemed to drag, yet when it
was over, to have been short.

'He's ready now, sir.   Shall I bring him in?'

'Yes, Briggs.   And then leave us.'

'Very good, sir.   Come in, Harvist.   Harvist, are you listening?   Come in.   Now.'

The Superintendent put the pencil down; faced the man before
him.   He looked steadily at him for several moments without
speaking.

No; not quite what he'd expected.   Shabby, ill-fitting clothes,
of course; his face marked by deep weariness.   But also—what?
The Superintendent groped for words.   Authority?   Calm?
Perhaps just an unexpected absence of fear.

'Well,' said the Superintendent, 'well.'   Harvist still stood before
him, silent in his shabby dignity.   'You'd better sit down.   Led us
quite a dance, haven't you?'

Harvist sat in the chair.   'I suppose I must have done.   I'm
sorry.'

How odd, thought the Superintendent, that this is Harvist

sitting there: the newspapers have made something different of the name, something larger than life, not quite human, so that one is surprised to see the grey in his hair, the ingrained dirt on his hands and the . . . gentleness, is it? in his eyes.

'But I've done my best,' Harvist went on, 'to make amends.'

See what Briggs meant, thought the Superintendent. And that air of confidence is—to say the least—at odds with his position at this moment. 'Saved us more trouble if you'd never gone.'

'Yes, obviously.'

'Think it was worth while?'

Harvist gave a slight smile; for a moment the Superintendent caught a glimpse of the man of whom it had been said that he gave comfort to those in distress. 'Yes, it was.'

'Difficult to see why. You lose——'

'The whole world.'

'Well not quite that——'

'I'm sorry. I was playing with an idea.'

Well, *perhaps* he's mad, thought the Superintendent: that would account for everything. On the other hand, the eyes are sane; you can usually tell from the eyes.

'Five days,' he said. 'Were they hard?'

Harvist looked in a slightly puzzled way at his hands. 'Yes . . . I suppose they were hard. They really are—difficult to describe.' A gentle glance, a small apologetic movement of the head. 'In fact,' Harvist went on in a sudden expansive burst, 'the whole thing is difficult, because while it was good for me that I went, I'm sorry to have caused so much trouble.'

Really, thought the Superintendent; apologizing like a traveller who's mislaid his ticket. Aloud he said, 'Did you sleep?'

'Sleep?' Harvist looked mildly surprised. 'No, I don't think I slept much. How could I?'

'No.' The Superintendent leaned back with a sigh. I begin to see what I expected, he thought, I expected that I'd be in some way *en rapport*; in his absence, he's kept me company here. But now I have him, here in this room, he holds me off. And at the same time, makes me want to get closer to him——

Oh, bother the man, he thought, in a spasm of irritation, and for a moment collapsed into an officer of the law with a criminal before him.

179

'We've reason to believe you had help in your escape. From a woman.'

The blue eyes showed pity, perhaps, or just the softening of a remembered kindness. 'She had no idea at first who I was. When she knew, she saw she couldn't help me any more.' For a moment the eyes lost the room and focused on some different point in time. They returned; glanced at the crowded desk. 'She advised me to give myself up. Which I have,' he added as an afterthought, giving a slight smile to the Superintendent, as if he might have forgotten. 'I can assure you that at first she knew nothing.'

The Superintendent frowned. Something not quite right about the story. Not exactly, he thought, that Harvist was lying; his voice carried none of the emphasis, nor the careful lack of nervousness, of the liar. But the words were thrown away, made to seem of no importance; yet somewhere in them, importance lay. 'Yes. I see.'

'I'd be glad to know,' Harvist said, 'that you won't bring any charge against her?'

The Superintendent was on the point of saying that that wasn't the kind of question he expected to be asked by recaptured prisoners: something stopped him. He drew a line or two on his blotting pad. 'I think you can rest assured that no charge will be made.' He frowned at the stiff, formal words; drew further on his pad.

'Thank you,' Harvist said. He seemed to look again into a distance. 'Yes, I'm glad to know that.'

Something here I don't get, thought the Superintendent; good Lord, this chap's a *parson*. Or was. He said, 'The climbing accident—the boy on Heel's Tor. You stayed with him?'

A placid turn of the head in recognition of the question. 'Yes.'

'What made you do that?' He felt that he trod clumsily.

'The boy was badly hurt. It seemed to give him some comfort.'

'I suppose it must have done. Not my line. Wouldn't make any difference to me, if I'd packed myself up below Heel's Tor, what any chap said to me, parson or no parson. What difference can it make?'

'A question of belief, surely? The way the wind blows in a man's mind. If he believes it's some good, it's some good.'

'Yes—but *really*? Apart from what he thinks—does it do anything?'

Again a gentle glance. 'They tell us so.'

The Superintendent gave a grunt; hunched himself over his desk. 'All a bit beyond me, I'm afraid.'

Harvist looked as though he was going to say more, then seemed to change his mind. 'What happens to me now?'

'Well . . . we give you a wash and brush up and a meal.'

'And then?'

'We have a brief wrangle with Scarside as to whether they send a car to fetch you, or we deliver you to them. Question being whether you belong to the police or the prison authorities.'

'How soon shall I be there?'

'Back at Scarside? Oh—say, within a couple of hours.'

Harvist nodded. He received the words with a certain indifference—at least, no, not quite indifference, the Superintendent thought: rather as if Harvist's mind was on something else of larger importance, and these brief facts would command only a small part of his attention. He said, before he could stop himself, 'You aren't what I expected.'

'No?'

'When you escaped it was a bit of a teaser. I mean—*why* you did it.'

'Yes, I suppose so.' Harvist frowned, as if he could only share in this speculation.

'And now you seem . . . well, unconcerned with the whole thing.'

Harvist looked directly at him; the tired face was fully open to him, if only he could read it. 'No, not unconcerned.'

'Then——'

'That's not how it is,' said Harvist.

The Superintendent went on looking into the blue, weary eyes before him; grasping and grasping for some fact that eluded him. His mind fumbled with ideas, such as suggesting a psychiatrist's report, though this didn't feel like the right track. . . . I'd give the devil of a lot to know, he thought, exactly how it is with Harvist.

§

Major Fellowes screwed and unscrewed the cap of his fountain pen, glanced towards the door. His Chief Officer entered. 'Here's his record, sir.'

'Thank you.' Major Fellowes turned the sheets of paper absently. 'When the doctor's done with him, I'd like him brought to me.'

'The doctor's already seen him, sir. Passed him fit for all forms of punishment.'

'Oh—right, then.' Major Fellowes seemed to be going to say something else, and the Chief Officer waited. 'Curious thing— *most* curious thing—but I feel rather excited. Anxious to see him again. Especially after that talk on the phone with the Superintendent. Couldn't get a thing out of him—you know the Super; cagey wasn't the word; he just grunted in that maddening way he has. And he sounded, of course, as he always does, as if he were in the last stages of melancholia. Reading between the lines it seemed to me that he'd got nowhere with Harvist. Nowhere at all. But then—without being vain—I don't honestly think he's got my ability to handle men.'

'Oh no, sir,' said the Chief Officer, having no idea whether the Superintendent could handle men or not.

'Not that Harvist was easy. Oh, God knows, he wasn't.' He returned to the cap of his fountain pen. 'Wonder what it's like for him to find himself back at Scarside again? To smell it, hear the gates closing and all that? Have you seen him yet?'

'Yes, sir.'

'How d'you find him?'

'He's . . . a bit quiet, sir.'

'Quiet? You mean, subdued? Defeated? That kind of thing?'

The Chief Officer puzzled over it. 'Well, no . . . not exactly, sir. More like . . . as if he was thinking about something else.'

Major Fellowes felt a twinge of doubt. 'Sounds as if he hasn't changed much.'

'He isn't *quite* the same, sir. He did seem anxious to see you. Said he wanted to see you as soon as he could. Said he had a question to ask you.'

'Oh, really?' Major Fellowes tried to conceal a certain pleasure. 'I hope—I must say I do hope—that I can make some sort of contact with him. It seems to me a case where the right word could make all the difference. He's got, after all, another two years. Somehow he's got to accept that. If he doesn't——' He broke off and threw the pen down. 'Oh, you'd better go and get him.'

In a few moments, the Chief Officer returned and showed Harvist into the room. 'All right, Woods,' said Major Fellowes. 'Wait outside, will you? I'll see the prisoner alone.'

His first impression was that the interview wasn't going to be an easy one. Harvist stood before him, already in the dress of the man who's tried to escape—grey suit with large, black clownish patches—and these clothes, which the Governor had seen on other prisoners often enough, seemed on Harvist a little incongruous, and to put up a barrier between them. Damn, he thought, and leaned forward on his desk. 'You can sit down, Harvist. This isn't an official do; that comes to-morrow, when you'll be charged with escaping. This is—well, just a little talk between the two of us. Go on—sit down.'

A slight smile. 'Thank you.'

Major Fellowes bit his lip, trying to think what to say next. Not much help so far; he gave a crisp smile. Help or no help, he could handle this better than the Superintendent. 'Well, now! Not a very sensible performance.'

'No, sir. I'm sorry.'

'You're clear, I suppose, what's in store for you?'

'I know I'm back here. . . .' The words were disconcerting; spoken with a kind of detached wonder.

'You lose ninety days remission, you lose your tobacco and you have fifteen days bread and water.'

'Yes, I thought it'd be something like that.'

Quite absurd, Major Fellowes thought, for him to feel a jab at his nerves as if he'd been cruel. 'That's fair, you'll agree? And that for the rest of your sentence, you're forbidden to go outside the prison walls. We can't take any chances, can we, after all?'

'No. On the other hand—you needn't have any fear that I shall try to escape again.'

That should have been encouraging, but the words were spoken away to the window, and seemed rather a private thought than part of a conversation.

Major Fellowes coughed. 'Glad to hear it. Learned a lesson, have you?'

'Yes, sir, you might call it that.'

'Rather a silly way of doing it, don't you think?'

Harvist was looking thoughtfully at his hands. In some way

he seemed quite independent of the ugly branded clothes. 'Yes. Yes, perhaps. Yet at the time . . . it seemed quite beyond my control. I *had* to go—to run into that mist.'

'What happens if this same sort of—ah—compulsion comes over you again?'

'Oh—it won't. I can assure you of that.'

A silence. Major Fellowes moved things about on his desk. 'After all . . . a man like yourself can rise above a thing like this. A man of education—a man of the Church; a so much better chance than most of the men here. . . .' He broke off, losing confidence; Harvist was listening to him with attention, but with a slight smile, as a man listens courteously to a companion who is making a fool of himself.'

'Yes, sir, I realize that.'

'I understand—' mild irritation gave an edge to Major Fellowes' voice—'I understand that there was a question you wanted to ask me.'

'Yes, sir.' Silence again while Harvist seemed to be working something out in his head. Major Fellowes waited. It was a curious silence; outside it he could hear the noises of the prison—steps and orders shouted, the closing of doors and gates and the rattle of keys. In his mind rose a picture of the prison, the stone floors, the bare cells, the kitchens, the courtyards; a walled, unnatural city with its own life.

'I was going to ask you,' Harvist said, 'if you'd make an enquiry for me.'

'What kind of enquiry?'

After another brief hesitation, Harvist said, 'Simply this. There is, I believe, an Anglican Community in Kilbrennan, in the Western Isles. The Society of Christ's Compassion——'

'Yes?'

'I'd like to know if—when I'm released—if they'd accept me.'

Major Fellowes felt as though he'd received a small but potent electric shock. Parsons were one thing, monks another. Monks were medieval, or foreign, or in some way not quite real. No one he knew had ever become a monk. He said cautiously, 'You mean . . . you want to go there for good? To—to take vows—all that sort of thing?'

'Yes, sir.'

'Retire from the world? Go from—ha!—one cell to another?'

'Yes, you might say that, sir.' He smiled. 'But there are cells and cells.'

'I . . . yes. I'll find out for you, of course, but . . . you're sure about this? You've given it thought, I mean? After all, it is . . . it must be . . . a tremendous step.' He paused, quite at sea. He supposed it was a tremendous step; he couldn't begin to conceive it.

'Yes, sir, I'm sure.' Harvist moved in his chair. 'As sure, at any rate, as any man can be, before he's taken the first step and lived amongst them for a time.'

'Well, yes. . . . I see.' Major Fellowes played unhappily with the cap of his pen. 'Shut away——'

Harvist was looking at him; the tired blue eyes were lit with the same smile. 'It's quite a bit different from a prison, you know. It's an Active Order, not Enclosed.'

'Oh, is it?' said the Governor, now finally defeated. He played with the pen, then threw it down. 'Oh, well. I don't suppose there's much I can say.' He was surprised to feel a weight of disappointment, as if some hope had failed him. Perhaps he'd hoped that Harvist would go back into the world on his release, saying that his prison sentence had been a good thing, and Major Fellowes was a good chap, and . . . 'Cut off,' he said, 'cut off from everything——'

'Well, not quite that, sir. They work, you know; work on the land; grow their own food. They go out helping people.'

'Yes. Yes, I see.' It didn't make him feel any happier, that they grew their own food. He had a deep sense of failure. 'Well, there it is. I'd just like to repeat what I said about making any further effort to escape——'

Gently, Harvist shook his head. 'You have my word, sir.'

Major Fellowes felt in some obscure way rebuked. 'Very well.' He glanced over his wide desk; he was still the Governor of Scarside; a defeat with one prisoner more or less didn't make all that difference. Still he felt heavy and sad. He tried to look forward to his dinner, with a glass of wine, and an evening by the fire in his own house, outside the prison wall, but he couldn't focus on it; he kept seeing how it would be for Harvist; he'd go straight back to his cell and the door wouldn't open again till the morning. Well . . . nothing to be done. No more, apparently, to be said.

He looked across at Harvist; gave him a little nod. 'That's all, Harvist.'

Harvist got to his feet; for a moment their eyes met. Something quite unreadable in Harvist's face—amusement? compassion? Clearly there flashed through Major Fellowes' mind a picture of the cell, of the days on a diet of bread and water.

'The doctor's passed you as fit,' he said, as if he argued with something in his mind.

'Yes, sir. So I understand.'

One last glance at that gentle, contemplative face; then, finally defeated, Major Fellowes rang for his Chief Officer.

'Woods, take Harvist back to his cell, will you? And then come and see me.'

'Yes, sir.'

'Well—good night, Harvist.'

'Good night, sir.'

Major Fellowes watched the figure in its clownish dress until the door closed behind it. He sat then, leaning on his desk, looking unseeingly at his pen-tray. When Woods returned, he gave a slight start, as if he'd pricked his finger.

'Ah, Woods. Yes, well, I've talked to him.' He drew one finger along his desk. 'Know what he wants to do? Join an Order.'

'A what, sir?'

'A religious Order—you know—wear a habit and all that sort of thing.'

'After getting out of *here*? He must be fair daft, sir.'

'Well, I don't know. . . .' Major Fellowes frowned. 'He says he won't give us any more trouble . . . won't try to escape again.'

'They all say that, sir.'

'Yes, yes. . . . Think he means it, though. Yes, I think so.' He sighed, and drew a line on his pad. 'Extraordinary business . . . don't get it. . . . He's back in his cell now, is he?'

'Yes, sir.'

'H'm . . . yes. Back there. After running off into the mist like that . . . all that palaver of hiding and being hunted . . . for five days. . . .' He looked down at his pen. 'What good did it do him? I don't see what he gained by it, do you?'

A000013166489